BLUE JEANS
AND
COFFEE BEANS

ALSO BY JOANNE DEMAIO

blue jeans and coffee beans

A NOVEL

JOANNE DEMAIO

Copyright © 2013 Joanne DeMaio
All rights reserved.

ISBN: 1479262773
ISBN-13: 9781479262779

www.joannedemaio.com

To my daughter, Jena

one

LONG ISLAND SOUND'S LAZY BREAKING waves chase her back onto the sand. She watches them carefully, believing they are truly after her. Upon the waves' retreat, her little legs dare to step back toward them, never to quite within their reach, while never far from her mother's reach, either. She is only a toddler, the girl in the blue and white ruffled bathing suit, her light brown hair falling with a salty fluff to just below her tanned shoulders. The last of an ice cream bar clings to its stick, melting slowly and dripping on her toes.

The woman looks on from her low sand chair. Long, slender arms loosely hold her knees pulled up close while she glances from her daughter to the sparkling expanse of salt water before her. Deep brown eyes level that gaze from beneath a wide-brimmed straw sun hat. She looks past the horizon, connecting with an influence far beyond the sea, closing her eyes as though seeing her sister over in Europe but as close as a wish.

Beneath the September sun, she stands and walks to her daughter, casual in loosely cuffed jeans and an embroidered tunic, a brown wooden bangle on her wrist.

1

"Look at the sunshine sparkling on the water. The sparkles look like ocean stars, don't they? Starlight in the daytime." Ever so lightly, her fingertips rest atop her daughter's head, moving through strands of salty hair. Life momentarily pauses in their brief seaward gazes, as though this forms the core of it. All else springs ever from this connection. She turns then, pushes her straw hat up a little and walks ankle-deep into the water. A flash of summer sunlight flares as the camera turns into the sun while her husband films her wading in the Sound. The scene flickers between washes of light and the fading woman, until a spray of dull white speckled with wavering black threads finally overcomes it.

Maris reaches over to the old projector and stops the 8mm home movie. She has become adept at imagining the words her mother might have once said to her, dreaming up a gentle voice reaching her ear. A lifetime of longing will do that.

And now this, another film to add to her collection. Maris has more video than memory of her mother, scenes she memorized long ago. Christmases, birthdays. But mostly, the beach. Her mother often planned seaside day trips with varying shoreline stops, a picnic lunch packed for them, sandals ready. There were rocky coastlines, dunes of beach grass, sunset walks. So this newly discovered scene seems a gift as her mother walks along a beach on a mid-September day. It brings her back to life with past images that Maris' eyes have never seen. Is it the last film ever made of her, the last time the movie camera was pulled off a closet shelf? Is it the last bit of lightness before an invisible patch of black ice descended upon them late the next year? Is the film intended to take her thoughts off the long-ago random, quick skid that threw the car into a large

2

oak tree? Even last week when she stopped at the damaged trunk out past the apple orchard, past the farm stand, a bouquet withered in the wind, the last of decades of bouquets her father must have tied there, maybe on her mother's birthday.

Tucked in an attic box for thirty long years, time has left its mark on this old reel of film that says so much, in so little, its colors fading. A quick scene, a look, a touch of her hair she can almost still feel. She knows what they mean though. A lifetime of watching silent home movies, of studying the nuances of the mother she'd lost, trained her eye. The body speaks volumes in the way it moves, listens, bends to touch a cheek. Now Maris captures the same quick feelings in her fashion sketches, the clothes covering human shapes that care, that move with feeling, that know love.

But after two weeks of going through her childhood home, room by room, placing in storage the furniture and household items she wants to keep, commissioning to the auction house the remainder, goodbyes are due. There are no sisters or brothers with whom to debate keeping a brass lamp or a linen tablecloth or a crystal vase. No one to consider living on in the family home. There is only herself, flying in from Chicago with a leave of absence to wrap up the loose ends of her father's estate.

It is time to leave. So on her last day here, with the boxes all packed, she finally set up the old movie projector and screen. But watching her family one last time together in their home, she doesn't count on the emotion. Doesn't even realize the simple beach images of her mother move her until she comes out of the kitchen with a glass of water, ready to watch the remaining film when her doorbell rings. Even then, not until her oldest and dearest friend comments on her tears does Maris realize she's been crying. Some longings never cease.

***

"Eva?"

"Surprise!" Eva shakes out her dripping umbrella. "Doesn't this beat email? Face-to-face, at last." She rushes out of the rain into the foyer, slipping off her wet trench coat. "I figured your car couldn't possibly hold all the boxes, so I brought the truck." She motions over her shoulder to the large SUV parked outside, then turns back to Maris. "Whoa, whoa, what's with the tears? I knew it. I knew this would be too much for you alone."

"It's not the packing. Really, Eva."

Taped and labeled moving cartons line the wall near the foyer. Beyond, floor to ceiling drapes still hang on the windows and a floral sofa fills the far corner. An old lamp, its shade yellowed with age, stands on an end table. Nails and light shadows remain on walls once decorated with paintings. Eva spots the movie screen and turns to her friend. "Are you seriously watching home movies? Alone? Today?"

"It's not what you're thinking. Really. I found a reel of film in an attic box and wanted to see what was on it before packing it up."

"Just one? By itself?"

"Honest, just one, and I've seen enough." Maris closes the movie screen. "Let's hit the road before it gets dark."

"Are you sure? We have time to watch the rest."

"Oh I'm sure. I've had enough emotion to last me a year at least. Your timing actually couldn't be better."

"Well hey, I want you packed and at my place as soon

as possible. Before you can change your mind about staying on a while. We've got so much catching up to do. And you'll have a little breather from all this, too." She gives Maris the lone reel of film. "Hold on to that."

"Let me take one last walk through, okay? I'll get the dog, poor thing. She's upstairs still waiting for my dad to come back."

Eva tucks the portable screen under her arm. "Take your time, say your goodbyes. It's okay. I'll call Matt from the car and let him know we're on our way."

Through the swishing windshield wipers and headlight beams illuminating sheets of rain, Maris considers the twelve years of time that stand between herself and her last summer at the Connecticut shore. Twelve years of building a career and maneuvering relationships as she relocated around the country.

When she exits off the highway onto the secondary beach road, her grip on the steering wheel loosens. Chicago seems far away, her life there, and Scott, only shadows right now. She opens her window and the thick salt air fills her car. Madison snorts the air from the back seat.

"You too, huh?" Maris asks. She wonders if her father ever took the German shepherd to the beach, if the dog has some beach memory of him.

The rain picks up again, bringing her focus back to the winding road. When a car pulls out in front of her, Eva stops her SUV at the curb until Maris catches up. While driving, she sees glimpses of the railroad track running along the coastline. On long-ago summer nights here, the train whistle floated through the dips and curves of the river valley and shoreline towns like a silver ribbon of sound. It is no wonder a train whistle always brings her back to her summers at the beach.

Only one narrow lane leads into Stony Point, forking in an easy curve off the winding main road. It is nearly hidden by the railroad trestle that runs over it and by the market and secondhand bookshop that sit on the trestle's hill before it. If you didn't know it existed, you could drive right by, completely unaware of a world unto itself. Now she follows her best friend around the curve, through the dark tunnel under the tracks. For the first time in months, her mind feels clearer and her spirits lift.

Someone once told her that the sea air and salt water are cleansing. They cure what ails you.

two

"MARRY ME," SCOTT SAYS.

"What?"

"Right away. Let's get married. At that chapel you like. Or a Justice of the Peace. I don't care where, just marry me. I love you and I was wrong and I want to be with you. Next week, right away."

"Scott, we're not even engaged." Maris presses the curtain aside and looks out the window, holding the cell close. The marsh spreads out past Eva's backyard, the grasses green and soft, rising from the mist. A heron stands on the bank, glistening white in the early sun.

"We're not kids. It doesn't matter. We'll do it right away, no engagement."

"Wait. Wait, Scott. What are you doing? It's not the right time. My father just died and I'm exhausted."

"Exactly. And you need me now. You need us together."

Maris turns away from the window, then turns right back.

"I love you, Maris, and I don't want it to come between us that I wasn't there for the funeral. Say yes to me."

"Oh, Scott." She leans against the window frame,

moving closer to the sea, the salt air. "I can't. Not yet, anyway."

"Of course you can. We've talked about it plenty."

She watches below as Matt walks outside to his car, his posture perfect in a state police uniform. She's been standing at this bedroom window since before anyone in the house had woken; now they are going to work. "Tonight. I'll call you tonight, Scott. I promise."

The walls grow close, the air closer. His proposal, if she'd call it that, hems her in somehow. And it makes her take a deep breath and push back by going downstairs to talk to her friend about it over a fresh cup of coffee.

"What are you looking at so intently this morning?" Maris asks, breezing into the kitchen.

Eva glances up from the laptop opened on the table before turning back to the screen. "Design ideas."

"Ideas for what?" Maris finds a mug in the cabinet and pours herself a cup of coffee.

"Decorating this place. It's great being back in my family home, but seriously? Sometimes it feels like I'm still in high school with this old wallpaper. Want to see some kitchen photos?"

Maris turns and leans against the counter, eyeing her friend.

"Or not," Eva says. She pulls a light cardigan close against the morning damp. "What's the matter?"

"Scott proposed."

"What?"

"He did. Just now."

"Wait. You're getting married?"

Maris shrugs.

"Whoa! Congratulations, Maris! That is awesome!" Eva rushes over and hugs her. "I'm so happy for you."

"Well nothing's definite yet." Maris takes her coffee over to the table and sits in front of the laptop. "He caught me a little off-guard with this."

Now Eva eyes her. "Uh-oh. This is good news, isn't it?"

"I guess. It just feels a little surreal. I mean, married? Me?"

"Yes!" Eva sits across from her. "You'll finally settle down! And Scott's a great guy. Aren't you happy?"

"Well. Sure I am. It just hasn't sunk in yet. Married!"

"You know what you need? A ring on that finger. That'll make it sink in."

Maris holds out her left hand, looking carefully at her ring finger. "I don't know."

"Can't you see it? A beautiful diamond glimmering on your hand? Listen. Just try this. Visualize it. You know, like I'm doing with these decorating images. Or better yet," she says, grabbing Maris' arm, "I have an idea." They run together up the stairs, Eva tugging at her halfhearted resistance.

"What are you doing now?" Maris asks when Eva lifts open the old hope chest in the upstairs hallway. Oh she can see it clearly in her eyes, that little bit of the rebel inspiring her idea, whatever it may be, as she digs into the blankets and scarves and sweaters.

"Visualizing, my friend. Visualizing. Trust me. I'll show you how."

<hr />

Time moves like the sea. Eva always felt so. Living right at the beach, time is placid and calm, soft waves of it rolling onto the shore of her days. One day follows the other, over and over, in a comfortable and reassuring way. No matter what she is doing, at any age, that awareness of the movement of the sea, and of waves of time, keeps her grounded.

But as volatile as the sea can be, so too is any hour, any moment. Washing ashore, overtaking her very self with its insistence, with its forward movement rushing over her so powerfully she can be knocked senseless by the force of time. Waves of the past have that way of pulling at her, leaving her gasping and struggling to get her bearings, to breathe evenly.

Like right now. Digging through old clothes in the hope chest, Eva remembers, crystal clearly, her own wedding memory from all those years ago. It was one of those days when so much happens, a day cresting with immense change. She could still hear her mother's words as she leaned close to the mirror the morning she got married, adding a smudge of eyeliner beneath her eyes.

"Look what you've done now," Theresa had said only weeks earlier, on a day when rain drummed steady on the house. Water streaked the windows, turning the panes fluid. "There's absolutely no going back now. And what about college? Did you two even think of that?"

Eva added more eyeliner almost in defiance of her mother's words. At least she'd finished high school. And it's not like she was the first teenager to ever get herself pregnant. But maybe what she needed was the definition of family that came with it; maybe it felt good to connect with a baby. She'd already begun whispering a few phrases, wondering if the baby could hear them. Because her baby would always know her, and its father, too. She and Matt would find some way to get married and stay together.

But fear of that uncertain future finally won out and had brought her to her mother for help. On that rainy day in the kitchen, her words to Theresa came like little riptides tugging at her heart, at her tears, at her throat, pulling her under and choking her up. *After a graduation party at Foley's* and *Usually we just hang out there, you know* were followed by a gasp as she was near drowning in fear. *We played cards* and *We were celebrating and drank a little* had her wiping tears off her face, tasting the salt and closing her eyes against the unknown washing over her. *Later we went to the beach, and I don't know, it just happened* she'd continued, her breathing ragged, her face wet, her youth drowned out by a clear reality now.

"Well you and Matthew made a bad decision. It's as simple as that." Theresa's voice dropped low. "And now your options are limited, so we'll make your next decision right now. You and me. And you'll stick to it, Eva. You'll get through this. You'll have the baby and live here. Dad and I will help you raise it, don't worry. It'll be okay."

Eva shook her head no as her mother spoke.

"What do you mean, no? You are not getting an abortion, and you are definitely not giving that baby up for adoption, tying up another generation in knots."

"We're getting married," Eva whispered.

"Excuse me?"

"We are. Matt wants to."

"Oh no. No, no, no. You are way too young for that. Maybe in a few years, if you're still together. It's bad enough there's a baby to take care of now. Marriage is out of the question."

"You can't stop us." At that point, she wasn't sure if her mother even heard her quiet insistence fighting tears, and fighting her mother's will. "I'm marrying Matt."

Theresa looked long at her, then reached forward and dabbed at Eva's damp cheek with a tissue. Eva wouldn't break her gaze, staring straight at her, her tear-rimmed eyes unblinking. After living a life shaped by moments she knew nothing of, moments that separated her from her birth mother, she'd resolved moments wouldn't decide anymore. She would.

So a few weeks later, on a late August Saturday morning, Eva stood barefoot in front of her bedroom mirror in the vintage gown she'd chosen. Embroidered lace flowers covered the sheer short sleeves, a white ribbon reached around her waist to a bow in the back, while the gown fell simply into a few lace tiered layers. She accepted Theresa's help now; she actually wanted it, desperately. The wedding would be small and simple, and she and Matt would live at home until they got their bearings. But still ... still. Eva would still do some things her way, would define her own path to motherhood. Her way meant the ceremony would be on the beach she loved. And remaining barefoot in the warm sand in her vintage gown became another of her own small acts of control, of definition. Because on the beach, in the sea breezes, in the sound of the waves, didn't other voices often carry, a whispered voice she missed all her life.

An embroidered lace bridal cap covered much of her long tangle of untamed dark hair, and looking at her reflection alone in her room on her wedding day, a fear rose in her eyes. No black eyeliner, no defiant attitude, no acts of rebellion could deny the fear of what she'd gotten herself into.

Every bit of that moment, the very one when she raised her arms, took hold of the veil and slowly but gently lifted it and draped it over her face, the whole moment that captured the unknown she found herself facing at eighteen, returns as steady and unstoppable as the tide, the rising wave of memory moving over her heart as Maris stands now in front of her bedroom mirror, the very same mirror as then.

Visualize, Eva softly suggests as she sets her old veil on Maris' head. And as Maris reaches up to lift the veil forward over her long brown hair, Eva sees her eighteen-year-old self in the look unbound in Maris' steady gaze at the mirror. It is there all over again, this time in Maris' dark eyes, that same pure fear of what she is about to do.

⁓

"I can't do it," Maris says.

"What do you mean? You'll make a beautiful bride. Look."

But Maris hasn't stopped looking, turning to the side, lifting the veil back over her face.

"My veil can be your Something Borrowed. It looks so pretty on you. And we can shop for a gown together. Or if you shop in Chicago, take pictures and email me the photos so I can see too. I'll let you know what I think of them. Here, hold this up, just for fun."

Maris takes the vintage gown from Eva's hands, feeling the detail of the fabric, of a life itself, in the complex threads of embroidery and lace. Oh the anticipation and tears and love and promise all stitched into one simple dress. It feels like playing dress-up, holding the gown against her body and seeing someone she isn't sure of. Someone she has to imagine, this bride. The delicate feel and faint scent of this aged cream gown long tucked into a cedar hope chest give it a tangible quality, an evidence of a life fully lived for one day within it.

"When will I ever find time to do all this? Gown shopping? A wedding?"

Eva stands behind her and adjusts the veil, resetting it over her dark hair.

"Can you do me a favor?" Maris asks, holding the gown's shoulders over hers, vintage satin and lace falling the length of her body, brushing her bare feet. Eva's reflected eyes in the mirror rise to meet hers. "Find me a place to stay here."

"Here? What do you mean?"

"Just for a little while." She turns back to Eva, giving her the gown. "The more I think about it, the more I want to do it."

"Do what?" Eva asks, laying out her gown on the bed.

"Oh, this idea so needs a fresh cup of coffee to mull over. Come on." Maris rushes back down the stairs to Eva's kitchen, feeling suddenly so hippy, barefoot in her skinny jeans, tank top and wedding veil. She sits in front of Eva's laptop again, glancing at her decorating inspiration. "I'll tell you what. I'll help you with your design plans in exchange."

"Maris, you design denim. Fashion design. Not homes."

"Fashion design. Interior design. It's all about having an eye for it."

"Wait. You said in exchange." Eva sinks slowly into a chair across the table from her. "In exchange for what?"

Maris adjusts the veil, lifting it and letting it fall back again over her shoulders, remembering Eva wearing it the same way when they'd found it all those years ago in a vintage clothing boutique. She looks around the kitchen now, seeing the faded country-print wallpaper, the Formica countertops, the tiny homework cubby filled with dictionaries and cookbooks, pencils and measuring spoons. Nothing has changed. So can Eva see the same memory she is seeing? The one of two teenage girls finishing breakfast and heading out for a day of tanning, or crabbing

14

on the rocks, or swimming out to the big rock? Right at this moment, it feels like she just arrived at her best friend's home, the same way she did all those years ago, suitcase bulging with tank tops and shorts and flip-flops. Suddenly they are fifteen again, beginning another summer when Maris stays with Eva and her family at the beach for two sweet months. When a smile breaks out on Eva's face, she knows her friend feels the same way.

"I need some time. There's so much going on in my life right now with the estate, and now this with Scott. Really, it's just overwhelming. Do you think there's some empty little cottage here that I can rent for a few weeks? I'll trade you my design skills for your realtor skills."

"Seriously?"

As soon as she asks, Maris feels the magic, the sense of a peaceful dove fluttering from an unfurled scarf. This beach has a way of casting its spell right through the windows under the guise of sun and salt, the call of the gulls, the sound of the waves. "It'll be like old times, one more time."

"For how long?"

"I can extend my family leave, I'm sure. A few weeks. Maybe a month." She stands then, spreads butter on a blueberry muffin and warms it in the microwave before turning back to Eva. "You game?"

Eva reaches an outstretched hand, her pinky poised in a hook, her steady, dark gaze time travelling back to their teens.

Maris reaches forward and hooks that pinky with hers, the silk tulle of the wedding veil brushing alongside her face.

~

Whispers, shadows. They are one and the same as far as Jason Barlow is concerned. Both have you turn at the hint of them. Both have you think someone is close by, watching. His life is their stomping ground, so much so that he begins answering them back if they get too close. Or if he can't make out the words. If he can't tell if it is the wind or Neil's far-off voice. Sunlight through tree branches, or his brother's soul visiting him.

Anything can spark them. Like now, driving past the still-empty guard shack. How many summer voices that sight can summon. "Don't even start," he says as he looks past the shack, steering down the old beach road. Abandoned homes have a knack for toying with voices and shadows, too. And he is on a crash course with one.

Jason drives past cedar-shingled colonials with windowed walls and porches facing ocean views. Tucked back from the road, small wood-sided bungalows with lattice-windowed front porches sit on refurbished stone foundations. His clients want all this, along with the swaying sea grasses, the sandy beach and gentle Long Island Sound waves, the swans in the marsh, the evenings on the old boardwalk. The cottages he renovates are all about architectural charm, and nothing about demons. As he pulls into the stone driveway of his family's deserted beach home, it is just the opposite.

"It's only for the weekend," he tells himself, or some shadow sitting in the passenger seat.

Inside the cottage, time stands still, like a museum. Or hell, depending. The faded walls, the seaside paintings, the musty furniture and framed photographs arranged on end tables, all pay homage to a family life. He sets two grocery bags on the kitchen table and plugs in the refrigerator. Opening the window over the kitchen sink, he sees the sandy pails and cluster of small fishing nets leaning against the outside shower enclosure. At low tides, he and his brother climbed over the exposed rock jetty, plucking mussels and snails from the damp stone surfaces. They cracked open the bait with a big rock and tied it on to their crabbing lines on the jetty and in the creek.

When he looks at the outside shower again, the pails and nets are gone.

Jason opens the cold water faucet and splashes a handful on his face. It seems so far away. Crabbing, swimming, hanging out at Foley's, rowing through the lagoon in summers that were endless, behind marsh grass that beckoned, beneath sunlight that nourished and starlit skies that calmed, forging friendships and memories. His fingers feel the long scar above his jawline. Whether he irritated it shaving or if changes in the weather bring it on, he can't be sure. But today the scar feels tender.

When he turns back into the living room, glass on the fireplace mantel catches his eye, the sharp slivers glittering on its brick hearth. If it hadn't all happened, he wouldn't have tired of seeing Neil in every shadow last fall, wouldn't have flung his glass of Scotch at the brick fireplace. He gets the dustpan from the broom closet now, sweeps up the mess and hears his father's voice complaining about the injustice of it all, of Neil not being with them anymore at the beach.

"Just shut up," Jason says under his breath. "Shut up or I'll leave."

But he never stays away for long; it is the only place he can find Neil now.

He picks up the phone and gets his sister's answering machine. "Paige, when you talk to Mom, tell her the house made it through the winter fine. But the outside window trim is peeling. I'll get someone to repaint it." He pauses a few seconds in case she might be rushing in, maybe running inside from the clothesline or from picking up her kids at day camp. Maybe she'll grab up the phone and talk a little. "Take care now," he finally says, holding the receiver tight to his ear a moment longer before disconnecting.

Then Jason Barlow walks out back to the barn like he did all those years ago with his father and Neil, the breeze carrying echoes of his father's low voice detailing his masonry craft and the work his hands did, building stone walls and patios and foundations. He swings open the barn doors and low golden sunlight sweeps into the dusty space. An old ladder hangs horizontally on high wall hooks. He lifts it down and finds a few spattered paint scrapers hanging with the hammers and screwdrivers and trowels on a wooden pegboard. With about an hour of daylight left, he has enough time to begin.

three

LIGHTS COME ON IN THE little shops outside, the morning gray with a lingering fog, its mist hovering low. It feels like Christmas, and Maris pictures twinkling lights strung along the storefronts and up the masts of the tall sailboats in the harbor. Elegant burgundy bows would hang from balsam wreaths, blowing in the snowy wind. Sitting in the diner's window seat, her laptop opened on the table beside a plate of scrambled eggs and fresh coffee, the morning is easy and comfortable. Until she reaches for the velvet box, the one holding a solitaire diamond on a platinum band. Scott had tucked it right into her laptop case before mailing it all to her. In his note, he tells her she is right. She deserves to be engaged. And her world stops cold at the sight of the ring.

He wants her back, soon. He wants them married. He wants a honeymoon before she goes back to work at Saybrooks.

She reaches for her cell phone and dials his, leaving a voicemail. "The ring, Scott, it's beautiful," she begins as she straightens the loose band on her finger. "Well, we definitely have to talk. But I'm not sure when I'll be back yet." She looks at his note, at the list of things he wants, wants, wants. What about what she wants? Does she tell him that mornings spent pressing wallpaper samples against Eva's walls and deciding on paint chips and having lunch outside on the deck all hold her back?

"It's just that I'm helping Eva with a project, and I have to get Madison settled."

How about what Madison wants? Does that count for anything? Does she mention all the driftwood the dog has stockpiled in a few days, carrying pieces back to the cottage from their walks along the high tide line, her tail finally swinging wide with happiness?

She is surprised at all she finds herself wanting here. Does she mention that coffee never tasted as sweet as it does on her front porch? And that she tucked tender seedlings into the flower boxes of the silver-shingled cottage she rented? Okay, it was on a whim, but still. The petunias reach skyward now, like nesting baby birds drinking in the nourishing late June sun. Sitting with her pastels and sketch pad, she'd sketched their deep azure color into her latest denim jacket design. And sleep. It comes so easy with a sea breeze moving in past the sheer curtains.

She pauses, thanks him again for the ring and disconnects. Then she slips the ring back into the velvet box, tucks it into her case along with the computer, grabs her check and walks up to the cash register. Customers sit at the counter stools; two cooks in white aprons work the kitchen, laughing and flipping bacon and eggs. This place is all about familiarity. She sets down her computer case when the waitress approaches, pulls her wallet from her purse, pays the tab and quickly leaves, feeling caught in a riptide between here and Chicago.

Jerry had wanted a boat all his life. He told everyone when he was a kid, *When I grow up, I'm getting a boat.* Then he did grow up and got married instead. *After we buy a house*, he told his wife, *maybe I'll get a boat.* Then she got pregnant. Three times. *When the kids get older,* he said to his family. *Maybe they'd like to have a boat, do a little fishing. After college,* he would mention to Kyle, *once their tuition's been paid.*

"You've got your boat," Kyle told him years ago when he washed dishes at the diner. It isn't necessary to die to go to heaven; Kyle Bradford finds heaven standing in front of the big stove, spatulas in hand, tending the eggs and bacon and home fries, sliding meals onto warm plates and turning the carousel for the next order. Cooking is his calling and his downfall, standing in the way of happiness and failure. A job at the diner can never support his family, so as much as he wants it, he can't have his passion. "You've got a big shiny silver ship right here, with lots of friendly people on it," Kyle told his boss back when he first worked there. That's how much Kyle loves the diner, as much as Jerry would have loved a boat.

And that's when Jerry changed the name of his diner to The Dockside. He added anchors and buoys to the décor and draped a big fishing net along one wall. Starfish and seashells dotted the net. At night, the new lanterns in the windows made the silver diner look like a ship out at sea.

Kyle glances over his shoulder as a woman leaves. Sometimes he wonders what life is like for his customers—if it is any better than his, when scrambling eggs and frying bacon to save his life, his wife is considering leaving him. He presses his arm to his damp forehead. When the diner door swings open a minute later, Kyle knows what this customer's life is like. He saunters out from the kitchen, wiping his large hands on a dishtowel.

"Hey, Barlow," he says as Jason takes a stool at the counter. "Haven't seen you around lately. How's it going, man?"

"Good. Busy, you know?" Jason asks. "How about yourself?"

"I'm hanging in there. Coffee?"

"To go, today. I'm pressed for time." Jason sets his elbows on the counter, clasping his hands in front of his chin, his thumb reaching for his scar.

Kyle pours a steaming mug of black coffee and sets it in front of him along with a plain doughnut on a plate. "On the house. Let me tell the boss I'm taking five." He heads back into the kitchen, returning with his own coffee, leaning against the counter across from Jason.

"Really, Kyle. I'm running late." Jason starts to stand until Kyle waves him down.

"Take a minute. So how are you, Barlow? How's the leg? Giving you any grief?"

"You ask me that every time I see you."

"Listen. After what you've been through? Get used to it. I'll always ask."

"Okay, then. It's fine, Kyle." He breaks the doughnut and dunks a half into his coffee. "It's fine."

"Just checking. I was reading somewhere that the limb actually feels pain with changes in the weather."

"It happens."

"The article said something about fluctuations in air pressure and temperature bringing it on."

"Okay, Doc. You've just about got my health covered today. You want to take my blood pressure while you're at it?"

"Just saying." Kyle sips his coffee.

"So, Jerry keeping you busy here again?"

"Yeah, cooking's a good side gig. There was another

layoff when they lost the submarine contract."

"It's tough, I know. Got any leads for work?"

Kyle shrugs. "Where you headed?"

"You won't believe it."

"Try me."

"Gallaghers'."

"Matt's?"

"They're back at Stony Point. Matt saw me scraping paint at my place. Stopped by and had a beer."

"No shit. Where they living? They buy a place there?"

"Eva's parents sold them the house, and I guess Eva took over her mother's old realty too. Now they want to move the walls around."

"Damn. Lauren wants to maybe rent a cottage there this summer. She'll be surprised to hear about Eva."

"It's late in the season, but she might have something." Jason finishes the last of his coffee. "I'm drawing up plans to redesign the porch." He stands for his wallet and picks up a leather computer case set on the floor against the counter. "Hey Kyle, someone left their merchandise here."

"Kyle," Jerry calls out from the stoves. "Let's go."

Kyle glances toward the busy kitchen, then turns back to Jason.

"Go ahead," Jason says, setting the case on the counter. "I'll take care of it."

Back at the stoves, Kyle grabs three eggs in one hand and opens them on the griddle. What he didn't tell Jason is that Lauren wants time apart this summer. A few weeks away at the shore. That maybe they can better sort things out separately. This round of unemployment rattled her bad and he can't stop worrying about how to bring her to her senses.

Jason opens the black leather case and finds a business card holder neatly tucked inside. Gold letters inscribe the word Saybrooks. His thumb slips out one of the cards.

"Well I'll be God damned," he says as he reads Maris' name.

A customer sits at the counter beside him. "Someone you know?"

Jason looks at the card again. "Definitely. A friend I haven't seen in years."

Funny how one name can erase time so easily. Way back in the day, old man Foley added a room to his local grocery for his grandson. The small store, with its screen door and creaking plank floors stocked bread, milk, juices and the like for the summer renters at Stony Point. Living quarters were above it, and in the back, on the second level, tacked on by a local handyman, was a good sized room with a jukebox, card table and a used restaurant booth, with an old pinball machine plugged in back in the corner. The kids wised up and pilfered a dorm-sized refrigerator to keep the beer cold. Still, the old man liked having his grandson hanging out at home, rather than God knows where, doing heaven knows what.

Not that he had reason to worry, because for the most part, nothing more than minor infractions ever went down in that back room.

All good things come to an end, though. The end of an era came when old man Foley sold the place. Though they had outgrown hanging out there, one last party gathered before it closed up.

Jason hasn't seen Maris Carrington since that summer night.

"Someday," she had said when they stood outside on the deck, Maris slowly spinning the ice in her glass.

"Someday, what?" He turned to watch her speak.

Springsteen's *Glory Days* drifted out from the jukebox inside, and they heard Neil keeping time with his old drumsticks, rat-a-tat-tatting on the tabletop. Voices reached out to the darkness on the deck, blending with bars of summer music.

"Someday we'll hear that song on the radio and we'll remember all this, the voices, the sea air, picturing the good times in Foley's. It's like we're actually living the memory, right now."

"It's a good summer memory, don't you think?"

Maris sipped her drink. "It's so weird that this is the last time we'll be here."

Jason almost hadn't made it. He and Neil were using the side porch at their Stony Point home as an office for a small design and construction business they'd started. When a contractor needed plans for Monday morning, Jason worked until the fine blue lines and tiny print wavered in front of his tired eyes. Leaving the drafting table behind, he finally walked over to Foley's, finding Maris alone on the deck.

"When do you start your job?" he asked, standing beside her while they leaned on the railing that night. A haze hung in the air, blurring the moon.

"Tuesday. In Boston. It's pretty exciting. I'll be cutting patterns and doing a little sketching."

He mentioned the remodeling projects he and Neil were lining up for the fall. Finally the last jukebox song came on and he turned to Maris. "How about a dance, then?"

He took her into his arms on the deck, in the hazy moonlight, and they had their first and last dance of the summer together. He held her close, his fingers touching her hair, skimming her tanned skin. Her body felt soft against his and as she rested her head on his shoulder, he breathed in the night, the salt air. And when his hands reached around her neck on that August night, he kissed her, giving her one more memory to keep.

Twelve years have passed. He'd been twenty-four years old with his whole life ahead of him with that kiss. Neil's life was nearly over.

He slips her card into his shirt pocket and returns the business card holder back to the laptop case, taking it all out to his SUV. As he drives to Stony Point, he calls a number on his cell phone. "Eva, hey it's Jason. Listen, is Maris Carrington in town by any chance?"

Sometimes before sketching a new design, Maris draws a silhouette shape first. It clears the details away and lets her visually see the idea of her garment, and the pose that will best depict it. In later sketches, detail, light and shadow will come into play. But a pure black silhouette helps her design eye begin.

So when someone knocks at her door and she steps onto the front porch to answer it, still in her sketching frame of mind, she sees a silhouette. He stands in shadow and all that's apparent is the shape of him, the stance he holds, the idea of his life. But as she opens the screen door and goes outside, light and shadow bring out physical details. If she were to sketch him, quick charcoal strokes would depict his hair, and strong, fluid lines would depict a lean frame dressed carefully but casually in khakis and a button down shirt, slight curves across the arm showing sleeves turned up at the cuff. There is more shadow than light in this sketch. More darkness than light in the stance and expression. But facial proportions are key in recognizing a person, and even after twelve years, she knows with one look at his that it is Jason Barlow.

And she wonders if he can see her life on her face, see the clothes she creates for others in her hands, see her insecurities and loves. She feels suddenly self-conscious and tucks her hair behind an ear.

"Maris," he says, like he can't really believe he is saying her name again.

And in the greeting that follows, the hug, the smiles, in his bending and retrieving her laptop case, in her relief at its return, not because of the diamond ring inside it, but more for her recent denim designs on the software using the blues of the sea, in the way Madison noses her way out the door and the way Jason's hands scratch the scruff of her neck, in his refusal of a cup of coffee, in his explanation that he is late getting to Eva's, in her asking if he is the architect designing their renovation, in his words asking if life's been good to her, in her glance at his leg, knowing about the accident he faced years ago, in the scar on his face that says so much about him, in the way he picks up her right hand and cups it in his hands as he backs away, saying "It's really good to see you again," and making vague plans to get together, in the way Maris watches him walk away, she has enough.

Yes. In the next two hours, sitting in her kitchen beneath baskets and bunches of dried flowers and herbs hanging from white ceiling beams, in the opened arched sash windows and the sunlight breaking through clouds, shining on the antique tins and small china plates lining pine shelves, and shining on a large sketch pad before her on the breakfast bar, Maris has enough detail, enough visual, to turn a silhouette of Jason Barlow into a detailed sketch, starting with graphite pencils and finishing with the smudged effects of soft pastels to create form with light and shadow, leaving off some actual lines of the sketch when she feels there is more there than he actually let her see.

four

LAUREN KNEELS IN HER FRONT yard beside the hydrangea bush. She turns over the rich soil near the roots and tugs at weeds and prunes around the new blossoms. But no matter how busy she keeps herself, she cannot get the rowboat out of her mind. Ever since seeing it this morning on Eva's front porch, when her hands touched the smooth driftwood, it's been in her thoughts.

It seems so long ago now, the summer she painted that rowboat. It was the first of her collection of driftwood paintings, of rowboats and seagulls and beach umbrellas and tall masts at sunset seas. She had gathered the paints and sketch pad she'd received for her sixteenth birthday and walked a wooded path winding through a patch of pine forest until turning a sharp corner where you always expected more woods, not a little beach laying open like a book. Little Beach. It was small and ragged, with flickers of silver mica shimmering along the shore.

Lauren had walked the beach and collected pieces of driftwood, plain and lifeless, but with a story to tell … of the ocean, its salty caress, its surrendering tides. All around her were seaweed and salt, snails and barnacles. Finally she pulled herself onto the back of a flat boulder and spread her paints to one side, the driftwood pieces to the other. A rowboat lay abandoned in sea-grass among the small rocks. Its aged wood showed through the fading white paint and brick red bottom.

She touched a brush into her white paint and began painting on the driftwood. At that moment, summer opened to her in a new way. Her light touch let the natural grain of the driftwood show through the colors. Her dabs of green and yellow and brown filled in blades of sea-grasses and the stones that moored the lost boat.

"Hey you," Kyle says now, coming up behind her. His hair lies flat on his head, wilted in the humidity, and his shirt is soiled from cooking all morning. "I'll get the rest of those weeds when I mow." He reaches out his hand and helps her to her feet, giving her a bottled water.

Lauren twists open the water and sits on the front step with Kyle. Keeping her gaze directed across the street at the row of small, sturdy ranches and capes, their yards filled in with tall maple trees shading the lawns, her voice matches the quiet of the old street. "I saw Eva today. She found a cottage for us."

"Really. For when?"

She swallows a mouthful of water, then turns to Kyle and sees his fatigue. His eyes are tired. "Last three weeks of July. The kids will love it."

"Three weeks? Out of the question. We can barely afford one."

Lauren lifts the bottle, then lowers it without drinking. "It's a late cancellation, so the first renters lost their deposit. That's one week's rent covered. And the owners decided they'd let the other two weeks go for half price, a thousand dollars instead of two, rather than lose the whole rental."

"A thousand dollars? That's all I need to know. You're wiping us out."

"Three weeks at the beach is all *I* need to know. I have to get away from here. So do the kids. I'll temp to pay for it if I have to." After a moment, she adds, "Besides, you and I can use the break from each other."

"So I'm not going on this vacation with you and the kids? Is that how it works now?" A bead of perspiration drips down his face.

Lauren wants to turn away, to not feel so suddenly sad. "I just need some time alone. We don't know where things are headed. You're looking down south for work and won't even consider changing jobs so we can stay here."

"Change jobs? To what? Cooking isn't going to support this family, and you damn well know it. Even with you working, it won't."

"What about culinary school? Or something at the casino? They're always looking for help."

"What? Get real. I'm going to have to work two jobs just to catch up from this bout. If you want to stay home with the kids, you have to stay home somewhere cheaper to live."

"What's the point?" Lauren asks.

"What do you mean?"

"What's the point? The sub base is restructuring, manufacturing is all done here. Your shipbuilding skills are useless. You're thirty-six and really, what's the point of chasing fitter jobs all over the country? More layoffs? You have to do something else." She finishes her water. "But how can you find anything else if you're at The Dockside every day?"

"Well I'm caught between a rock and a hard place, then. Steel work's all I know. And as long as I'm in Jerry's kitchen, money's coming in. If I tell Jerry to forget it, the well is dry. The diner and your temping are barely getting us by. They were, anyway, until you went and broke the bank with that lousy cottage. And I'll move south before I deal cards part-time at the casino just to make a living. Got it?" He waits for her to answer, and when she doesn't, when she closes her eyes against the stinging tears, he stands and goes inside the house.

Where did it go, that feeling of sitting at the edge of summer? She had hoped that she could gather enough driftwood at the beach to begin painting again once the kids went back to school in September. Just a little, here and there. Instead, the way things are going, her paints will sit untouched on the closet shelf, collecting dust.

Her children come around the corner to the front yard. They step lightly and bicker under their breaths, treading on that taut line strung between Kyle and herself. Lauren gives them a leaf bag she'd found in the garage.

"Hey guys, how about stuffing those weeds into the bag?"

Hailey's four-year-old hands gingerly pick up the leaves, while Evan dives into the pile with open arms, as only a six-year-old boy would.

Kyle opens the front door and calls out. "You doing laundry?"

She looks up, shielding her eyes from the bright sun.

"It'll be the last load for a while. Water's all over the laundry room floor." He closes the door and disappears back inside the house.

Lauren stares at the closed door as though it has the last laugh, pulling her to the edge of something much different than summer. She thinks of Eva living the beach life now in that big cottage. It is old and needs work, but it is grand

and within walking distance of the beach. Oh if she could just find that little abandoned rowboat again, she just might paddle far, far away.

⌒ᴗ

"What do you think, guy?"

Jason steps back from his cottage and looks at the windowsill. After scraping off the pale gray, he had spread three different shades of trim paint on the wood. It is the end of the day, he feels tired and hasn't moved around enough, and his leg shooting whispers of pain warns him to take a walk, at least. Or else remove the prosthesis and use his crutches.

He stands and scrutinizes the paint samples.

"The beiges are good. White's too bright."

It doesn't matter if the words are imagined or if they are pieces of old conversation from when he and his brother worked side by side, their hands and minds finding aesthetic beauty in restoring the cottages by the sea. He still hears them clearly.

"Maybe the beiges are too bland though," Jason says.

"No way," his brother answers. "Listen. Pack it up. I want to show you something."

An offshore wind scatters clouds from west to east. Is that all he hears, sounds carried on the wind? The murmur of the sea? He presses the tops onto the paint cans and washes his brushes in the sink in the barn. Shadows grow long now, giving the barn a perception of life, as though the old tools spread on the worktables were suspended overnight, not over years. As though someone will return early, beneath morning's clear light, and sand and score and cut and hammer. A short board is clamped in a vice and he wonders if Neil's hands had touched it last.

"What?" Jason asks. "Talk to me, guy." The barn is silent, the silence erasing the memory of the hands and words and minds once at work here. He looks up at the vaulted ceilings, picturing new skylights letting in natural light, the space housing his drafting tables and computers, with lots of shelves on the walls to hold his archives of books on old cottage designs. The wide interior walls have space enough to showcase his photographic display of completed cottage restorations. As an architect, he knows that the best designed buildings outlast their original use. The barn has. Can he pull off working right here?

He closes the big double doors and walks down to the beach.

"You can do it." He hears the voice when he steps off the boardwalk onto the sand. "You'll never go wrong here."

Jason looks at the beach, at the glow of the sunset casting its hue on the sand.

"It's the sea's palette. These colors always work with what we do. Can't you picture them?"

Twilight spreads violet across the eastern sky; the salt water deepens to evening gray. An old white rowboat dips just offshore, the waves lapping at its reddened bottom. Someone anchored it just within swim's reach, to take it out for a paddle, maybe through the creek to the lagoon. But the sand, holding onto the deep gold of the sunset, is what strikes him. It is the same color as the deep beige paint sample on the window trim at the cottage.

Jason walks down to the water's edge. The firmness of that packed sand feels good beneath his legs as he walks the length of the shore. Neil had walked it, too. Contemplated it, read about it and felt it. He'd even kept a journal of his beach observations, filled with notes and sketches and photographs. They defined his carpentry as he'd work elements of the sea and sands right into Jason's cottage designs with color, texture, essence.

Tomorrow he'll buy enough of the sandy beige paint to trim the windows, doors and eaves.

"The barn, too," he hears. "Start on the barn."

He stops at the water's edge. Seven years have passed since the wreck and he feels stronger now. He stretches his left leg straight and looks at the prosthetic limb attached below his knee. "Okay, Neil. You win."

~

I have light freckles and green eyes.

Eva scrolls down the screen. Maris just emailed her the detailed itinerary for their Fourth of July reunion barbecue. Leave it to Maris to design the perfect columns of their beach friends' names, phone numbers and RSVP check-box, then bullet the food menu, the yard games, drinks and even a schedule of tasks for the days before the event.

Eva saves the email and quickly returns to the other screen she has opened. Her fingers rise to her hair, stroking the auburn strands as she reads along. This is the reason she stopped lightening it. She needs to see its real color, to recognize herself and, okay, maybe her mother in her reflection. All her life she's wondered and looked for her, being quietly alert and open to possibilities of her true identity. Since she couldn't find her birth mother anywhere else, maybe she has to look no further than her own face. Women say that spark of recognition jolts them when they recognize their mother in their reflection. Who will she see when her features take their natural form? Whose eyes are hers? She desperately wants to see her mother in the mirror. And on the computer screen, each trait belongs to a different adoptee on the very same search.

I have light freckles and green eyes or
Birth Name Baby Girl Deborah or
My grandparents wear eyeglasses or
Adopted one month after birth.

The words look like small stars, lost in a vast sky moving through cyberspace. They have so little—in some cases, only their date of birth.

She clicks on the link to the Registration Form. Surprisingly, this one is pretty straightforward. Matt says she isn't fully with him and their daughter Taylor when she starts up with her searching. So she just takes a look, scrolling down and returning to the top. Then, taking a deep breath, she looks more and reads the instructions advising the adoptees to fill in any and all information they have. The words are kind, advising that it is okay if they are missing details. She finds her birth year in the drop-down menu.

Most prompts are easy to answer.

You are the? Adoptee.

Searching for? Birthparents.

Your date of birth? February 11

Other prompts she can't know the answer to. Birthparents' Names, Hospital. She checks her watch and glances out the window at the night. Will Matt really mind if she tests the waters? She doesn't have to tell him if she just dips the paddles and sets her search sailing, like a little rowboat moving through time. She won't let it get to her like before, bringing her down. And what if all her answers come with this one online search? Knowing has to be better than wondering.

The air is calm outside her window and the distant sound of waves breaking on the beach reaches her, as it often does on still nights like this. She glances at Lauren's rowboat painting, picturing the old boat bobbing in the gentle waves.

And quietly, so quietly, she begins to type.

five

EVA REACHES FOR THE PENDANT Maris wears. The etched star hangs on a braided gold chain and has a way of catching the light. Maris' name is inscribed in cursive on the back. "You still have this? I remember you wearing it back in high school."

"I've never really stopped wearing it. It came in the mail a few years after my mother died," Maris says, biting into the last of a devilled egg and wiping her hands on a paper napkin. "It's from her sister in Italy. She actually moved there after studying abroad in college."

"Is she still there?"

"I don't know. I used to ask my dad, but some bad blood came between them after Mom died and he wouldn't talk. I'm surprised he even gave me the necklace. There was a letter with it, telling me sweet things like how my mom loved to walk on the beach in the evening."

"So that's where you get it from."

"Maybe. I guess she and Mom were really close and she hoped when I looked at the stars over Long Island Sound, I'd think of my mother looking at the stars, and of her too, across the Atlantic. It would be nice to talk to her, but whenever I Google her, I can't find anything."

"Sometimes I wish Taylor had a sister, someone to be close to. If I ever had another baby, they'd be so far apart in age now."

"Age doesn't matter. If you're in that sister club, nothing can come between you. Not even the Atlantic Ocean. Or time."

"I suppose I could have a sister and not even know about it."

"What?"

Eva walks over to the stove and lowers the flame beneath the corn on the cob to a simmer. "Want to know a secret?"

Maris reaches out her hooked pinkie and catches Eva's, remembering the time Eva made her *Promise, promise, pinkie swear* not to tell anyone their first secret, that Theresa and Ned had adopted her. The salt water spun their tubes languidly that long-ago afternoon and when they drifted too far apart, their arms would reach for the other, pulling back close again while imagining the royalty, or celebrities, who might be Eva's birth family.

Eva glances out the window at Matt and Kyle setting up the grill for barbecuing. Maris moves beside her and sees Taylor and Lauren busy at the badminton net with Lauren's kids. "What's up?" Maris asks quietly.

Eva looks to Maris then. "Follow me," she says, leading her to the office in the front room, locking the door behind them and sitting at the desk.

Maris had snagged another devilled egg off the kitchen table and now watches over Eva's shoulder while her fingers fly over the keyboard. Lines of text scroll down the computer screen. Finally, Eva pushes her chair back. "There I am."

Maris finishes the egg and reads the highlighted lines.

I was nearly one year old at adoption. Adopted family relocated from Mystic Connecticut to Stony Point Connecticut. I have auburn hair. Eva is searching.

"You're looking for your birth parents again?" Maris asks.

"Just a little, here on this site."

"Have you heard anything?"

Eva shakes her head no. "I only registered a few days ago. Today's actually the first day it's posted online."

"I thought this got you all stressed and you weren't going to search anymore."

"I wasn't. It's kind of because of Taylor that I am. She's a teenager now and I see so much of myself at that age in her. And that whole mother-daughter recognition, well it makes me wonder about my own mother."

"Are you sure about this?"

"Honestly? What I'm sure of is that the wondering never really goes away, and if I don't do something about it, it drives me crazy."

"What does Matt say?"

"He doesn't know yet," Eva says. "And for now, what he doesn't know can't hurt him."

"I'm not so sure about that. Little secrets between friends are one thing, but Matt should know. This is big. What if, like, your *mother* responds?"

"Then that's when I'll tell him."

"Oh, I hate surprises."

Eva turns back to the screen and Maris recognizes the look, the familiar obsession. Over the years, it rose to the surface in the current of Eva's life, significant times when she deeply missed her real mother's presence: Christmases when you want to look up from opening a gift and see your mother's teary eyes; walking down the aisle in a white gown, seeking a glimpse of your mother's assuring smile; a quiet summer evening when all that shapes the day is warmth and a lone robin's song and all you want is to be sitting on a front porch with Mom; times when the phone rings and you just wish to hear that voice. *Heidi is searching.* And *Birthmother was very young.* And *I have red hair and blue eyes.* Her friend's eyes stay glued to the screen on some solitary, enduring hunt. *Private adoption through Catholic charity.* And *Birthmark on my right forearm.*

"Don't you see?" Eva asks as she continues to read. "I belong to this. Here on this site. No one else has as little as we do."

"Wait. Excuse me?"

Eva turns quickly. "What's wrong?"

"We should go," Maris says then, turning to the door. "Your guests are waiting."

"Whoa," Eva answers. "I thought you'd be excited for me."

"I'm not, Eva. I'm sorry, but I'm actually not."

"Why not?"

"Why not?" she asks. Maris opens the office door and grandly sweeps her arm to all the life outside it. They hear Taylor calling for her mother. Fourth of July peals of laughter and voices come in through the open windows of Eva's old beach home as the barbecue gets underway. Thin white curtains fill with a sea breeze. Yellow sunlight pours into the big kitchen and the scent of cooking food hangs in the air.

Maris turns back to Eva. "I never had a mother to speak of. My father just died. I have no family except for some distant aunt somewhere in Europe, and I have no marriage, no children. Seriously, Eva. No one else has as *little* as you do?"

"Maris, wait! That's not what I meant," Eva says as she logs off the site and clears her toolbar history. Then Taylor interrupts to tell them that Matt and Kyle need more hamburger buns to toast, and Jason's sister Paige comes in, asking what she can help carry outside, and Theresa pokes her head in the office, saying they need the serving utensils.

Maris gives Eva a long, piercing look before heading to the kitchen to lift the steaming corn out of the pot.

⌒〰

What are photographs, really? The merest memories we put corners on and paste into an album, one whose pages we slowly turn and brush a finger across in wistful moods. We are driven to hold some memories in permanence, but isn't that like trying to pin down a spirit? To trap some ethereal feeling that has a way of slipping by, just out of reach, ever elusive? That's what Lauren thinks by the day's end, with Eva's camera still clicking. Eva had photographed the whole reunion barbecue, from the grilling to the badminton to everyone eating at the picnic table. Not a moment missed that roving lens. Her camera seemed to be mining their histories in search of friendships from nearly twenty years ago when every summer day was spent together hanging on the beach under the sunny sky, every night on the boardwalk beneath the stars. Lauren doesn't need a photo album to remind her. Memories are enough. And seeing her friends all day, one took shape, one from another July Fourth. A memory that captured so much, fading little over the years.

"Let's take out your boat," Kyle had said that night, holding a bunch of bottle rockets. The sun had set and the beach was crowded with Fourth of July revelers walking along the high tide line. "Less people in the way."

"It's too small for all of us," Jason answered. "We'll never fit."

"And the gas tank's empty," Neil added, picking up a flat stone and skimming it out over the dark water. His jeans were cuffed and he waded in the shallows.

"We'll take another one then." Kyle turned to face them, walking backward in the dark, the waves breaking at his feet.

"What. Like steal one?" Eva asked, her thumb linked through Matt's belt loop as they lagged behind.

"More like borrow one," Kyle suggested. "You know."

"Right," Maris said, bending to pick up a small conch shell from the high tide line. "Because if we're returning it, it's not stealing?"

They all quieted then, but somehow their ambling at the water's edge shifted up toward the boardwalk and the boat basin behind it, filled with moored, idled boats.

Lauren hung back, unsure about liking the subtle shift happening, the change beneath the surface of the night. "You guys are crazy. We'll get arrested if we get caught."

Neil turned to her, smiling in the moonlight. "Get caught?" He shook his head and jogged up to Vinny then, putting an arm around his shoulder. "Hey, Vincenzo. Your old man got any brews around?"

"Let me run back to the cottage and see what's there. He won't know the difference."

"Hurry up," Jason called after him, squinting into the darkness to survey the pleasure craft docked in the marina. They followed the circular walkway around the boats, quietly arguing the possibilities until deciding on a small cabin cruiser docked near the entrance. One by one, while Neil kept watch, they jumped aboard and headed down inside the cabin, calling out to Vinny when he trotted back with a six-pack in a paper bag.

"Shit, you guys." Vinny climbed aboard, tripping on the dockline and nearly falling over until Jason caught his arm. "Do you know whose boat this is?"

"What difference does it make?" Paige asked.

"A ton. It's Lipkin's." Vinny pulled the beer from the bag while watching Kyle hot wire the ignition at the helm. "The Beach Commissioner, guys."

No sooner were the words out of his mouth when the engine kicked on and Neil whooped and took the wheel. He backed the boat out of the slip and very slowly, with the engine quietly chugging, maneuvered through the shadowy marina out into the open water.

"I want to get off," Lauren whispered, watching from the cabin as the empty slip faded away.

"Shit, this is crazy, man," Matt said, snapping open a beer as he left the cabin and sat in an upholstered rear seat with Eva. "Crazy." He took a long swig and passed the can to Eva before joining Jason at the wheel with Kyle and Neil.

Maris and Lauren emerged from the cabin and sat with Eva, sharing another can of beer. Lauren looked out at the Sound, as black as the sky, the only difference being the motion it brought beneath her. She'd never been on the night water and tipped her head back, feeling the rise and sway of the sea, seeing the starlit black sky far above unfurl as vast as the water below. The immensity of it all made her own self seem diminutive and she thought that all the twinkling blackness could swallow her whole.

Paige stepped out from the cabin with a bottle of wine and a few cups. "Lucky us, the fridge is well stocked."

"Par-tay!" Eva called out, holding her beer up in a toast to the holiday night as Paige opened the wine and poured herself a cup.

"Cheers, girls!" Paige tipped her cup to their beer. "To another amazing summer together. Bottoms up."

Lauren poured herself a cup of wine, glancing at Neil as he carefully steered the boat out to the open water, headed toward the Gull Island lighthouse. Feeling the boat rise and fall over the Sound's surface, without actually seeing the water as it blended with darkness, unnerved her. The murky sea slapped against the side of the boat, their voices were quiet. Kyle was on the bow of the boat with Vinny, the two of them plotting something together. "I don't like this, Maris. Don't you think we should go back?"

"Let me see what the guys are up to." Maris went to the helm and Matt moved over to let her have a look. When he did, he caught Eva's eye behind him and motioned for her to follow him into the cabin.

"All right," Eva whispered. "A little bit of heaven down below." She took her beer and disappeared into the cabin with Matt.

"Whoa," Lauren said. "This is getting out of control now." When Neil told Maris to take the wheel, Lauren reached for the wine to refill her cup. "My parents will kill me if they find out about this. If I don't get lit, I swear I'll have a panic attack."

"Wait," Paige said, pulling the bottle back, spilling some of the wine as she topped off her glass. "Me, first."

"You ever steer one of these before?" Neil asked Maris. Jason reached past her and turned the wheel, adjusting the boat's direction.

45

"No!" Maris answered. "Is this safe? I can barely see where I'm heading."

"Just take it real easy, no sudden turns. Move the wheel in the direction you want to go, and keep it smooth." From behind, Jason steered with her. "Let's head her toward the beach." He pulled back on the throttle as they began to turn parallel to the shoreline. Together they navigated the vessel to a spot just beyond the big rock that vacationers liked to swim out to.

"Easy does it," Neil said. "Slow her way down now." He turned back to Lauren. "You want a turn at the wheel?"

"Shit, no," Lauren answered, downing her wine and standing to look out behind them at the sea. The sky above was heavy with thousands of tiny stars and a nearly full moon painting a swath of amber light across the water.

Once the boat stopped, Neil threw the anchor over and nodded to Kyle, who kicked off his sandals and dove right in.

Lauren yelled out, racing up to the bow, then carefully walking alongside the cabin, holding onto the rails and following along as Kyle swam. "What the heck are you doing?"

Kyle headed for the rocky outcropping, then called out for Neil to throw over the bottle rockets. "Fireworks, Ell. On the water. Just for you."

"Let's get this show started," Vinny said from the bow. He peeled off his shirt and dove in too, making his way over to Kyle with an empty bottle to set the rockets in. They lit off three, one by one, streaming them high into the night sky.

Floating on Long Island Sound this summer night, and floating in time, Lauren thought it's all the same somehow. Both give a sense of unseen motion moving them along together. The rockets' reflection illuminated the still water beneath the anchored boat, doubling the red, green and gold sparkles until they were surrounded by trails of color wavering in the sky and sea.

"Hey!" A voice rang out at the same time a spotlight beam caught them in its path. "You kids, what are you up to over there?"

"Shit," Kyle said, jumping off the rock into the water as Vinny lit another rocket. "Let's get out of here, man," he called out as he swam back to the boat. The smaller boat with the light approached theirs so quickly that Kyle barely made it aboard before Neil took the helm, opened up the throttle and ripped through the open water.

"Hey man, Vincenzo's not back!" Kyle called to Jason.

They all turned to see Vinny treading water in the dark. "What's going on?" Matt asked as he climbed out of the cabin, Eva trailing behind wearing his long sleeved denim shirt over her tank top and shorts.

Matt and Jason leaned over the side of the boat watching Vinny, while Kyle, dripping seawater all over the deck, walked closer to Neil. "Quit horsing around and go back," he said.

"And get busted?" Instead Neil tossed Kyle a life ring. "Throw it to him!"

"What? You're crazy! He's in the water!"

Neil steered the boat a little closer to Vinny. "Throw it, Kyle. Now!"

As Kyle flung the life ring, Neil turned the boat away and expertly gunned it, slicing through the water faster than the small boat in pursuit, quickly losing it behind them.

Lauren looked at Paige when she began laughing on the bow of the boat. "You think this is funny?" she asked.

Paige's laughter grew until she doubled over with it, then

leaned over the side rails with a groan. "Oh, I'm not feeling too good now."

"I *knew* this would happen with all that wine. What a mess." Lauren looked from her to Matt and Jason sitting on the rear seats, snapping open cold beers and leaning back without a worry. "And what's wrong with you guys?" Lauren asked. "Vinny will drown out there."

"Someone had to be sacrificed," Jason answered in the dark, looking out in the direction of Vinny.

"Neil!" Lauren called. "Go back!"

Kyle took over the helm and Neil headed to the cabin, emerging in a minute with two shot glasses and a pint of tequila. He poured a shot for Lauren. "Here. Drink this. You'll stop worrying fast."

"You're kidding, right? I mean, Paige is sick, and what about Vinny? If he drowns, I swear, Neil." She took the shot glass from him, ready to toss it overboard.

"Hey, it's all right. Vinny's the friggin' captain of his swim team. He's just at the rock and can make it to shore in five minutes, no problem. Relax." He touched his glass to Lauren's and downed his shot, holding her gaze until she did the same. "Cheers," Neil mouthed, raising his hand to her hair, tangling his fingers in it for a long moment before turning back to the helm.

"Shit," Lauren said under her breath, touching her hair where Neil had before turning to see Matt and Jason sitting side by side at ease, watching her fret. They looked from her, to each other, before tipping their cans together in some toast of collusion.

Nearly two decades later, moments, expressions, phrases of that epic July Fourth night take shape in her mind like images under the wash of a chemical developer. Lauren puts away the ketchup and mustard and wipes down the kitchen countertops with Eva still taking pictures of everyone. If they had snapped photos that long-ago night, would they see a hint of what was to come? Of her and Kyle sitting at either end of the picnic table, miles apart? Of Matt formally shaking Vinny's hand when Vinny arrived today with Paige and their kids? Would there be a premonition of the group photo caught in a gaping silence mid-conversation with no one really meeting the other's eye? Can they ever go back? Can they ever be who they were to one another on a different July Fourth? Now one of their circle is dead; another unemployed; still another missing a leg; while Eva is still missing a mother, ever seeking some connection she longs for from behind that camera of hers, every click a search.

"Well, well. Look who's finally arrived," Maris says while washing a few serving pieces in the kitchen sink. "I wondered if he'd show up today."

Lauren looks over Maris' shoulder out the window to see Jason sitting at the picnic table beside Matt. His dark hair is still damp from a shower as he talks to Kyle across from him. She lets out a low whistle. "My oh my. Looks just like his brother. Those Barlow boys were always so easy to look at." Eva and Maris turn to her in a stony silence, with Eva giving her a flick of a dishtowel. "What. I can look, can't I?"

"No, you cannot," Maris insists. "You know, I haven't seen you guys in years, and I noticed that you and Kyle seemed tense today, Lauren. I hate to think you're having issues, so maybe you should think about your husband, who, for your information, isn't too hard on the eyes either." Maris takes her by the shoulders. "Keep your focus. And sheesh, eat something, would you? You're skin and bones."

49

"Yeah, yeah." Lauren, wiping a pot dry, walks over to the back door and looks out as Jason opens a beer and toasts it to Matt's. And there it is in that one moment, that one snapshot, that glimpse of the past filled with all their story. "Remember the time we stole that boat?"

"Huh," Eva answers. "What I remember is spending the rest of the summer sweating it out sanding and painting fresh whitewash on the boardwalk after we got caught."

"Oh man," Maris says. "And wasn't it the hottest summer ever?"

"Vinny had the last laugh, didn't he?" Lauren asks. "The only one not on the boat when we got busted. He got off free as a bird."

And somehow, Lauren knows. There'll be something of their friendship in those photographs Eva will surely post on Facebook. Some reminder will be caught in a flash, some memory of a seventeen-year-old Maris in her tie-dye jeans, mid-leap jumping onto that cabin cruiser. There will be dripping Kyle looking back at Vinny in the dark water. Lauren holding Paige's long hair as she got sick over the boat's side. Neil uttering *Shit* when they pulled back into the marina to find Lipkin and the police waiting there. And Kyle taking her hand, helping her off the boat, then not letting go all night that summer they began dating. Oh there will be a photo album of memories, of spirits, in the July Fourth moments Eva caught today, if they look hard enough beyond everything else that has happened since.

six

STARS EMERGE FROM THE BLACK cocoon of night far over Long Island Sound. Vacationers walk past on the boardwalk, and on the beach the last of Kyle's bottle rockets blow into the sky. He runs backward a few steps, unsure of its wavering course, until it whistles into multicolored oblivion over the dark waters.

"Show's over, folks," Matt says when he and Kyle return to the others sitting together on the boardwalk. Matt sits beside Eva, slipping his arm around her shoulder. "This is just like old times."

"Not really. Twenty years ago," Kyle says, running his hand back through his hair, "we'd be headed to Foley's right about now."

"Instead we're all ready to go to sleep," Vinny answers. He leans forward, elbows on his knees. A glow-in-the-dark Frisbee he found on the beach hangs loosely from his fingertips.

Paige stands and looks at them all sitting there, the boats in the marina behind them shining in the moonlight. "Well come on people. What are you, a bunch of duds? I've got some rock and roll left in me. How about a drink or

51

something? A beach toast on the boardwalk? Hm?" Her gaze moves across their faces. "Like a summertime Auld Lang Syne? For old acquaintances, guys."

"I'm game," Maris says, punching the air. It's what she and Eva had hoped for, connecting somehow with everyone again. Jason sits beside her and she gives his shoulder a nudge. "What about you?"

He looks first at her, then past her at everyone else. "Shit, let's do this then."

"Where do you keep the good stuff, Eva?" Paige asks. "I'll go back and get it."

"Plastic cups are in the cabinet over the fridge, and there's a bottle of wine right on the kitchen counter. You can't miss it."

"I'll help," Lauren says. "I want to check on the kids, anyway."

"Use the canvas tote on the porch," Eva tells them. "Put everything into that."

Kyle stands and steps onto the sand, watching them go. He kicks off his sneakers and heads down toward the water.

"Hey," Vinny calls out, standing on the boardwalk. "Heads-up." He flings the Frisbee to Kyle, who barely catches it flying over his head. Vinny runs onto the sand and Kyle throws the Frisbee back to him. On the night beach, it softly glows between them.

Maris watches for a moment, then slips out of her sandals. She joins Kyle and Vinny and when she does, the others follow. A few groans and stretches come as they jockey for position in a circle on the beach. The Frisbee wobbles and does a few dives and loops.

"Hey, Officer," Vinny calls out. Matt leaps and makes the catch, immediately turning around and spinning the glowing Frisbee to Jason. He catches it easily and considers

Vinny waving his long arms wildly for it before sending it in his direction.

Vinny dives, landing in the sand. "Damn. Good throw." He stands, sweeps the sand from his shirt and eyes the group. He squints into the night, takes aim at Kyle, then flies the Frisbee to Eva. "Ha! Faked you out, Kyle," he yells.

When Eva spins it over all their heads, Vinny and Kyle chase it until Vinny lunges and hits it out of the air, whooping and falling on top of it.

"You're a maniac, Vincenzo," Kyle says, retreating back to his space in the circle.

"What's that, sour grapes?" Vinny stands and gives it all he has, whistling the Frisbee over Kyle's head. Kyle goes for it but stumbles over his own feet so that the Frisbee heads for the water, directly between Maris and Jason. They both run for it.

"Look out!" Vinny covers his eyes and sinks to his knees.

Maris calls "I got it!" just as Jason yells "It's mine!" right when they trip on each other and fall hard. Maris turns on her back, lying flat on the beach and laughing as Jason pulls an arm from beneath her.

"I got it," Jason tells her, catching his breath and laughing at the same time.

"You cheated." Maris looks over at him, grinning. Her clip has come loose from her hair, which now fans out in the sand.

"Cheated? How?" He brushes a strand of hair from across her forehead, his face close to hers in the dark.

"You tripped me," she insists.

"I did not."

"Did too."

"So are you all right?"

She squints at him in the darkness. The touch of his fingertips lingers on her forehead, but she had felt the prosthesis against her leg during their tumble, too.

"Are *you* okay?" she asks in all seriousness now.

"Barely." He sits up and wraps his arms around his knees, the Frisbee hanging from his fingers.

"Well," she says, her grin returning. "Serves you right." She sits up beside him then, still winded. "I haven't had this kind of fun in years."

"What's going on over there? We playing Tag now?" Vinny calls out.

Jason stands and brushes himself off. "Matt, catch! You're it." Jason whizzes the Frisbee to Matt and Eva moving away from the boardwalk, away from the friends, effectively ending the game. Matt and Eva run after it and don't return.

Kyle looks back to the boardwalk, then sits in the sand near the water. "I was watching The Weather Channel," he says, his voice steady in the dark. "They predict a hot summer on the East coast. It's something to do with the waters in the Florida Gulf being warm this year, and that warmth will move north. Kind of like El Niño, but it's not. El Niño is in the Pacific region and they referred more to the Gulf."

"Some people say a warm summer means an active hurricane season," Jason says.

"I read somewhere that scientists can track El Niño by studying tree rings. Depending on the tree's location, they find evidence of El Niño in ring patterns that mean a rainier or drier season than normal."

Jason sits beside Maris on the sand. "He'll talk about anything but his life," he says under his breath.

Maris looks over at Kyle explaining weather patterns.

Everyone saw the way Lauren kept her distance from him today, and the way Kyle watched her, their words tense. He goes on now about the details of the weather phenomenon, with no sign of Lauren returning to the beach.

Jason presses his fingers against his eyes before sliding them down his face and behind his neck as he drops his head.

"Hey," Maris asks. "You okay?"

He looks out over the Sound. "Yeah, thanks," he says. "I had a nice night."

She looks to see what he is watching over the water. The moon throws a golden path across the Sound and in its light, a tugboat moves across the horizon. Lighthouse beams flash on opposite shores and the waves retreat with the outgoing tide. She jumps a little when he reaches over and presses his hand over hers before withdrawing back to himself. All the while, his eyes never leave Long Island Sound, as though he's boarded a distant ship taking him somewhere far away from Stony Point.

~

Farther down the beach, a few boats are moored just beyond the swimming area, their cabins glowing with yellow light. Beyond the boats, the lighthouse at Gull Island faintly beckons. An occasional faraway call of a foghorn moves through the night.

"We really can't go back, can we?" Eva asks as they walk at the water's edge. Something about the very act of doing that, walking at the edge of the sea, always stirs her questions. "Once we've left a place, or a time, it's gone, isn't it? It's just a memory."

"Maybe we didn't really want to go back to that time."

"Not even for a day? It seems sad not to." She stops near the end of the beach and sits in the sand. The shadows of the patch of woods reach beside her.

Matt sits with her. "Sad? If we have good memories, at least we have that."

Eva considers what Maris told her about having so little. But sometimes happiness is simply all about the memories. And Maris comes from a home of memories where she at least knew her family; she knows that love existed, even though her mother's love was cut short. But still, it happened, that love. She has the memory.

Matt stands and takes her hand, walking back near the lagoon grasses.

"Matt? What are you doing?"

"Time travelling." He leads her to long shadows on the beach where no one will pass.

"We can't do this," Eva says, resisting a little, knowing exactly which memory he wants to travel to. "Come on, we're not kids anymore, Matt."

"I've got a pretty good memory of being a kid, though." The lagoon grasses whisper behind them, the waves break and the shadow of the forest hides them. Matt tangles his fingers through her hair and kisses her once, twice, then again. His hands move to her face and she feels his lips touch her eyes, her cheeks, her throat.

The black sky spreads over them, stars twinkling. It is amazing how the sadness, the longing, always leaves when she turns to him like this. Under the cover of a summer night, she takes the teenaged memory of love he offers. At that moment, she no longer cares where or who she really is, wanting only to lie in the sand and feel each soft grain against her skin, feel the damp sea air, the heat of the July night, feel everything physical, nothing emotional, every pore of her skin covered by Matt and the beach and summer. All that matters is the sensation.

~

Maris opens the door to the telephone ringing in the kitchen.

"Where have you been?"

"Scott?"

"I've been calling all day. Your cell, the cottage. Haven't you been home at all?"

"It's the Fourth of July. I was at Eva's barbecue."

"This late?"

Scott would never understand hanging out on the beach, walking on the boardwalk, the spontaneous game of Frisbee. He's lived in the city all his life. "It's such a beautiful night here, we took a walk on the beach. That's all."

He exhales a long breath. "I'm sorry, Maris. I've just been trying to reach you all day and I worried when it got late."

His worry isn't about a cookout or her being out all day. It is that she hasn't given him an answer, hasn't told him how beautiful the ring looks and that she can't stop showing it off. Oh, she knows exactly where his worry stems from—that one velvet box sitting on her dresser.

"Well, I'm fine," she says. "Really."

"Good then. Okay." A second passes. "So how was the cookout?"

Maris sits on a wicker stool at the breakfast counter. She reaches up and opens a white shutter over the window. The evening sky fills her view. "Eva invited some old friends. We all grew up together here and it was nice to see everyone again."

"Anyone I should be concerned about?"

"What? No, Scott. Just old friends with lots of catching up to do. It's been twelve years since I've been here."

"And almost a month since you've been here. I'm going crazy missing you. You'll be ready to leave next Friday, right?"

Her car will be tuned up for the drive, this rented cottage will be closed up, Matt and Eva will help her ship the packed boxes she kept from her father's estate and will temporarily take in Madison. "I will." It is Thursday night. She has seven days left. Seven days of tending flower boxes brimming with red geraniums and snow white petunias. Of throwing windows open to sea breezes and walking her dog along the high tide line. Of finishing Eva's redecorating. Of sitting in a sand chair, sketch pad and pastels beside her.

"I made my airline reservation. You'll be busy packing, so I'll get a ride to your cottage from the airport, okay? Then we'll drive back together. Take my flight number down."

Maris opens a drawer for a piece of paper and bumps into the dog. "Let me call you back, Scott. I can't find a pen and Madison has to go out. She's been inside all day."

"I still can't believe you got a dog."

"I didn't get a dog. She was my father's. What else could I do? Abandon her?"

"No, but a dog won't really work here. I thought your friends found a home for her."

"They're working on it." She finds a pen in the third drawer and takes down the flight details. A dog won't work. A garden won't work. The touch of plants and cool dirt won't work. Designing on the porch to the sound of breaking waves won't work. There.

Here, her sketch pad overflows with new denim designs, all inspired by the sea, the cottage. Maybe she can have a potted garden on her townhouse balcony, a place where she can draw outdoors and feel the sun warm on her back. Madison sits in front of her, ears erect, eyes happy. When she hangs up with Scott, the dog follows her to the porch, dancing in place as Maris reaches for the leather leash hanging on a hook before deciding that she doesn't need it at this hour.

Paige and Lauren never returned with the wine earlier. Wine or not, friends or not, all Lauren wanted to do was go home. But walking the beach road, Maris wishes she had that wine now to loosen Scott's tension knotting her shoulders.

Along the beach, the Sound's waves roll onto the shore. From the boardwalk, the sky, heavy with stars, subdues her. She remembers her mother's long-ago touch. Or maybe she only remembers the video of it, lighting on her hair. But the thought of her mother lifting and stroking salty strands of her hair seems so real. The closeness of it has her reaching for her gold pendant as she looks out at the water.

Madison runs down the beach along the high tide line in search of driftwood. Maris follows, walking barefoot to the water's edge when a figure emerges from the shadows on the beach. She knows by his gait that it is Jason.

"It's not safe to be out alone at this hour," he says as he nears her. He had put on a black sweatshirt over his tee.

"I've got my dog for protection."

"What, this beast?" Madison trots behind him, tail swinging, her face filled with anticipation as she waits for him to toss the driftwood. "Madison, right?"

"And you have just discovered the key to her heart."

Jason tosses the driftwood up the dark beach toward the boardwalk. "She's a beautiful dog." He stands beside Maris and they watch the German shepherd lope after the driftwood. "Come on, I'll walk you home. Unless you wanted to walk on the beach still?"

So he understands walks on the beach. And salt air therapy, curing what ails you. And lingering at the water's edge listening for voices in the breeze. He even understands random games of Frisbee. "That's okay, I'm ready to go." She falls in step with him.

"Eva and Matt went all out today," Jason says.

"They did. It was so good to see everyone. Too bad about Kyle and Lauren though. They hit a rough patch."

"The economy's not helping them. It sucks he's laid off again."

Maris notices his gait and wonders if he needs to rest. "Is your leg okay, Jason? Do you want to sit for a while?"

"It's better if I keep moving actually."

A distant train whistle floats through the night. As they step onto the beach road, Madison catches up and walks beside Jason. Her nails click on the pavement and she holds her head high, driftwood clamped in her jaw.

"She'll carry that all the way home," Maris says.

Jason laughs. "She's all right. Loves the beach just like the rest of us. Have you had her long?"

"She was my father's dog. Eva and Matt are trying to find a home for her before I head back to Chicago."

"You'll miss her," he says after a moment. "When are you leaving?"

They near her rented cottage. Not one detail, made softer by the light of evening and the thought of leaving, escapes Maris' notice. Dim lamplight casts a glow on knotty pine paneling inside. On a porch table, pale lavender heather spills from a blue vase, the color of the morning Sound. The outside lamppost illuminates the stone walkway, shadowed with large pots of geraniums. "Next week. I'll be driving back on Friday."

The dog trots to the side of the cottage where she sets the driftwood down before returning to Jason's side. He reaches down and strokes her head. "You're a good dog, Maddy."

Maris opens the porch door and lets the dog in ahead of her. "I hope I'll see you before I leave?"

Jason watches her for a second. "You bet. Have a good night now."

She goes inside and turns off the porch light, walking around the dog still standing at the front door watching Jason walk away.

seven

S TOP THE PRESSES," MARIS TELLS her assistant.

"What?" Lily asks. "But the fabric samples just arrived. And the trade shows are in a couple weeks."

"I know. And I'm still going." At Saybrooks, initial design to final production happens over eighteen months. So she is shy a few months and will have to sweat this one out. Her team will need to pull a few all-nighters to meet the deadline. "But I'm trashing the fall line and starting fresh."

"Maris, wait. After we've already cut the patterns?"

Maris turns and looks into the living room. Sketches cover every surface. A zip-front jacquard denim jacket with notched sleeves and a collar turned up against a sea breeze. An ocean-blue colored cardigan with marled yarns. Bootcut jeans, the bell embellished with appliquéd leaves the color of sand touched by a sunset. A chenille jacket with princess seams and high lapels, the chenille color reminiscent of autumn's beach hydrangeas, purples and blues fading to brown. A midnight-blue denim vest, detailed with time-lapsed shooting stars.

She couldn't stop earlier this morning. Ideas flowed like

the tide, never-ending. Her sketches are textured with pastels, highlighted with gel pens, detailed with ink, beach colors blended with watercolors.

"Lily, don't worry," she says into her cell. "I'm taking full responsibility for this. Just go ahead and scrap all the designs for the fall line. All of them."

"But the trend reports. The way we analyzed them, I thought we nailed the next look."

"Oh I did now. Believe me. When I finish the basic conceptual development, I'll get it to you right away. It's got a new campaign name, too. Blue Jeans and Coffee Beans."

One of the tenets of design is that it blends reality and illustrations. The aim of a designer is always to give the illusion of reality. To capture moments in time with each sketch, rather than posing figures. Everyone from the marketing team to the consumer has to see the fashion fitting into their lives.

She disconnects the call, takes off Scott's diamond and sets it on the counter, then returns to her epic design madness filling the cottage. Funny how since she moved one step closer to commitment with Scott, she finds herself halfway across the country from him. She's put on the diamond ring three times already today, taking it off after only minutes each time. Nothing seems to make that ring a permanent reality in her own mind.

And yet, in the sketches spilling off the end tables, lined along the couch cushions, propped against the wall and leaning on the fireplace mantel, she sees clearly the day, the moments her artwork captures. The reality that she can't seem to get enough of. The sketched figures of her new fall line sit on a penciled boardwalk, toss driftwood down a long watercolored beach, skim stones over the pastelled

Sound, catch Frisbees mid-air, ink strokes freezing the moment, and walk along the high tide line, sipping coffee side by side with old friends.

~

Jason hasn't come this close to calling his doctor in more than a year. Nothing seems to be working today. He wonders if he's developed an infection and feels his neck for fever. Maybe a virus is settling in. He took a walk. He wrapped his leg in a warm, soft towel. He removed the prosthesis and prosthetic sock, thinking maybe a nerve was being pinched, then put them back on a while later. Still the phantom pain hangs on. The last time it hurt like this, his doctor's shot of morphine was all that worked.

But he's trained himself since then and put those lessons to use now. First, distraction.

Scraping the trim around the barn door helps at first, but standing in one position only increases the pain. So he moves inside the barn and takes down old rusted tools hanging on one of the pegboards beneath the big stuffed moose head. If this is going to work, if the barn can be renovated into his architectural studio so he can stop working out of his condominium, the debris has to be cleaned out. A rickety lobster trap sits on the floor below the pegboard and he moves it to his workbench.

"Jason?"

"Yeah." He leans his left arm on the lobster trap to pry open the jammed latch and the entire trap, dried out and fragile, caves in on itself. A thin nail slices his palm as the wood gives out. He gives his hand a shake.

Paige walks into the barn. "Wow. This definitely has potential." Her gaze moves over the walls, the cluttered workbenches and dusty wooden shelves covered with masonry tools. "What do you suppose Dad did with this?" She touches a strung rope with clothespins randomly clipped on it.

"I don't know." Jason presses his palms together to stem the bleeding. One way to stop pain is to introduce a new one. "Maybe he hung his work gloves there when they got wet with mortar."

"Huh." She flicks a clothespin with her fingers. "Hey. The kids loved sleeping here last night. We all did." Paige turns to him. "Are you coming down to the beach with us?"

He shakes his head.

"Why not? It'll do you good to get some sun."

He holds out his hand, the red gash already swelling. "I've got to take care of this."

She takes his hand in hers. "How'd you do that?"

"Screwing around with a lobster trap."

"You should go to the emergency clinic. It might need a couple of stitches."

"Maybe." He pulls his hand back and shakes out the sting again.

"Do you want Vinny to drive you?"

"No, I'll be fine. I've got to stop back at my condo anyway. I'm backlogged with work." He looks around the barn. "This old place is slowing me down."

"Why don't you hire someone to clean it out? They have companies that haul all this away."

"No. It's Dad's stuff. I'm going through it myself." He points to the wall shelves that he's already cleaned and given a fresh coat of wax; Paige walks over to them, running her hand across the wood. "A small dumpster's coming next week," he adds. "I need somewhere to throw the trash."

"Well that'll help." She turns back to him. "We're leaving before dinner, grabbing a bite to eat on the way home. Will you be back here later?"

"Not today."

"Oh. Okay then." She walks the vast barn space. "Eva and Matt had a nice cookout yesterday. It was good seeing the whole gang. Maris, Kyle. You know."

"Neil should have been there, too."

"Don't start blaming yourself again." She stares at him for a long moment. "Is that what this is all about?"

"All what is about?"

"This." She motions in a wide circle to the space around them. "Hiding out here in the barn."

"I'm working."

"No you're not. You're stewing."

Jason looks at his hand, then back to his sister. "More of it came back to me yesterday."

She sits in a wooden chair. "After all this time? What'd you see?"

Paige's words seem lost in the barn, in the vast space of memories and echoes and images that fill it if he turns a certain way, or when the lighting shines low at the day's end. When he hears Neil's voice talking up some renovation plan using the white sand as the cottage canvas, the colors of the harbor boats brought in with paints, starfish cutouts in the eaves and an elevation looking out to sea.

"The reflection," he says. "In the rearview mirror. Now I can't get it out of my head."

"That means something, when the memory comes back. Doesn't it?"

"It means being back at this cottage is a mistake. I was doing fine until I decided to move the business here." He looks up at the old rafters. "This is all a mistake."

"Can't they give you something to speed your memory?"

"No. I've got to do it myself."

"But if you're under a doctor's care," she persists. "Or therapy maybe."

"Damn it, Paige." Jason sweeps the old lobster trap onto the floor. "Just leave it alone already."

"Okay. Okay, I get the message." She holds up an open hand and backs away. "Well it was fun spending the holiday here, and we'll be back in a couple weeks. I'll have the kids stop in to say goodbye. Try to be nice to them, would you please? You're their uncle."

"Yeah." He looks down at his hand, then reaches for a clean rag from a worktable, pressing it against the gash. If only it were that easy. Bandage it and let it heal. Medication, alcohol, exercise, time. They are all bullshit bandages. He's tried them all, and yet when he walked on the beach alone late last night, he'd heard it in the waves. It sounded far away, just like then, that engine opened all the way, a ton of metal bearing down on them from a distance. He's never forgotten that sound. But last night, a flash of the *image* finally returned when Kyle's voice talking about the weather became Neil's voice behind him on the bike. Memory triggers, his doctor calls them. Moments. Moments that bring it all back.

He kicks the broken lobster trap aside, his leg feeling better now. The same way one pain displaces another, one thought does the same thing. He turns to go inside and wash out the stinging cut on his hand, knowing that it was Maris Carrington beside him on the beach who had displaced the vision of the accident last night.

eight

ON A HOT JULY SATURDAY, all Lauren thinks about
is painting driftwood on the beach, while all she actually
does is take summer inventory at Bayside Department
Store. But it is a temporary job from the employment
agency, and at least it brings in a paycheck. The store is
closed to shoppers while the help tickets and inventories
the summer merchandise. She uses idle time to collect
empty cartons from the storage room. They are perfect for
vacation packing, and she thinks she just might toss her
paints in one.

At noontime, she settles in her car and directs the air
conditioning vent at her face. The store isn't far from
home, and it's easy to add ten minutes to her lunch hour
without much notice to drop off the boxes. Driving down
her street, the house looks deserted with no bicycles in the
driveway, no kids drawing chalk games on the sidewalk.
The drapes are drawn against the sun's rays and the grass
wilts beneath the heat. She lifts the cartons from her trunk
and sets them in the garage, keeping them out of the oil
that leaked from Kyle's pickup truck. After neatly stacking
the boxes along the back wall, there's enough time to make

a quick sandwich for lunch. When she opens the garage door into the kitchen, Kyle is coming in through the front door carrying a mixed bouquet wrapped in cellophane.

"Hey, Ell. These are for you."

Lauren leans against the closed door to the garage. "For what?"

"It's a celebration. We'll take the kids out for burgers tonight. They'll love it." He reaches for a glass vase from the cabinet beside the refrigerator and fills it with water.

"Mom's got the kids and I'm working till six, so she's feeding them dinner." She still leans on the door, not moving in the heat. "What are we celebrating anyway?" Watching Kyle, she thinks that even if he finds a permanent job, it might not help them at this point.

"Sit down." Kyle slides out a kitchen chair and Lauren sits while he peels off the plastic and sets the flowers into the vase. "Listen to this," he says as he arranges the flowers. "Jerry's going away for a couple weeks. To Maine."

"Maine."

"His son lives there. Somewhere on the coast. Jerry and his wife are taking a two-week vacation there. And before he goes, he's taking a few days to finish up some chores around his house. Painting his porch, that kind of thing." Kyle swings a chair around and sits backward, his hands clasped over the top.

"So?"

Kyle stares at her.

"What?" she asks, hands turned up.

"Come on, think about it. He's leaving me in charge of The Dockside for almost three weeks. He was never comfortable leaving the diner before and always closed up on vacation. But he wants me to handle it. I'll be running the whole show."

Possibilities run through Lauren's mind: of Kyle turning this stint into another management job, of the money Jerry will pay him. She relents and goes to the refrigerator, pulling out the bottle of wine. Kyle stretches behind him and grabs two juice glasses from the counter. She fills them, feeling him watching as she pours herself only enough for a toast.

"More money?" she asks.

"Of course."

"Well congratulations then. It's nice to have good news for a change." They touch glasses and drink the wine.

Lauren tries not to, but still, in the back of her mind, she waits for the bomb to fall. For the refrigerator to break. For the furnace to quit. For the pickup truck to break down. Good news never comes alone into their home. Something always sneaks in on its tail. She looks at the flowers and notices one white daisy has snapped. Its head droops.

"When's Jerry leaving?"

"Next Thursday. I'll start Monday so he can show me around the office."

Her mind calculates that the first two weeks of their vacation, Kyle will be working full days and some nights, what with the food ordering and paperwork. He'll be exhausted. By the third week, he'll be done and want to be with them at the cottage. They'll cross that bridge when they get to it. For now, she plans to go on vacation with or without him. With him for a little while won't be that bad.

Kyle tops off his glass and takes a long swallow. "Listen, Ell." He reaches across the table, taking her hand in his. "I know it's not much, but it's better than nothing. Let's celebrate." He hitches his head toward the staircase, a question on his face.

Lauren reads it. It asks her not to think that he found only three weeks of full-time work. That funds are getting low and he's feeling nervous. Every line, every shadow on his face comes from that worry. But with a glass of wine downed and Kyle's attitude filled with optimism, she could give in.

"Come on," he says. Half standing, Kyle bends over the table and kisses her on the mouth. His hands embrace her neck and lift her hair off her damp skin. She likes that she has no time to think. He just leans over and she can only feel: the warm air in the quiet house, the perspiration beneath her hair, his hands moving down her back, her mouth opening to his. The cicadas buzz outside in the trees and Kyle slips her shirt off her shoulder. As the kiss deepens, he leans closer, knocking over her empty glass so that it rolls off the table, splintering on the floor. Lauren pulls back at the sound.

"Don't stop," Kyle says.

"I can't do this, Kyle." She glances at her watch. "My lunch break's up."

"Who wants to take inventory in this heat? We've got a little time," he says.

Lauren stands and straightens her shirt. It's probably better to move away from him. If he reaches for her again, if he holds her right, she just might stay. It will take a moment, but she can let him persist, let his mouth cover hers, let his hands slip off her clothes. But then he'll think everything turned out all right. He'll think he can stay at the cottage. That they can laugh again. That he can love her all the time. Too much feels wrong for that to happen. She doesn't know what to think anymore. He needs to turn his energy to meeting the mortgage on time, to finding work. Not loving her. She screws the cover back on the wine bottle and returns it to the refrigerator, then starts sweeping up the glass. "Maybe later," she says.

Kyle finishes off his wine, watching her silently. "Forget it."

"Forget what? Money? Bills? Your truck leaking oil all over the driveway? Give me a break, Kyle. There's so much on my mind, and I've got to get back to the store." The marriage won't stop unraveling, like a stray thread on a sweater. When they pick at it, at the thread, whether it is money, or sex, or work, a whole row of stitches unwinds with it.

"I'm out of here." Kyle swings his chair around and topples it over. "I am so gone," he says as he bends and rights the fallen chair. Grabbing his keys from the table, he walks out of the kitchen.

"Where are you going?"

Kyle heads outside to his truck. He starts it and rolls down the window.

"Kyle?" Lauren follows him out into the sunshine, the dustpan still in her hand. "Where are you going?"

"I can't take it here anymore."

"But where are you going?"

"Matt's."

"I'm sorry, Kyle." She sees the way he doesn't want to talk to her. He won't meet her eye when he speaks.

"Right. Matt's got a socket set I'm borrowing to work on my truck."

She stands there, close, just waiting. "It really wasn't a good time. Just now."

"Yeah."

"What about the kids?"

"What about them?" He looks out at the house, then glances at the rearview mirror.

"Are we taking them out later for burgers? Or an ice cream or something?"

Kyle puts the truck in reverse. "You take them," he tells her and leaves her standing in the oil-stained driveway. The tires chirp as he switches gears and takes off. Lauren turns away, locks up the house and goes back to work without lunch.

⁓

"Maybe the valve covers need to be tightened," Matt says as he rolls down the passenger window in Kyle's truck that evening. "Or else the gasket might be bad. You'd have to bring it in then, if it's the gasket."

Leaving Stony Point behind them, Kyle eases the pickup into traffic. "I'm down a quart of oil, too."

"Well, we'll tighten the valve covers, add the oil and see what we can do. Pull in at the gas station there and pick up a quart."

Kyle downshifts and turns into the station at the light. "Need anything else?"

"No. I'm good." Matt spots Jason's SUV across the street when Kyle returns and sets the can of oil on the seat between them.

"Isn't that Barlow's truck over at the bar?"

Kyle shifts into gear and carefully crosses the lanes of traffic to The Sand Bar, parking beside Jason's vehicle. "Let's have a quick one and see what he's up to."

Inside, a lone jukebox stands near the door. Occasionally someone drops in a few coins and plays Jimmy Buffet or a slow Dave Matthews. Booths lining the side wall have high backs, forming deep pockets of privacy. The entrance door is propped open and the hum of passing cars comes in piecemeal with the warm summer air. Someone tuned the television to the evening news, the anchor's voice filling the room like a thin haze of cigarette smoke.

Jason sits at the far end of the bar, wearing jeans and a ratty college tee, looking like he needs a shower and a shave. He nurses a drink while a short woman with red hair makes small talk beside him.

"It's not good to drink alone, man," Matt says from behind Jason, putting his arm around Jason's shoulder. He takes the empty stool just past him.

Jason turns, eyes Matt and Kyle, and nods toward the woman. "I'm not alone."

They turn to her. "He a friend of yours?" Kyle asks.

"He's keeping me company while I wait for my ride. Is it true he's an architect?" she asks.

Matt leans on the bar in front of Jason. "He told you that?"

Jason watches the television, looking only half interested in the talk around him.

The woman turns to Kyle standing beside her, sizing up all six feet two inches of him. "Well? Is he for real?"

"Oh he's the real thing," Matt assures her. "And I'm a Connecticut State Trooper." He watches her check out his worn jeans, docksider shoes with no socks.

"And I'm a chef," Kyle adds. Jason glances up at him.

The woman stands and shakes her head. "I think my ride's here." She lifts her purse to her shoulder. "Nice talking to you, Jason."

"Same here," he tells her. "Take care now."

"That was easy enough." Kyle turns and watches her go. A car idles outside the door. "You really need to find someone more challenging."

Jason motions to the bartender for another drink.

"Make it a pitcher," Matt tells the bartender. "He's

buying. We'll take it over there." He points to the booths. "Come on, guy. Let's grab a seat." Matt reaches for the basket of pretzels. Kyle leans against the bar until Jason stands. They shift in the booth, getting comfortable until the beer arrives with three frosted glasses. Jason lifts the pitcher and pours a round of drinks.

"Why don't you get yourself married?" Matt asks him, pulling a glass close. "What the hell are you doing picking up broads in a bar?"

Jason takes a swallow of his drink. "She was picking me up."

"Well knock it off. Don't you have yourself a nice girl hidden away somewhere?"

"Nope. No one," Jason tells them, taking another taste of the beer.

"Maybe you're better off," Kyle says.

Matt looks at Kyle. "Trouble in paradise?"

"Paradise, like shit." He drags a hand through his hair, then finishes off his drink. "If you call no sex, no money, no fun, paradise."

"Paradise is open to interpretation," Jason answers.

"Not in my house, it isn't." Kyle pours himself another glass. "Something's got to give. It'd help if a job came up before I have to tap into my severance money."

"Watch it, Kyle," Matt says. "It's easy to piss through that money. All of a sudden you'll be wondering where it went."

"A little here, a little there. Next thing you know, nothing's left," Jason adds.

"Moving's not the answer," Matt says. He doesn't like the way Kyle is drinking and slides the pitcher to the other end of the table. "It'll be the same down South. You might get a job and get settled there, lulled into a false security with that overtime cash. But sooner or later there'll be a fucking pink slip with your check. No warning. Contract's up, the sub's built. Only you'll be a thousand miles away from here. It's your line of work. Shipyard welding, pipe-fitting. It's up and down, man."

"Can't you get a job at the casinos?" Jason asks. "They must need chefs in the restaurants there. They're busy."

"I don't have that kind of experience. You know," he says. "I've got The Dockside." Kyle pauses. "I need a cigarette."

"That's bullshit. You haven't smoked in years," Jason says.

"I think I'll start up again, what the hell. I read it's easier to quit the second time around, okay?"

Jason gives him an irritated look. "Where'd you read that shit?"

"I don't know. I just feel like a smoke. You got a fucking problem with that?"

"Yeah, I do," Jason tells him. "Just calm down already."

Matt sips his drink, watching Kyle put his away before reaching over for the pitcher, topping off his glass and adding more to Jason's. Kyle perspires the whole time. "I don't know how you do it on one income," Matt says, shifting in the booth. "Eva's taking over the real estate business pays a lot of bills. It's a good thing you've got Jerry giving you some work in that diner in the meantime."

"What a goldmine he's sitting on," Kyle says. "He bought that place for next to nothing back in the day. You could do shit like that back then."

"It's different today," Jason says.

Matt turns sideways and leans against the window ledge, looking Jason dead on. The heavy curtains behind him block out any sense of outside life. "And what about you?"

"What about me? I have a job."

"You need someone to keep you out of dumps like this one."

"How about Maris?" Kyle suggests.

"Maris?"

"Yeah. Why not?"

"Maris got away a lifetime ago. The small town girl went big city." Jason turns his glass on the table.

"Then what the hell's she doing hanging around here all summer?" Kyle asks.

"Doesn't matter," Matt says. "Eva says she's got some big job offer in New York, and some corporate dude waiting for her back in Chicago."

"Maybe she does, maybe not," Kyle says. "She didn't seem spoken for on the Fourth."

Jason stands. "Let's shoot some pool."

"Grab another pitcher," Kyle tells him.

Jason turns and sizes him up when Matt catches his eye. "One more," Matt says, sliding out of the booth. He walks behind Jason to the bar and puts a hand on his shoulder, holding him back a step from Kyle. "He's screwed up tonight."

⌇

"Is everything okay?" Eva asks when Lauren calls looking for Kyle.

"I hope so. I just want to be sure the guys are all right. Kyle left here really pissed off."

Eva hears the worry in her voice. "Did you call his cell?"

"Yeah, right. I wish. We cancelled our service. Would you have him call me if he shows up there?"

So Eva checks in with Matt, but he can't talk and tells

her he'll call back when he gets a chance. And when Kyle's pickup pulls into the driveway, Eva definitely knows something is wrong when she sees Matt driving, with Jason pulling in behind them. Kyle practically falls out from the passenger side and trips coming through the doorway.

"Easy, man. Easy." Jason grabs Kyle's shoulders from behind and steers him to a chair on the porch. "Sit down and stay down."

"Eva. Place looks great," Kyle says, motioning to the freshly sheetrocked wall. "Really great." Then he sits back and closes his eyes. His face looks pasty and his brown hair disheveled. Jason stands beside him, as though blocking him from going inside the house.

Matt walks in and motions her back into the living room. "Would you put on a pot of coffee? Kyle's so shot, man, he's not going anywhere tonight."

She heads to the kitchen with Matt following her to the counter. "What are you doing risking a DWI for those two?" she finally asks, not turning around. "You put your job on the line for them."

"It's not like that. I'm fine, really," he says, turning her and taking her hands in his.

"Well where the hell have you guys been? Lauren's called everywhere looking for Kyle."

"We ran into Jason at The Sand Bar."

"The Sand Bar? See? I knew I smelled liquor on you."

"Come on, you know me better than that. I only had a couple."

She checks his eyes. They are clear. So are his words. "The designated driver?"

"Something like that."

"Why didn't you at least call me?"

"We had our hands full with Kyle."

"We?"

"Jason, too. He's fine. It's Kyle who's a mess. It's taking the both of us to keep him relatively conscious."

"Well what about Lauren? She's waiting up for him."

"He can't drive, that's for sure." Matt glances over his shoulder when Kyle starts moving around on the porch.

"And I don't want him here, waking up Taylor," Eva says harshly.

Jason leans into the kitchen doorway. "Hey, Matt. Kyle's going outside to clear his head. Give me a hand, would you?"

"I'll catch up. Don't let him get far." He turns back to Eva. "Can you call Lauren? Tell her his truck broke down or something and he's spending the night here. Or at Barlow's."

"What if she wants to talk to him?"

"Make something up. Tell her we're outside working on the truck." Matt starts to leave, looking over his shoulder. "I've got to help Barlow."

"Want me to make something to eat? It'll soak up the alcohol."

"Not now," Matt says, rushing out. "Maybe later, with coffee. Just call Lauren."

Eva fills the coffee pot with water and measures in the scoops of coffee. The house is still, so still, now that the guys left. It's that same kind of stillness that falls upon a steamy, humid summer day, the kind that makes you alert, that draws attention to something happening that you can't really see yet.

～

"Hey! Wait up," Jason calls after Kyle heading down the beach.

Kyle spins around once, eyes Jason, then keeps walking.

The beach is dark and the waves choppy with the high tide coming in. Kyle sits himself in the sand near the water, kicks off his work boots and rolls up his pant legs. All the while, he never stops talking to himself.

Jason catches up to him. "What the hell are you doing?"

"Taking my shoes off. What's it fucking look like?"

Jason hears the words slur. "No swimming," he warns him. It's bad enough that Kyle is drunk. Drunk and drowned they don't need.

"Shut up and leave me alone," Kyle says under his breath.

Jason watches him for a second before trying just that. He walks down the quiet beach, and just like he thought, it doesn't take long for Kyle to spook. He pulls himself up and jogs barefoot to catch up.

"Hey. It's Lauren who wants to be alone. Not me."

"Yeah, right. It's all Lauren's fault, guy."

They walk half the length of the beach. Kyle sloshes ankle deep in the breaking waves, but Jason stays on the packed sand further up. The firmer sand eases his gait. As long as he hears Kyle talking to himself and wading in the water behind him, he'll be all right. Kyle just might walk it off and sober up that way.

"Hey!" Matt eventually calls from behind them. "Eva's making coffee, let's go."

Jason turns back and heads toward the boardwalk. "You ready for a coffee?"

Kyle tries to follow, but stumbles and falls in the shallow water. "Damn it," he says, moving out deeper, splashing and falling again as he struggles to stand with unsteady feet pulled by the waves.

Jason turns to see Kyle wet head to toe, on his knees in

the water. "Come on, you idiot," he says as he wades into the dark water. The worst thing for his prosthesis is to get it wet, but Kyle needs serious help. With the rising tide, the water nearly reaches his knees by the time he gets to Kyle. He lifts him by an arm, pulls it around his shoulder and tries to stand him up without losing his own balance. Kyle stands taller than Jason and is clumsy in the water, nearly falling to the side. They stumble through the waves back onto the beach.

"That's enough already, Kyle. You're really screwing up my leg. Now stay out of the damn water!" Jason gets him far up onto the sand and shoves him in the direction of the boardwalk.

~⁓

Lights illuminate the long boardwalk at either end, and Matt sits waiting for them. He watches the two men emerge from the shadows. "Jesus Christ, what'd you do now?" he asks. "Go swimming?"

Kyle climbs up onto the boardwalk and sits dripping beside him. "I fucked up, man."

Kyle smells like the ocean and it is enough to move Matt over a few inches. Jason sits on the edge of the boardwalk itself, rather than on the bench that runs along it. He looks exhausted. "Hey Barlow. You clean out that barn today?" Matt asks.

Jason turns sideways while brushing sand off his prosthetic leg, glancing up at Kyle, too. "All afternoon."

"Must be shaping up. You need a hand with it?"

"Anytime." He bends over, still trying to clean off his leg. "There's a lot of paint scraping left to do."

"I think Lauren's leaving me," Kyle says. He sits back and drops his hands in his lap.

81

"She's not going anywhere," Jason tells him.

"You don't understand," Kyle continues. "She doesn't love me anymore."

Jason leans back on his hands then, looking at the Sound spread out in front of them, the moonlight catching ripples in the water. "She loves you just fine, Kyle," he says over his shoulder. "Who could resist?"

"No she doesn't," he says. "I can tell." He turns around and looks at the boat basin behind the boardwalk, his hands hanging over the seat back.

"You're going through some hard times," Matt adds. "She'll come around."

"She won't even sleep with me. I heard on a talk show that fifty percent of marriages end in divorce today."

"Never mind those talk shows." Matt stands and turns then, resting a knee on the seat. "You've just got to straighten up, man. Fly right, you know. Take control." He runs his hand over the names and initials carved into the boardwalk's weathered wood. Behind him, the boat basin, a pretty good-sized marina, holds about fifty boats in a circle. At the far end, it narrows to a wide creek that feeds the lagoon, and on the other it widens and flows out to the Sound. But the marina itself is a safe harbor for the boats and the swans. He looks over the top edge of the rail, directly down to the concrete walkway below that the boaters take to get to their docked vessels. A fine layer of sand covers the concrete. If he squints a little and focuses, especially on a night like this, oh there are ghosts down below too, images from the past, shadows running by the boats, hushed voices whispering.

Now, in the dark, rising and falling imperceptibly against their moorings, the subtle pull of the current brings the boats to life as they creak against the pilings. Matt turns to

Jason. "Hey. Remember when we were about twelve?"

"I don't think I was ever twelve."

"Yeah. You were. It was a long time ago, but I remember. You and Neil had that little Boston Whaler. Remember we'd take it out and horse around on the Sound?"

Matt takes a step, listening to the boats creaking and those hushed voices and laughter from the past. As he walks, his hand runs along the damp top rail of the boardwalk. Like reading Braille, the initials, dates and messages carved into the wood speak to his hand. Somewhere along the way, he knows he passes over MG & E, knicked deep into the wood. He takes his time walking down the boardwalk, giving Kyle a chance to sober up. At the far end, Maris walks up the granite stairs with her dog.

"Maris, hey." Matt stops and pats the dog's head. "You're out late."

"Matt? What's going on? Is Eva with you?" Madison pulls on her leash, sniffing the salty air in noisy bursts.

Matt motions behind him. "No. I'm sobering up Kyle. He's in rough shape tonight."

"Kyle?" She looks past him. "What's he doing? He's going to hurt himself, Matt."

Matt turns around, but Maris reaches for his arm. "Don't yell," she says. "He'll look up at you and lose his balance." She pulls Madison in and holds the dog close beside her.

Kyle, still barefoot, sits on the top rail of the seat back. He has turned sideways, lifting one foot at a time to the top rail. Then, just like mounting a balance beam, he slowly rises to a standing position, his arms wavering in an attempt to keep his balance. One foot moves in front of the other while he walks the beam not quite eight inches in width, with no barricade to prevent him from falling twenty feet to a concrete landing.

"He's going to kill himself. Jason's got to do something."

"Jason?" Maris looks around him.

Jason stands in the sand and motions to Matt to help before turning back to Kyle.

"He knows," Maris says. "If Kyle turns, he'll fall. Just how drunk is he?"

"Man, he's wasted."

Kyle takes a step, his arms wavering, his focus on the long board ahead of him. Jason moves silently onto the boardwalk, and then hesitates. He presses the heel of his palm to his forehead as though he can't see clearly. Matt watches him bend at the waist, hands on his knees, like he's struggling to breathe. "Something's wrong," he tells Maris. "Jason's not right."

They both watch Jason now. He lifts his head, still bent at the waist, and eyes Kyle. "Is he drunk?" Maris asks.

"No. And I don't like what I'm seeing." He starts to walk but Maris pulls his arm.

"Wait. Look." She points to the shadows in the boat basin. "A swan!"

Matt looks toward the west end of the marina, beyond Kyle's viewpoint. A lone white swan moves through the creek into the darkened harbor. It moves slowly, its unseen webbed feet paddling beneath the black water. "Don't they sleep at night?" he asks Maris. The large bird heads for the center of the marina.

"If Kyle loses his focus, he'll go down," Maris insists quietly.

"Shit. Come on, Barlow," Matt says under his breath. He knows Jason. They've been friends all their lives. No way is Jason drunk, so something else is happening with him, except Matt doesn't know what. All he knows is that this long, hot night has finally done its trick. It's pushed each one of them to their limit. Jason, unexpectedly, reaches his first.

~

The waves breaking on the beach, splashing over and over, wash over Kyle's thoughts of Lauren, of a steady job, of meeting the bills, of his old pickup and his kids. He can't make his life work, no matter how hard he tries. The waves keep rolling along the beach. Salt water, the waves, the rhythm, are so comforting.

His left foot shimmies on the wet board and he lurches to the right to keep his balance. When he looks up, he sees Matt at the far end of the boardwalk and suspects Jason's presence behind him now. "I know you're there, Barlow. Leave me the fuck alone," he says without turning. His voice is thick and he blinks back tears. Those sweet waves, he hears them breaking on the beach, they keep washing over his troubles. Tears blur the board in front of him. It's weird because this doesn't feel like the scaffolding he climbs at the ships. This board feels cold and slippery under his bare feet. Where are his boots? He doesn't remember taking them off and thinks he should try to sit, but loses his balance again. His outstretched arms dip to the right. Finally he manages to lower himself to his knees, both hands holding the board in front of him. But somehow this feels worse. If he moves at all, he might not be able to stop himself from falling in the wrong direction. His legs feel too big crouched beneath him. He drops his head and listens to the waves still breaking on the beach. They never stop.

Jason moves closer when a rush of lightheadedness passes over him. He strains to hear; there is that sound again. Something more than just the bike's engine idling. It leaves him cold. Perspiration soaks through his shirt.

Now he sees it coming out of nowhere again. He straightens and runs his hands through his hair. Out of nowhere. Wreaking havoc in its path. His chest hurts as he wrenches the Harley Davidson with all he has, twisting his whole body to escape the impact barreling down on them. He bends at the waist again, hands on his knees, sucking in air.

He shakes his head and looks up from the swan to Kyle. Not Neil.

Kyle.

The big white bird gracefully paddles directly into Kyle's line of vision and Kyle falters. He is too big to stay crouched on top of an eight-inch-wide plank. Suddenly he freezes and Jason knows he's caught a glimpse of white movement. Kyle turns toward the wayward bird and his arms swing frantically as he loses his balance.

One last second. The second Jason needed seven years ago finally arrives. With it comes the screaming engine, filling his head so that he covers his ears to block it out. Every muscle knots again in resistance to the collision about to happen.

Kyle's feet slip out from beneath him.

"Jesus, go!" Matt yells as he bolts down the beach to Kyle.

Kyle falls in the wrong direction, toward the concrete, his arms flailing, and Jason lurches forward, barely catching his arm. Feeling the impact, feeling his brother slam into him. He turns and wrenches Kyle toward him for all he is worth, never letting go.

~

The strength with which he wrenches Kyle drives Jason backward until he trips off the edge of the boardwalk, falling hard. Kyle, still in his grip, hits the wooden planks of the boardwalk first, then falls off to the sand. On his back, he hits the ground hard, too. Matt thinks the wind is knocked out of him until he sees Kyle sit right up and look over to Jason.

"You stupid bastard," Jason says in a low voice. His chest heaves; tears wet his face. "What the hell is wrong with you?" He stands himself up, shifting his stance on the beach, reaching down to where his prosthetic leg attaches to his knee, while the others watch. His shirt is drenched. He shakes. Perspiration runs down his temples while he struggles to brush the sand off his leg again.

The beach is quiet except for the waves breaking. Maris steps off the boardwalk to help Kyle to his feet. She reaches for his hand, dropping Madison's leash to do so. The dog sits on the edge of the boardwalk, watching Jason.

"Don't you ever, *ever*," Jason shoves Kyle in the chest, "pull a fucking stunt like that again." His eyes are wild and when Kyle steps back, Jason moves right with him, staying within inches of his face.

Maris backs way off and Matt moves in closer. "Do you understand me?" Jason yells, shoving Kyle again. Seven years of rage surface and Matt sees it. He knows they all do.

"Do you?" Jason asks, moving closer, his voice ragged. "You want suicide? Next time leave me out of it." He pushes his hands hard against Kyle's shoulders.

Matt has seen it all in his work. Rage does funny things. It can go off at any time, at anyone. He comes around behind them and hooks his arms through Jason's, pulling him off Kyle.

"Come on, guy," he says, knowing what this is all about. "Let it go."

Jason shakes him off hard. Eyeing Kyle one more time, he wipes his face with the heel of his hand before turning and walking toward the water.

Maris hurries past Kyle to catch up to Jason.

"Leave him alone," Matt says to Maris, blocking her from getting by. "He's got his own demons to deal with."

She turns, ready to argue, but Matt cuts her off. "Trust me, Maris. Let him be."

But no one is quick enough to stop Madison. She quietly jumps off the boardwalk and runs down the beach.

"Madison!" Maris calls out. The dog runs faster, shadowing Jason, the leash dragging behind her.

～

Maris and Matt walk with Kyle back to the Gallaghers' house. Eva makes a plate of club sandwiches to go with a strong pot of coffee. No one wants to relive the incident at the moment, particularly Kyle. Maris knows it scared the daylights out of him. Or Jason did. Kyle's face is white; he doesn't talk.

"Matt will fill you in later," Maris tells Eva in the kitchen. "When Kyle sleeps it off, if that's possible. I don't know how he'll be able to sleep at all tonight."

"It was that bad?" Eva asks.

Maris nods. She pours an extra cup of black coffee.

"Where's Jason?" Eva asks.

"He disappeared down the beach. If you think Kyle had it rough, you should've seen him."

"Jason? He looked fine earlier."

"Well this was awful. He really had a breakdown. I'm going to see if I can find him."

It is after midnight and the timers have turned off the lighting. Maris can make them out on the dark boardwalk, though, Jason and Madison. The dog's tail thumps the sandy boards as she nears.

"Hey," Maris says softly. She stands beside Jason, unsure if he wants anyone with him right now.

"Maris," he says. "I think this is yours." He hands her the leather leash.

She takes it and sits beside him in the quiet night, setting the coffee mug between them on the seat. He must have splashed salt water on his face, his head. His hair is dripping wet and slicked back. Shadows and whiskers cover his face. Even the darkness can't hide that he looks a wreck. Maris can smell the salt, the perspiration, the night, on him. She leans over the coffee and gives him a quick hug. "Here, I brought you something hot to drink."

"Thanks." He takes the coffee. "I planned to drop the dog off at your place. But I never made it that far."

"That's okay." They sit at the very spot where Jason had saved Kyle's life. He sips the coffee while Maris talks. "I wanted to go after you," she tells him. "But Matt stopped me. He said to leave you alone." Jason doesn't look at her. "Are you okay?"

He reaches into his shirt pocket and pulls out a nearly empty pack of cigarettes, taps one out, lights it and takes a deep drag. His other hand presses against his injured leg, as though it aches deep inside.

"Jason." Her hand takes his, the one pressing his leg.

She holds it, easy, warming it. "I have to know that you're okay."

He looks at her beside him. "I'll be all right."

Maris finds it hard to believe, because he looks like every single ounce of his body, every muscle, every bone, is spent. It looks like he'd gotten sick on the beach afterward. Not from drinking, but from the night.

"Do you need anything?" she asks. She can't remember ever being so worried about someone.

"No."

"Can I help somehow?"

"No thanks, Maris." He sits up straighter, taking a long breath. "Really. I'm fine."

"Well." A moment passes. "I'll just sit with you here, then." She reaches over and pulls the cigarette from his fingers, taking a drag herself like they did when they were teenagers short on smokes, then returns it. His hand trembles as he takes it back.

"What a night," he says.

"No kidding. How about that swan?"

"Jesus." He glances behind them at the boat marina. "Out of nowhere."

nine

J ASON PLACES A SHEET OF tracing paper over the sketch on the drawing board. Two new clients need preliminary designs soon. Eight by ten photographs depicting the cottages in their current form are tacked in front of the table. It would be easy to scan them into his computer and engage his software to rework the designs, but instead he uses a roll of tracing paper to overlay sketch, adding detail and bringing the cottages further back in time with each new layer of paper. Neil had accumulated scrapbooks of old cottage photographs, and one lays open beside his drawing board as Jason replicates the white-painted columns supporting a porch overhang.

Time passes quickly when he works like this. He'd stayed up long into the night, cleaning and drying sand and salt water from every component and crevice of his limb. And still, he'd been up with the sun. Now, after three hours, he sets down his pencil and walks to the window, letting himself feel what sketching and planning have supplanted since early dawn. It will take more than ten miles of distance in an air conditioned condominium to rid the salt air from his lungs, to blind the panic from his eyes, to erase the regret he feels that Maris saw him out of control.

It's bad enough so that an hour later, he walks along the flagstone path to the front porch of her cottage. Geraniums stand like bright red flags in clay pots alongside the flagstone. White and purple petunias cascade from window boxes. When he stands outside her front porch, the scent of brewing coffee floats through the screen door. Noises come to him as he stops there: dishes clattering in the kitchen, water flowing from the tap, a pan placed on a stove burner. On the porch, a novel waits open on a white wicker table. A copious spray of cattails reaches from a tall ceramic vase in the corner and hurricane lanterns and starfish lean on a high shelf. *Paradise is open to interpretation.* A life like this, as close as the other side of a screen door, is as far removed from him as a ship on the horizon. The chink of silverware being pulled from a drawer and Maris' voice talking to her dog has him move closer. He reaches for the lighthouse knocker and gives three good raps.

Madison rushes to the porch, a growl rising from her throat until she sees him there. "Jason?" Maris asks, following behind the dog. When she unlatches the screen door, Madison noses herself outside and presses her muzzle into his hand while her tail never stops wagging.

"Hey there, girl," he says, scratching her neck. When he looks up, Maris stands holding the door, barefoot, wearing denim cutoffs and a white tank top. A gold star pendant hangs around her neck and her hair is clipped in a low ponytail. "Maris," he says. "I hope I'm not interrupting anything."

"No, not at all."

"I know it's early, but I wondered if we could talk."

"Sure. Have you had breakfast?"

"I'm good. How about a walk instead?"

She hesitates. "I just poured my coffee." She holds the screen door open and he steps onto her porch with Madison close at his feet. "Come on in the kitchen," she says as she walks through the cottage.

He follows Maris through the living room, looking for any familiarity in the décor. A sofa is slipcovered in navy and white stripes; fashion sketches cover an old cherry drop-leaf coffee table; a white painted cabinet sits at the stair balustrade and large square paned windows line the staircase wall.

"This is a great place you're renting," he says as he walks into the kitchen.

"I love it here." She motions for him to take a seat at the breakfast island. Bunches of dried herbs hang from exposed ceiling beams. Soft strains from the local jazz station rise from a countertop stereo. "I've got crumb cake," she says over her shoulder.

"No thanks. Just coffee."

"Are you feeling better today?"

"Yeah, I'm okay." He takes in the details of the kitchen. It all fits perfectly with the sounds he listened to outside its door. Vases of sea glass and heather, white shuttered windows, a lazy ceiling fan. "My brother and I had signed on to do the renovations here."

"You're kidding," Maris says, turning to him with the coffee pot in one hand, a mug with a seashell design in the other.

He notices the architectural details in the kitchen windows and exposed beams. "But we got in the accident before I even drew up the plans."

She fills the mug and sets it in front of him.

"Naturally they used someone else," he says. "I haven't been in here since."

Maris sits across from him and sips her coffee.

"He's kind of why I'm here now, Maris. Neil is. And last night and everything that happened on the boardwalk. It was crazy, and I want to talk to you about it."

"You don't have to explain."

"No, I do." Madison settles on the tile floor beside him and he takes a long swallow of coffee, thinking how to begin. "It's been good seeing everyone this summer."

Maris reaches over the breakfast bar and clasps his hand. "It has, and we're all friends. We understand, Jason."

He pulls his hand back and stands, ready to thank her for that, for letting him off the hook so easily. He can quickly finish his coffee and be on his way. But when he sees the coffee pot and the dishes in the sink and her digital sketch tablet with a recent design on the screen, when he looks back at her and sees the way she watches him, he pulls out his stool and sits again. "Friends, Maris, also explain."

She slides her coffee cup to the side. "Why don't we take that walk outside then? I've been cooped up in here all morning."

⁓

"They call it hysterical amnesia," Jason explains at the water's edge. July's sun bleaches the sand before them. "My doctor says it happens following a traumatic incident."

"You don't remember the accident happening then?"

"No, I actually do remember most of it. This type of amnesia blocks only parts of the trauma." He stops and picks up a stone on the beach. "It's a psychological defense, suppressing the emotion from, well, from a day like that."

"And last night something came back?"

Jason throws the stone out into the water. "It did."

"You mean you remembered something for the first time after all these years?"

He nods and begins walking again. "The scope of the amnesia depends on a lot of things. How severe the trauma was, how physically close I came to it, how psychologically close, post-trauma care."

"I'd guess you rated pretty high in all those."

"You'd be right. Most of that day is clear to me, but lately I've been remembering some of the missing pieces."

Maris puts her hand on his arm. She thinks of his frenzy right after stopping Kyle the night before. Visions of the collision had flashed in his mind. He was back in the accident that killed his brother. "The emotions flash back too, don't they?"

"That's what you saw last night. It can get pretty intense."

They reach the rocky ledge at the end of the beach and Jason bends to pick up a conch shell, its inside whorls of pink.

"I wish there was some way I could have helped," Maris says.

"You did. It helped just to have you there." He puts the seashell in her hand. "You kept me from completely losing it with Kyle."

Maris looks up at him. Hidden somewhere behind that pain, can she still find some of the beach friend she once knew, and danced with, and said goodbye to on a deck twelve years ago? His whole life can't stem from only one day now.

"What?" he asks.

"So that wasn't your normal temperament then?"

He laughs and she is glad to see a little of the old Jason return. "No. I haven't felt like that in years. I thought the memory loss was permanent. It's really sudden the way it's coming back."

"Why now?" They turn and walk back down the beach. The sun rises further in the sky and families stake out their spots on the sand, setting up bright umbrellas and opening sand chairs. "After all these years."

"I know exactly why. My doctor warned me this could happen under the right circumstances. The first circumstance is that I'm tired."

"Rest is so important, Jason."

"I know. But I've been looking for a place to move my studio and thought I might move it here. It's a big job cleaning out the old barn. And I'm bogged down with work. So fatigue plays one part. The rest is that for the first time, I'm spending the summer here at my brother's haunts."

"Facing memories?"

He nods. "The doctors call them cues. They trigger my mind to remember. There's really no way to control it, except to get through it." He stops and throws a piece of driftwood far out into the water.

"Or leave it behind?"

"That's always an option."

Maris crouches down and lifts a piece of seaweed from the high tide line. Sea glass glistens amidst a few stones and sun-bleached shells. "When I was in high school, I went through a phase when I was really missing my mother. And I'd get so sad and couldn't focus. There was a horse stable in town, and my father would take me horseback riding, to help." She stands, squinting into the sun.

"They say animals are therapeutic."

"It's true," she says as they continue walking. The boardwalk stretches before them. "Shadow took me places, not only physically, but in my thoughts. We rode miles and miles of trails through the woods, when I saw through his eyes."

"Shadow?"

Maris smiles. "He was a huge black horse, and very old. Every single time I rode him, as soon as he caught sight of the barn at the end of our ride, he would break out in a gallop. Nothing could stop him from rushing to get home."

They step onto the boardwalk. In the morning light, it looks different. What had pushed two men to the brink only hours ago is now a mirage beneath the sunshine. But still, it is there.

Jason kneels a leg on the seat and faces the boats behind the boardwalk. Maris stands beside him. She hears him take a long breath.

Today the beach will fill with families and conversation and suntan lotion and sandcastles. People will linger long into the afternoon, lying in the sun or swimming out to the raft. He needs some of this beach easiness.

"Hey," she says. "Let me show you the designs I'm working on. I think you'll like them." He turns and looks at her. "Seriously. They're inspired by Stony Point. Come on."

"It depends."

"On what?"

"Do you have any of that crumb cake left?"

And she knows that, for him, breakfast on the porch will be so good, just like that horse ride through the trails.

⁓

"Mom?"

"Not now, Taylor," Eva calls over her shoulder, annoyed at the interruption that comes as soon as she sits at her desk.

The whole day has been like that. By the time Kyle left and Matt went in to work, the breakfast dishes needed cleaning. Two clients called about Open Houses listed in the Sunday paper and her mother called over her morning coffee. "I'm busy." She clicks on the adoption site, wondering how many days have passed since she last checked. Her eyes search the screen.

"Mom."

This time the voice is right behind her. Eva minimizes the screen and turns in her chair. "What is it now?"

Taylor rolls her eyes. "What are you so crabby about?"

"I'm not crabby. I'm really busy with work. Now what is it?"

"What were you working on?"

"It's business, checking out houses."

"Oh."

"Is there a problem?"

"Kind of."

Eva takes a quick breath. "Well am I going to have to pull it out of you?"

"Who were you looking at houses for?"

"What's with the questions, Taylor?"

"Mrs. Curtis? The one who signed papers when the baby was three days old?"

"What?"

"Or Denise Gorman."

Eva turns quickly to the screen. Taylor had read it over her shoulder. She saw the desperation, the scraps of identity clung to, the years of wondering.

"The teacher. It said she's still searching and hasn't stopped crying in twenty years."

Eva turns to her daughter. "I don't like it when you sneak up on me like that."

"Well you said—"

"Never mind what I said." She jabs her finger toward the door. "Get out of here."

"But Mom—"

"Now!" Eva yells.

Taylor's eyes fill with tears before she turns and runs upstairs to her room. A few moments later, Eva hears the thumping of her stereo, the volume cranked to the limit. She looks back at the computer and finds the Birthparents Searching screen, scanning for any new entries posted since she last checked. None fit her criteria. Her identity. None say that every February 11, their hearts break once again. None say their beautiful girl has auburn hair. None say how special the name Eva is. Or that she has her mother's wide smile. Or her father's eyes. They give no clues, no names to whisper when she studies her reflection.

She glances up at the ceiling, getting madder with each thumping intrusion into her quiet search. She finally pushes back her chair and marches up the stairs, finding Taylor sitting on the bed, arms wrapped around her knees, the stereo suddenly off.

"You know how I feel about playing music that loud," Eva tells her.

"I turned it off, so leave me alone." Taylor turns her head away.

Eva holds out her open hand. They don't speak as she stands there, her outstretched arm not moving.

"What?" Taylor finally asks.

"Your cell."

"Why?"

"You lost the privilege, playing music like that just to get me mad. Give it to me."

Taylor slaps her cell phone into her mother's hand and

without looking back, Eva returns to her office and closes the door. The house is quiet enough to hear Taylor rushing down the stairs in her flip-flops, through the kitchen and out the side door, slamming it behind her. Eva looks at the computer screen and shifts a vase of faux marigolds beside it. She and her daughter both need a little time to settle down.

She stops seconds later, in the middle of typing in the next site address. Taylor was dressed to go out. Eva pictures her standing behind her. She wore khaki shorts, a new green tank top, beaded flip-flops, and had slung her straw butterfly purse over her shoulder. A seashell necklace looped around her neck. "Damn it," she says, dropping her face into her hands. "I forgot about the movies."

Maris closes up her front door and sees Taylor walking from a block away. Her sandals flip briskly, her gaze glued to the road ahead of her. "Hey you," Maris says, but she walks past without noticing. "Taylor?" Maris calls after her. She checks her locked doorknob with a quick jiggle before catching up.

"Oh, Maris," Taylor says. "I didn't even see you."

"I know. You're a million miles away."

"I wish I *lived* a million miles away. From my mother."

"Your mom? What happened?"

"We got in a fight."

"About what?"

"She said she would drive me and Alison to the movies but instead she's cruising through all that adoption crap on the computer. *Oh my heart breaks. Oh where is my baby? Still searching, searching, searching.* I can't stand it when she gets into that weepy stuff. Then it makes *her* all weepy."

"Are you sure that's what she was doing?" Maris remembers how Matt didn't like Eva searching out her parents online. So this is why.

"I saw her. I read the sob stories."

"Maybe she was almost done?"

Taylor shakes her head. "When she starts, she sits in there for hours. She keeps pulling a gross tissue out of her pocket, sitting alone and staring into space. I mean, what about Dad? And Grandma and Grandpa? And me? She has us, but she acts like if she doesn't have the people who gave her away then everything sucks."

"Taylor. I think she's curious about her other parents," Maris explains. "Like she's just wondering if they loved her at all or if they didn't care. I mean, you know your mom loves you. But imagine if you didn't know? I'm sure she doesn't mean to ignore you like that."

"But she promised to take us to the movies. The beach will be too hot and crowded today."

"When does the movie start?"

"In an hour."

"Well I was just on my way to see her."

"Huh. Good luck."

"Listen, let me talk to her. Here's my key. Go get Alison and wait on my front porch, okay?"

"Why? I don't even feel like going now."

"Let's just see what I can do. If she can't drive you, I'll give you a ride there."

Taylor looks over her shoulder as though gauging the day. Beach versus movie. Bright, oppressive heat versus dark air conditioning. She fidgets with her seashell necklace. "Okay," she finally agrees with a long breath.

"Good. I'll talk to your mom."

"Can you come with us? It would be more fun."

"Oh, Tay. I'm leaving in a few days and I have so much to do. A ride I can manage, okay? Maybe an ice cream later on?"

Taylor nods easily. "Cool. That works for me."

～

Maris knocks at Eva's door. Her SUV is parked in the shade near the garage, so she's definitely home. When Eva doesn't answer, Maris walks inside, leaning against the doorjamb to Eva's office, amazed that she doesn't even sense her standing there. The computer screen scrolls through adoption listings until she taps lightly on the door.

"Taylor," Eva says with annoyance. "What now?"

Maris raises an eyebrow. "We really need to talk," she says.

Eva spins around in her chair. "Maris? I didn't hear you come in."

"I know. I knocked, though. Twice. The door was unlocked."

Eva checks her watch. "I better log off. I didn't realize how much time has passed."

"So I've heard."

"What?" She puts her hair behind her ears, pushing it back twice.

"From what Taylor tells me, once you start with that," she hitches her chin to the computer screen, "she loses you for hours. Sometimes it's days before you're yourself again."

"When did you talk to Taylor?"

"Just now. Outside."

"She's so moody lately. It must be hormones. Let me

sign out here," Eva says, turning back to the screen.

"Wait." Maris reaches down and covers the mouse with her hand. She glances at the online messages. "Maybe Matt is right."

"Matt?"

"You said he doesn't like it when you do this." Maris pulls a wooden chair up to the desk and reads the screen. "It changes you."

The sky is bluer, the grass is greener, now that I've found you. The world is sweet, my days are heaven on earth. Maris glances at Eva before reading the next story, the next reunion. *I've been crying for twenty-one years. Now that I've found you, they're tears of joy.*

She looks at Eva again, longer this time.

"Taylor's being ridiculous," Eva insists. "She gets me so mad lately. Like, I had to punish her and take away her cell phone. Do you know how long it's been since she's made me that mad?"

"Yup. I'll bet it hasn't happened at all since the last time you were searching for your birth parents."

"What? You think *this* makes me mad?"

"Well it's not Taylor. You know it isn't. So don't put it on her."

Eva looks at her, then at the screen again. Maris sees that she really can't stop. Her need to know the truth about her parents shows in the way she cannot tear her eyes away.

Eva scrolls down through the success stories. "Sometimes I'll read the same screen over three times, just to be sure I didn't miss something, some clue, or reference to my appearance. I analyze every circumstance to see if it fits with what I know." She looks back at Maris. "And you're right. Each time I reread a line, I get madder and madder."

"Why though?"

"Because no one cares enough to wonder, I guess. To validate to me what they did."

"You spoiled brat. You know what you need?"

"No. But I have a feeling you're going to tell me."

"You need your ass kicked, seriously. You keep saying no one cares. No one cares. Well Matt and Taylor couldn't care more. And if I'm not mistaken, when you were placed with Theresa and Ned, that became their job. To care and want you. And they've never *ever* stopped."

"No they haven't. But there's still some emptiness there, they all talk about it online. Empty spots, empty hearts. And it seems so great when they fill it. I want that too."

"But you only see the happy stories. You don't see the reunions that go bad. You know, the ones that need a therapist or third-party to moderate. Those happen, too, Eva. Don't kid yourself. So why don't you let *your* beautiful family fill your emptiness? You'll feel even more empty if you keep snapping at Taylor like you did today. One day, she might keep on walking."

Eva glances at her watch and stands. "Taylor."

"She's at my place with Alison. I told her I'd drive them to the movies."

"We'll both go." Eva grabs her daughter's cell and half runs into the kitchen. She finds her keys and picks up her handbag. Maris watches from the porch. "Come on. We'll get them to the movies and then work on this redecorating." She motions to her living room. The furniture is pushed into the center of the room, all the pictures have been removed from the walls and rolls of new wallpaper line the baseboard molding.

Maris shakes her head. "You go fix things with Taylor. Your very real birth daughter who you have in your life every single day."

"I don't think she even had lunch yet." Eva checks her watch again. "If I hurry, we can stop for a quick bite on the way."

"Go," Maris says, motioning her to the door.

Eva first stops and gives Maris a hug. "Thank you."

"For what?"

"For the kick in the ass I needed." She hurries outside into the bright sunlight and rushes to her car.

ten

EVERY MORNING NOW, KYLE SITS alone at the kitchen table before the sun rises. A ceiling fan paddles the still air, the curtains hang limp at the open window. He's never felt like this before, this scared. No way can he tell Lauren about his boardwalk jaunt. His marriage is screwed up enough as it is. His hair, drying after a shower, clings to his head; a cup of coffee cools in front of him.

That night winds its way through everything he does. Jerry will be showing him the delivery schedules and he pictures falling off in the other direction. Jerry discusses menu preparation in the heat and Kyle rubs the bruise beneath his shirt sleeve. Jerry explains estimating food requirements, anticipating the amount of perishable food needed on hand, and Kyle hears Jason telling him off. His days start before dawn and last until evening and he hardly stops thinking of how close he came to dying. The sensation of Jason's iron grip on his arm stays.

After a second shower Wednesday morning, he combs out his damp hair, dresses in a T-shirt and black pants for work and finds his shoes near the nightstand. Lauren is still asleep, the sheet twisted around her legs. He sits on the edge of the mattress and watches her. Finally, he touches her shoulder. "Hey," he says.

She opens her eyes and looks at him sitting near her. For a moment, he is certain their life hasn't come back to her. They are in that window of time before she has to get ready for work, dress the kids, make breakfast and think whatever it is she thinks lately. He had only told her that he'd gotten drunk the other night. But for this moment, in the dim bedroom, with the air conditioner humming and sunshine outlining the blinds, that life isn't there yet.

"Don't you have to get up now?" Kyle asks. "It's almost six-thirty."

Lauren turns her head to see the alarm clock. Her blonde hair fans out behind her neck and he wants to touch it, to stroke her face and stop the time on that clock right there. His eyes close for a long second and it feels hard to breathe.

"Kyle?"

He opens his eyes. Her voice still sounds sleepy, her bare legs are still twisted in the sheet. It is all he can do to not climb onto the bed and wrap his arms around her, to imagine her murmurs, to slip her nightshirt off her shoulders and make love by the low morning light. To imagine how things used to be.

She raises her hand and touches his arm. "What happened?"

His whole life abridges beneath her fingers on his skin. He glances at the purple bruise she touched and sees the evidence of Jason's strength. "I don't know. I must have bumped into something."

"Oh. Looks horrible." She sweeps the sheet off her legs and lifts her robe from the end of the bed. "I'm taking a shower. I guess I'll see you tonight."

She walks out of the bedroom leaving behind only a possibility still hanging on in their lives. For a second, he had thought it possible her touch could move up his arm and say something else. It still could stop on his shoulder and pull him close. It could wish him good luck at the diner. Anything. Instead he has Jason's grip. He stands then, straightens the sheet, smoothes the wrinkles and makes the bed before leaving for work. Jerry expects him by seven. He bought a spiral notebook and pen to take notes this week. Twenty-five years of experience drives Jerry. Kyle takes down every word of it, as though his life depends on it.

❧

Just after breakfast, Lauren stands in front of the mirror and slips on her seersucker blazer. Even in the heat of summer, she still needs a jacket in the air-conditioned office.

"Come on, kids. Your backpacks ready?" Her shoulders hitch the blazer into place and she turns halfway around, studying her reflection. Tan skinnies, tapered at the ankles, black cami and the jacket define her closet in one word. Functional. Her hands reach behind her neck and clasp on a sterling silver necklace. A sparse wardrobe works, being basic enough to cover temporary assignments where no one would notice how little she actually has. She brushes her long-overdue-for-a-cut hair off her face and spritzes it with hairspray. It falls in a wave just to her shoulders.

"Let's go, Grandma's waiting!" Lauren calls out as she leans close to her reflection. The kids are thumping around in their bedrooms. She puts on foundation, blush and light lipstick.

"Hurry, hurry!" Hailey scoots past her door, lifting a backpack. "Get your stuff into the car." The kids know the routine. So does her mother, babysitting for her. Everybody pitches in, keeping them going. Lauren will miss this if they ever move south. They will be alone.

"The money will help," she told Kyle when he argued that he'd be working full-time all week learning to manage the diner, so she didn't need to temp. "A little to pay down the credit card, a little for at the beach. Ice cream money," she answered. Most to pay off the new washing machine. There is no getting ahead, just catching up.

"Stenil Insurance, please hold. Stenil Insurance, may I help you?" Monotonous, but a distraction, at the very least, from her thoughts. It keeps her marriage in limbo, and therefore alive. The job is tolerable except for that phone. Everything she does there, all her office tasks, are interrupted by the telephone. When it rings, which seems to be whenever she steps away from her desk, she knows what a dog on a leash feels like, doing an about-face all day. *Come Lauren. Heel.* And she sits back down and puts paper clips in the drawer, straightens a pile of folders, stacks pens neatly in their cup and aligns the damn phone with the edge of the desk, all while taking a message.

The office is two blocks from the diner, but Lauren packs a bag lunch and walks to The Green every day at twelve o'clock. She knows it would mean the world to Kyle if she stopped in, just once. If she took a stool at the end of the counter and ordered a grilled cheese sandwich. It would mean they had something to work for. Hope is as close as a sandwich.

Today Lauren sits on the shaded bench beneath the old maple tree. Cars drive past behind her, and a town employee pulls down the red, white and blue holiday streamers from a bandstand to her left. She finishes her juice and packs her wrappings into her brown lunch bag when she hears footsteps, and Kyle's arm reaches around her with a double scoop chocolate ice cream cone. She looks up at his face first, because, well, it is either that or let a memory wash over her, and those aren't helping her much lately.

"Shouldn't you be working?" she asks, taking the cone. "It's your busy time."

"Hey, I'm the boss," he asserts with feigned seriousness. "Jerry's got everything under control," he adds then. "I told him I needed to run an errand."

"Oh." She licks the melting ice cream around and around before it dribbles down the side of the cone. "When's he leaving?"

"Today's his last day. But he'll be home for a couple of days, if I need him."

"That's good."

"How's Stenil?"

"Boring. What a long week." She wants to take the kids swimming, not sit at that desk all afternoon. It is Wednesday now, and she still needs to stop the newspaper delivery for their vacation. And buy sunscreen. She bites into her cone.

"You look nice today," Kyle says.

"Thanks." His words make her feel funny. Modest even. A piece of summer slips between them then, traffic sounds, people's voices, birdsong. Summer becomes palpable in their silence.

"Well. I've got to get back," Kyle says. He leans forward, elbows on his knees, nervous hands fidgeting in front of him.

"Okay." Lauren studies his back, taut beneath his shirt.

"I just wanted to see you, that's all." His head turns back to look at her and she is glad she wore her sunglasses. Sometimes her eyes feel so sad. After a moment, he stands and touches her shoulder. "Take care."

If he looked back, he would have seen her turn on the bench, imagining him pulling the thick white apron over his head, flinching when it touches that massive bruise on his arm, firing up four griddles, his hands reaching for spatulas and orders and food and dishes. When she reaches for her handbag, she notices his notebook on the bench. She opens it in her lap, reading his notes on planning menus for two weeks—who not to buy tomatoes from, keeping the meals light if the heat wave continues. And there are coffee things, too, things he'd like to try. Lattes and cappuccinos. Coffee flavors, and an outlined menu of pastries. She looks back up, but Kyle is gone from sight and in his place comes the memory she resisted before, of Neil coming up behind her with an ice cream cone, one day on the beach, not too long before he died.

~

"Is this ethical?"

"Yes," Eva says. "Well, no. But it is, kind of." They walk along a tended, flower-lined stone path to an imposing shingled two-story cottage perched on a rocky outcropping facing Long Island Sound. Eva punches her code into the lockbox on the front door. "I mean, I told the owners I have a client I wanted to show their home to. And I do." She turns to Maris behind her. "You're my client. Right? I did rent you a cottage."

"But I'm not looking to *buy* a cottage. Though this charmer could definitely tempt me." Two white

Adirondack chairs sit on a grassy side yard facing the sea.

"I just want to show you their furniture, quick. It's what I want in my redecorating." Eva unlocks the door and they go inside. "Come on, you have to see this."

"It feels a little like we're breaking in though. Snooping around illegally."

"Hey, it's not like we're Bonnie and Clyde. I did list the house for sale. So we're kind of window shopping, admiring the goods. They'll never know the difference."

"Wow!" Maris says as they turn into a dining room anchored with a large painted table, around which white wicker chairs are set. The built-in hutches are painted the same sea-green as the table, which has a huge vase of hydrangeas filling its center. A stained glass chandelier hangs from the ceiling.

"Now we're talking," Eva says.

"Oh yeah. Casual beach chic. This stuff is top shelf, Eva."

They move into the living room, walking past the blue and white striped upholstery on the chairs and sofa. Lace table runners line the coffee and end tables, topped with huge shallow bowls filled with perfect seashells. Knotty pine paneling lines the wall with the stone fireplace, and tall French doors finish the far A-frame wall looking out at the blue waters for as far as the eye can see.

"I like the way they bring lace into the look. With that view, it makes me think of sea breezes. Pretty lace curtains and things like that," Maris says. They walk through the kitchen with its mix of old and new. Granite countertops and beadboard walls. Stainless steel appliances and painted glass-front cabinets. She turns around in time to see Eva lifting her cell phone at the room. "You're taking pictures?"

"Just getting ideas. I want to show this to Matt. Do you

think I can pull off something like this in my decorating?"

"Actually," Maris says as she looks into the bedrooms at the whitewashed picture frames and lighthouse lamps, "a lot of clients will be coming into your home office to make their summer vacation rentals. Or to buy summer homes. So the office has to be business, but you can give it a cottage flair."

"Exactly," Eva agrees. She opens a dresser drawer and takes a quick look, then lifts the top of a jewelry armoire beside it. The earrings inside are a jumbled mess.

"Hey, what are you doing?" Maris asks a few seconds later.

Eva turns to Maris, a little startled and holding a pair of amethyst stud earrings to her ears. "Pretty, aren't they?" she asks casually.

"Pretty and not yours. Really, Eva. Put them away already, what if someone sees you?"

"Fine," she says, turning her back to Maris and catching another glance inside the armoire. Seeing things like this, this treasure of a life all contained, intrigues her. How many Christmas mornings are held in this jewelry box? Or moments of an anniversary, or a quiet birthday celebrated over candlelight, a velvet box wrapped with a bow on the table. So many memories must unfold with each glimmering piece. She raises her hand to the armoire as though returning the earrings, but closes her fist around them before slipping them into her pocket. A long glance around the room then is more to still her heart than to observe the decorating. Finally, with a decisive breath, she walks through French doors on the other side of the room and lets out a low whistle at the balcony's rattan chairs with overstuffed cushions, throws casually draped over the arms. She grabs her cell to snap another picture. "I found a great shop in Westcreek. It's used furniture, all stripped and redone. Which is basically what—"

"Cottages are furnished with. Secondhand stuff."

"Want to take a ride there? Taylor's with Alison until dinner, and I'm showing a home in a half hour and have to fly. But if you can stop by my place at two, that'll work."

"Sounds good. How is Taylor doing anyway?" Maris asks. "Have you patched things up?"

"Definitely. We played Bingo on the boardwalk last night and she won a jigsaw puzzle, which we worked on till midnight. Matt, too. Hey, have dinner with us tonight. She loves talking to you and we're all going to miss you—"

"When I leave, I know. Dinner sounds really nice. Maybe we'll finish that puzzle too."

Eva locks up the front door and they walk the beach roads back toward Maris' cottage. Tall oak trees throw pools of shade on the warm street. "And I want to show you some picture frames Theresa gave me. She said they're from my birth family. I guess they gave her a few family things during the adoption."

"No kidding. Well that's nice to have." Her cell phone rings and Maris checks the caller id. "It's Scott. I better see what's up."

"Go ahead, I've got to run. See you at two?"

Maris nods and answers the call.

⌒〜

"Are you wrapping things up?" Scott asks.

"I drove to my dad's house yesterday. It's all in order and locked up there."

"Good. Now what about that dog?"

Maris opens her porch door and heads inside, the dog

prancing with happiness at seeing her. "*That dog's* name is Madison, Scott." *That dog* that follows her around with hoping eyes ever since she arrived in Connecticut. Hoping she'll keep her, hoping she'll go for a walk, hoping she'll throw a driftwood stick. She looks at the German shepherd sitting on the tiled floor. The heat has her panting now.

"Madison, all right. But there's no way we can have a pet here. It's too much."

"I know. Eva and Matt promised to hold her until they find her a home."

"So you're ready to leave Friday afternoon then?"

"Listen, I was thinking." She's been thinking about her new line of beach denim sketches, about Eva's decorating, about the pretty marina and the salt marsh. Thinking about everything but Chicago. "I'd love to show you around a little. How about if we leave on Sunday? There's a seafood place you'd like here. I'll ask Eva and Matt to come with us."

"It won't work, Maris. I've got to be in court Tuesday."

"Oh. I guess we won't have time. All right, then." She turns around and her eyes sweep the kitchen. She sees the hours spent there with Eva, talking and planning. And the times she watched the sun come up with her coffee. And the morning with Jason. Where has it all gone? Time seems like such a dream, the way it eludes her.

Maris walks through the living room past the plaid overstuffed chairs and painted end tables. On the porch, she listens to the birds and a distant boat motor, to footsteps behind a baby stroller, its tires gritty on the beach road. Two women walk side by side, their voices deep in conversation. She doesn't know how she can ever sit herself in her car, fasten her seatbelt, turn the ignition and drive away.

One thing is certain. She can't drive away this afternoon to shop with Eva. Her last hours in Connecticut have to be immersed in walking the boardwalk, taking an afternoon swim, breathing the salt air. She goes back to the kitchen, to the sun streaming in through the white shutters, to the mismatched cottage dishes stacked on the kitchen shelves. She picks up the phone and leaves a vague apology bowing out of shopping on Eva's answering machine.

And the afternoon opens up before her. It will be a long time before she can feel so close to her mother again, can feel her presence here at the edge of the sea. It's one of the hardest things about the thought of leaving, the thought of some sort of goodbye to even memories. Going upstairs to change into her bathing suit, she passes the painted cabinet at the bottom of the staircase and sees the DVD there. Her father had transferred all their home movies to it, and she had asked the local camera shop to add the 8mm footage found in the attic in a box of baby things. All that is left of her childhood home are scenes to watch on a screen now. She decides against going to the beach, and brings the DVD into the dining room and slides it into her laptop.

During the next hour, the home on Birch Lane comes to life, as do the day trips to state parks and Stony Point. One long-ago Christmas Eve, her mother sits on their brocade sofa with Elsa, her sister who lives in Italy. Their eyes sparkle, their heads tip close together in the telling of some delightful secret. They are definitely sisters, with the same facial features, the same strong jawline, the same wide-set brown eyes. Watching them feels like looking in a mirror, though Maris has more of her aunt's dark brown hair rather than her mother's auburn.

Time unfolds on her as a toddler wearing a red velvet Christmas dress, sitting on her aunt's lap. A beaded necklace hangs around Elsa's neck and Maris reaches her small fingers to it, lifting the beads and letting them fall again. Behind them, a cherry clock sits on the fireplace mantel, nestled in the greens of Christmas.

She pauses the movie to study her aunt's face on the computer screen. This woman tried to sustain a fragile tie with her after her mother died. Maris touches her gold star pendant. Too fragile, apparently, to withstand the emotional swells of a broken family. The lifeline became lost at sea.

Time stops after her mother died, with no one filming for a long time then. Which, in a way, only extends the sadness of the death, keeping it central until Halloweens and birthdays finally return several years later, leading to Maris' graduation. And the DVD closes with the early scenes the camera shop added at the end. Though they come out of sequence now, they are still new to her, and what matters is that the two scenes bring her mother to life once more. Moments together are captured. Maris and her mother on the beach that breezy September day, followed by her Christening. Every seat around the dining room table is full. The men wear suits, their ties loosened and their jackets off. The women wear dresses and jewelry. Dinner plates have been cleared away; wine and coffee remain behind as the film silently animates laughter and conversation.

But something doesn't make sense. She reverses the disk, backing everybody up. The dining room glitters with the crystal chandelier twinkling over the table, dessert plates and flickering white candles set in place. A large wall mirror with beautiful etched scrollwork curving around its corners hangs behind the table.

Yes. There. A woman's reflection passes over the mirror.

Maris pauses the image on her computer. Reflected off to the side in that mirror is her Aunt Elsa. She wears a suit of rich brown, with the same color silk scarf wrapped beneath the jacket and up around her neck. A large gold pin accents her lapel and her thick hair is pulled back in a low twist.

A young girl in a navy nautical dress perches on her hip, her little arms reaching comfortably up around her aunt's neck. A little girl with a blue ribbon tying back her wispy brown hair. The scrolls etched into the corners of the mirror frame the image in an ethereal way, making it all seem dreamlike.

"Oh my God." Maris leans forward, squinting. "That's me." She backs the film up to the scene of the christened baby in her mother's lap. The baby who is obviously someone else then. Is it a cousin? Elsa's child?

Maris replays the entire Christening segment, then pauses it to be absolutely sure. Old photo albums hold snapshots of her wearing that same nautical dress at her second birthday party. There is no mistaking that this little girl framed by etched scrolls is her.

She stands and walks around the room, back and forth, back and forth, all the while staring at the frozen scene of her aunt holding her. Finally she hits Play and the film ends with the christened baby held lovingly in her father's arms, the gown beautiful against his navy suit.

The baby who is *not* Maris after all. The home is hers, as are the parents. She even recognizes the gown as a family heirloom, so the baby has to be family. If it is Elsa's child, why would her father keep the reel of film in an attic box? And her aunt is never filmed holding the baby; it is always, always her mother. The way she holds her, the way she fusses over her with such mother-daughter affection made

Maris think *she* was the baby.

But she obviously is not. In the last scene, her mother leans close to her father holding the infant while she smiles intimately at someone behind the camera. Probably, Maris now realizes, at herself. Maybe holding her aunt's hand, maybe rubbing her tired eyes.

It takes every bit of effort to stop looking at the movie, to tear herself away from the second child her mother apparently had. Maris goes up the stairs to her bedroom, ties back her hair, puts on gold hoop earrings and slips on sandals. All her life she has done this, moving around, never staying too long in one place, and now she understands that it is to keep one step ahead of some shadow, some fear. It always comes to this. She has to leave.

Snatching her car keys from the dresser, she knocks the conch shell from Jason off the edge. Her hands barely catch it, shaking the same way they do when she opens the velvet box and puts on her diamond engagement ring, a ring that holds a life far away from here. An escape. Because this is too much, it is all too much. Grabbing her purse, forgetting her cell phone on the nightstand and running down the stairs as though the house is haunted, she runs outside and without stopping, gets into her car and drives off.

So her whole life has been a lie. She wipes her tears and drives at the same time. Secrets, surprises, they never come to any good. Never. Still, her mind tries to deny the truth she just saw. It has been more than a missing mother who haunted her life, who woke her up at night with vague dreams, who moved her to always run away and leave a certain sadness behind.

She understands now that she is actually more than she ever knew herself to be.

She is a sister to someone. Or was a sister. There had been another child, and that sibling, until now only a suggestion in memories and fleeting voices in the wind and visions in starlit, wish-filled skies, has finally, finally caught up with her.

eleven

AS FAR AS WEDNESDAYS GO, Jason Barlow's has been typical.

Up at the crack of dawn, he submitted and reviewed blueprints with two clients before taking on a new job renovating an old bungalow the next town over. Later he caught up on his voicemails and finally, at the end of the day, checked on the Gallagher remodel.

Matt had just woken up, having to work the graveyard shift that night.

"How do you do it?" Jason asked him, imagining working around-the-clock shifts.

Matt sipped his black coffee as they walked around the outside of the house, inspecting the new wood siding.

"You acclimate, I guess. I like the change."

Acclimate, Jason thinks now. Some might call him an expert at it. Following the accident, he couldn't live in his family's beach home. He tried, but every day back there was a souvenir of the past, every room a mirror, every scent a memory.

So he acclimated by buying the condo and keeping Stony Point within reach.

After the accident, he knew he was crippled. Half of his left leg was gone. But he acclimated with the help of time and doctors and physical therapists, learning to walk again using an artificial limb. Now he'd be damned if he let that leg slow him down.

But the most difficult acclimation came from working solo. The two brothers had meshed like the fine gears on well-oiled machinery. Neil was the carpenter and the historian. Far into summer nights, he sat on the front porch getting ideas from old yellowed plans, reviving cedar shingles and lattice windows and bungalow styles. Those ideas shaped Jason's blueprints restoring the architectural details of another era. Then Neil and his crew completed the seaside porches, gingerbread trim and windows looking out at the sea.

So Jason had acclimated again. He kept Barlow Architecture small and manageable, doing what he had loved since sitting in that barn, listening to his father's mason tales of what two hands had built. They built his life, those hands. Now they build Jason's life. And Neil's historical influence shapes Jason's blueprints to this day. The business keeps Neil's spirit alive; Jason owes him that much.

To cure pain, one has to feel it first. That's what acclimating is for him, dealing with some sort of pain. And that's what eats at him now. Either pain has to be felt, or escaped from. He pulls out of Stony Point and drives to his condo knowing that the pain of one flashback drives him away. Some invisible threshold challenges him to stay, or go. To face Neil's memory, or leave it behind. And he'll be damned if that one day of the accident will win again. It is early enough to pick up the designs at his condo and return to the cottage for a couple hours of work.

"Where do you think she is?" Taylor asks.

Eva looks up from the eReader she holds in her lap. "I don't know. I hope she's all right."

"Huh." Taylor continues flipping through her magazine. "Are you sure she said she'd come for dinner?"

"Yes, I listened to the answering machine two times. She cancelled shopping, but not dinner."

Taylor turns a page. "Maybe you should check again. And could you get me a pen? I want to take this quiz."

Eva walks into the living room. Though the carpenters haven't finished the front porch, she and Taylor like to sit out there in the evenings, reading and talking at dusk. She checks the answering machine, then dials Maris' cell phone and leaves another message for her to call, no matter what, no matter when. Then she grabs a pen and a bottle of gold nail polish, keeping an eye on the road for Maris' car as she paints her fingernails beneath the glow of the porch lamp. The evening air coming in through the screens begins to cool.

"What's the quiz you're taking?"

"How Romantic Are You?"

"And how'd you do?"

"Wait, let me add up my score."

Eva sets the nail polish aside and looks out at the street for any sign of Maris.

"I'm True Blue, which means romance lies deep in my heart and my boyfriend will have to know all the nice things to do for me."

"Like what?"

"Like holding hands on the beach, and having old-fashioned manners like holding open a door. And he'll do little things, like maybe not bringing a bouquet of flowers, but just one. Or sharing an ice cream with two spoons."

"Sounds nice," Eva says. She wishes Taylor, in her heart, all that sweetness.

Taylor closes the magazine and pulls her chair opposite Eva's. She takes the nail polish bottle, lifts her mother's bare foot and starts painting her toes. "Was Dad ever like that?"

"Like what? Romantic?"

"Yeah," she says, carefully filling in the gold color.

Eva thinks of their night on the beach after the barbecue. "What do you mean, *was*? Can't he still be romantic?"

"Dad?"

Eva smiles. "He's romantic. Sometimes it can even be the way someone looks at you, or the words they say, that are sweet."

"I guess," Taylor answers. "The guys at school aren't like that. It's like it's all backwards. They want the girls to ask *them* out."

It is getting late with still no word from Maris. "Well, some day when you least expect it, you'll find a romantic boyfriend. You have plenty of time."

"Maybe I'll read some of those romance books. Can we download one?"

"Sounds like a plan," Eva says as she takes the polish from Taylor and begins painting her daughter's toenails. "What time is it, Taylor?"

"Almost eight."

"I wish she'd call. Maybe I should walk to her place and check things out."

"After our nails dry. I'll come with you," Taylor answers. "Don't worry, Mom. You're the first person she'd call if something was wrong. So she must be okay."

Outside, the shadows grow longer. One lone bird holds

on to its song still. "You're probably right. But we'll take a walk over anyway. Just to be sure."

～

The black sedan with Illinois plates catches Jason's attention as he nears The Sand Bar. It is parked right in front. And that's when his Wednesday stops being typical. He signals, slows and pulls in beside the car.

Inside the tavern, the drone of the television falls across the dim room. Maris sits alone at the bar, wearing faded jeans and a black tank top, her hair pulled back.

"People get in trouble when they drink at this bar, you know." Jason settles on the stool beside her. "This is where Kyle got all wound up."

"Hey, Jason. Don't worry, I just got here." The bartender sets a glass of wine in front of her. She reaches for her wallet, but Jason stops her.

"It's on me." He turns to the bartender. "Coke. On the rocks."

They wait for his drink, Maris folding her hands on the bar, her fingers toying with the wine glass.

"Eva's looking for you."

"Eva. Darn it. I was supposed to stop by."

"I was over there a while ago checking on the job. She was worried about you."

"I went to Addison and got tied up at the house there."

"You should probably call her. She's keeping your dinner plate warm." He sips his soda. "Closing up your father's place?"

Maris nods. "Pretty much."

"Is everything okay? You're a little quiet."

"Just something on my mind."

"Seems like a pretty big something. Can I help?" he asks. When he does, he remembers his sister's words. She said them a few years ago, when his temper was short and the accident still close. *Someday*, she had said, *maybe you'll care about someone other than yourself again.* She had been fed up with his whole lack of enthusiasm for life after the crash, with the time he spent in bars, with his third corporate job in two years. He had told her to go to hell.

Maris shakes her head. "Thanks, but it's complicated. I've got to work this one out on my own."

He can't help noticing the diamond on her finger and wonders if that is her complication.

"Well, I'll just sit with you here, then." He lifts his soda glass to her wine glass and tips it gently.

⁓

Maris isn't used to being in a small town where people know her. Where they know exactly what to say. She glances at Jason. He looks tired at the end of a long day. The humidity has brought out a wave in his dark hair and he needs a shave.

"I'm not keeping you from anything, am I?" she asks.

"Just dinner." He checks his watch. "Have you eaten?"

"No."

"Come on then. Let's blow this joint." He stands and holds out his hand to help her off the stool. "We'll drown your sorrows in seafood."

Maris finally smiles. "You know something? That actually sounds really good."

"Okay then. Let's take a ride and find somewhere nice." He pulls his wallet from his pocket and turns to the bartender. "Thanks, guy," he says and leaves the bills on the bar.

"Have a good night, kids," the bartender tells them.

Jason holds the door for Maris and they head outside into the warm evening. The midsummer sunset casts a pink hue to the sky. "Why don't you leave your car here?" he asks. "We'll come back for it later."

Maris slows a step. "I don't mind following if it's too much trouble."

Jason stops and turns to face her. "You? Trouble? You're a piece of cake," he says, opening the passenger door for her.

She watches him settle in the driver's seat, buckle his seatbelt, check his mirrors. Her car, his SUV. He has no idea that she can't make a decision, can't answer a question, can't get her mind off a baby her family had seemingly hidden from her.

Jason backs out of the parking space and opens his window, letting the seaside air fill the truck. Eventually they cross the Baldwin Bridge spanning the Connecticut River. The sun sits low in the western sky in front of them, a red fireball on the horizon.

"Another scorcher tomorrow." He motions to the sun. "Red sky at night."

"Sailor's delight," Maris finishes.

The first exit after the bridge leaves them in the center of a small shoreline town. Maris thinks it's one of those places where time stands still, one decade indistinguishable from the next. Main Street is a mix of historic homes, small boutiques and an old fashioned general store. Beyond are roads lined with old estates, their sloping manicured lawns overlooking a river cove. At this dusky hour, the scenery has a pastel feel to it, soft and smudged around the edges. Sailboats look like pages from an artist's easel, docked in the cove in front of a violet sky. They follow a road that takes them to the mouth of the river where its waters empty into Long Island Sound. There, alongside a large marina, Jason pulls into the parking lot of a restaurant with a miniature golf course beside it.

"You should really call Eva and let her know you're okay. She'll be worried about you."

"I would, but I left my phone at the cottage," Maris says. Jason gives her his phone, and she stands off to the side and calls while he places their orders at the walk-up window of The Clam Shack. "Two large orders of clams, one strips, one bellies," she hears him say while dialing Eva's. "Two large fries, two lemonades and a side of coleslaw."

⌒〜

They eat at a stone table near the water, swapping bellies for strips until Maris refuses Jason's offer of another belly with a sincere "Yuck." A sea breeze lifts off the Sound, and after eating they bring their coffees to the iron railing, looking out over the water, commenting on passing pleasure boats, imagining which one they might own. It grows dark beneath a starry sky and Jason thinks back to a night long ago, leaning on the railing at Foley's. Maris has made a life for herself since that night. She's built a career moving around the country identifying fashion trends, learning fabrics and designing clothes, hooking up with someone back in Chicago while she was at it. A corporate attorney, according to Eva.

But fate brought her back here this summer, to Stony Point. Standing beside her now, if he isn't mistaken, there might be some bit of unfinished business between them. He rests his arms on the railing, the night sea unfolding before them. "There's nothing like being at the water to put life into perspective. To help uncomplicate things?"

"Oh, if only it were that easy. Some complications run as deep as those currents out there."

"Well, you know what they say. The sea air cures what ails you."

"That's what your brother used to say, all the time," Maris says, leaning her arms on the railing too, close enough to touch his. "Neil loved the summer."

Jason glances at her. "Did he ever. If he wasn't on the beach, he was rowing in the lagoon, or sitting out on the porch half the night."

"Does it ever get any easier? I mean with Neil, do you still miss him?"

"Every day." He looks out at the choppy water. Distant harbor lights twinkle along the black horizon. "Every day."

Maris is quiet beside him then, looking out at the Sound, too. "I hate to leave here," she finally says, in almost a whisper, "but Madison's been inside all afternoon."

"That's okay, we'll head back. I've got some plans to finish up for tomorrow." They walk to his SUV and Jason wonders if she feels as reluctant as he does to leave this place beneath the stars, on the water.

On the ride back, she tells him about being Saybrooks' Senior Denim Designer. "It's not like the old days. So much of my work is electronic now. I use a stylus to design on my tablet and I read the digital trend reports. But I still begin with paper sketches. The day I stop visiting vendors and touching the fabrics, going to shows and seeing the runway fashions is the day I pack it up." She pauses as they near The Sand Bar. "I envy you, in a way."

"Me?"

"Yes. You've kept your work personal, and *here*, of all places."

"Not always, though. I tested the waters with corporate work."

"And what made you come back to restoring beach homes?"

"Mostly Neil. When I worked in the city, a day would go by without a thought of him. Then another, and it felt like I was losing him all over again. Then I took a side job renovating a cottage porch and there he was. In the design. This was our gig together before he died, and it brings him back, in a way."

"Wouldn't he be proud." Maris leans back and considers him. "A local architect restoring beautiful old beach homes on the shoreline. Yup, I'd say I'm a little jealous."

"Don't be. You've worked hard and done well for yourself." He pulls into the parking lot and stops beside her car. "Are you sure you'll be okay now? If someone's giving you problems, I can damn well straighten them out for you."

She squints at him, her head tipped. "You would, too, wouldn't you?"

"You bet."

"Thanks, Jason. For everything. I had a great time."

He watches her fish around in her bag for her keys before opening the door. And he knows her complication, whether it is diamond-induced or not, is bad. She wouldn't talk about it all night. "Maris, wait."

She looks up at him. On the one hand, he wants to leave now, to go back to Stony Point alone, to check his messages and finish a preliminary drawing.

But he wants, too, to reach over, to put his arm around her neck and pull her to him. He wants to kiss her, to taste the salt air and clams, to taste summer on her. Like that night at Foley's. One kiss.

He hesitates, though. Because where does he get off thinking that he can love a woman, can feel her kiss and touch her skin, when his brother will never have that chance again? He hasn't deserved the entire evening.

Instead he quickly opens his door and comes around to the other side to help her out. "You let me know if you need anything," he says, standing close and watching her.

She pauses as though to say something, then turns, opens her car door and gets inside. "Good night, Jason. Take care," she says, waving as she drives away.

⌒〜

Maris holds the DVD. She can light a fire in the cottage fireplace and toss it in, never to consider its contents again. The flame would melt all evidence of it. Or she can fling it against the stone hearth, but then she'd only kneel down in tears trying to salvage the pieces. Instead she slides it into the laptop.

Understand the body first. With each design she sketches, Maris has to perceive a body's curves beneath the clothes it wears. The body is the main structure and comes before all else. Clothes only enhance it. So she turns that eye on her mother's body on the added beach scene and sees the full breast and swelled stomach that she missed before. She wears her clothes well. The early pregnancy is concealed beneath her tunic and loose jeans as she stands beside a nearly two-year-old Maris on the beach, her fingers fluffing her salty hair. A baby.

Her mother had given birth to another baby, probably that winter. A baby girl wearing her Christening gown. Who is this baby? What happened to it? Did it die in the car with her mother and nobody told her? She ejects the disk then and immediately Googles her mother's name and date of death, searching for any information. She tries every variation of words, date, location. But it all happened so long ago, there is no Internet record of the accident.

Upstairs in her bedroom, the white lace curtains fill with a sea breeze. Her gaze moves back and forth between the window and her bed until she grabs the foot of it and swings it around before reaching for the white-painted headboard and pulling it even. She inches the heavy bed over to the window this way, pushing and pulling until perspiration and tears cover her face, until her hair is a mess. She looks out at that sky and thinks of Jason's words. *Every day.* He misses his brother every day. It never goes away.

She knows that feeling of missing someone. Now it seems she has missed someone more than her mother. Someone else, maybe a sister, has left a mark on her life.

Every day, Jason said, standing in front of the sea.

The night sky over Long Island Sound bursts with stars and memories and words of the past, words about the sea and its sky and finding comfort in their enchanted presence. The constellations are a crisscrossing network of love, filled with stories as old as time, stories about love and pain, about family and home. The stars glimmer at each special connection, and she knows that one connection, somewhere over the sea, belongs to her and her sister.

twelve

SOMETIMES IT TAKES YEARS OF living life to understand a situation fully. Maris doesn't have years. She has days. The next morning, warm sea air spills in the bedroom window and glances her skin like a mother's touch. She sits up and pulls the sheet over herself, nowhere near ready to pack and leave.

Scott will be here tomorrow. "No," she says, "no, no, no," before grabbing the phone from the nightstand and punching in his number. It's early and he'll still be asleep in Chicago, but at least she'll catch him before he leaves for work.

She stops dialing, though, and hangs up. What would she say to him? *Oh, by the way, my parents had another baby thirty years ago. Give me a few days to find her?* He would think she was crazy, or at the very least he'd scoff at her story. The bottom line dictates Scott. Contracts and projections and negotiations.

And that's when she knows how to buy more time. She dials the number again.

"Can't you handle it long distance?" he asks when she makes up a story about multiple offers on her father's house. "Your agent can fax the offers to you here. You sign off on them and fax them back. It's legal."

"But there could be a bidding war. It'll be easier to handle this way. From here."

"In this day and age, distance isn't an issue. She can email you any details."

"I know. But then there's the home inspection. What if the sale is contingent on repairing some plumbing problem or patching the roof?"

"How long?" he finally asks after an uncomfortable pause.

"I'm not sure. A couple of weeks maybe?"

"Maris."

"What?"

"Is that all it is?"

"What do you mean?"

"Selling the house. Are you sure you're not rethinking things with us?"

"No, Scott." She still slips the engagement ring on and off, more than once a day. "My father died. You know I have legalities to take care of. And I might head into Manhattan one day for that job I've been offered. They want an answer, and if I can work out of Chicago, it's something to consider. Seriously, I'm not rethinking us." She takes a long breath, thinking of the home movie and rethinking a different kind of love. Or maybe all love. That film has her doubt everything now. "I'll call you when I hear something. I promise."

"On one condition. I'll postpone my flight, but I'm not cancelling it. I'll reschedule it for two weeks from tomorrow. If the house is still under negotiation, it'll push your agent to sign off on it knowing you're leaving soon."

"Two weeks. I think that should work."

As she hangs up the phone, what feels a lot like relief brings tears to her eyes. Two weeks.

⁓

"What are you doing?"

Kyle jumps at the sound of Lauren's sleepy voice. "Ironing." He presses the iron down in a cloud of steam without looking at her.

She walks into the kitchen. "This early?"

He had opened the wall unit ironing board and spread his white apron over it. "It's late, for me. I've got to be at work in twenty minutes."

"Why so early? The diner doesn't open until seven."

"Two deliveries are coming. Why don't you go back to bed?"

"I'm up now."

He looks at her standing there in her nightshirt, her robe hanging loose, her hair sleep-mussed, then turns the apron over in silence.

"Why would you iron your apron?" she asks while plugging in the coffee pot.

His arm moves back and forth over the white fabric. "I read a book on effective management. It said image is important to show authority. You know, like keeping appearances professional makes you look confident. And that translates to authority." He glances down at his new shoes. "I'm trying to look professional."

"How do you check in the deliveries?"

"It's not bad. I confirm the delivery against the requisition. If it doesn't match up, we've got a problem that management has to work out."

"Oh. And management would be you."

Kyle folds the apron in half. "Why don't you leave for work a little early? Stop by for a coffee?"

Lauren shakes her head. "I'm going to pack some

135

kitchen stuff before I go in to work. Maybe when we're on vacation and I'm not so busy."

He unplugs the iron and drapes the pressed apron over his arm. Jerry expects the cooks to dress in black pants and shirts, with white aprons. "I'm late. Can you put away the iron?"

"Sure. Go on." She motions him away.

They talk only because if they don't, the silence asks that they reconsider their relationship. Which he does, in his own silence in the predawn hours, and during the ride to The Dockside, and in the minutes waiting for his morning deliveries. His chest feels heavy and driving to work, he wonders if he is having a heart attack so he takes long, deep breaths and it feels like he can keep inhaling, like the air isn't reaching the right place.

At the diner, he leans around the packages in his arms, turns the key in the double locks, walks in and locks the door behind him. When the packages start slipping, he hoists them but doesn't turn around. Turning around means seeing the empty room and picturing every single table full by seven-thirty. Instead he keeps his eyes to the floor, walks quickly past the napkin dispensers, the salt and pepper shakers, the menus standing straight at each table and heads past the kitchen to the office, where he drops his keys, notepad, the brown paper bag and a couple of library business books on the desk, before carefully hanging his white apron on a hook behind the door. Then he grabs a cloth in the kitchen and wipes down all the tabletops again. Last night, he stayed late and sprayed clean the glass doors and the inside of the windows. Anything to not screw up.

Someone raps loudly as he bends over a long table, wiping it in a sweeping motion, and he turns to see Matt on the other side of the door, dressed in full uniform.

"Hey guy," Matt says. He comes inside and waits for Kyle to lock up the door again.

"Matt. What's up?"

"I'm on my way home from work. Thought I'd stop in and see how it's going."

Kyle grabs the cleaning rag from the table. "I'm running the show today."

Matt takes off his State Police hat. "You nervous?"

"Nah. You know. Come on, I'll give you the grand tour."

He walks him through the freezer, the back office and the kitchen, past spotless stovetops, and utensils lined up precisely, and tall towers of napkins.

"Have you talked to Barlow?" Kyle asks as he turns on the coffee at the front counter. The pot gurgles and coffee aroma rises from it.

"I saw him last night." Matt sits on a stool at the counter and slowly spins around. "He stopped by to check up on the crew at my house."

Kyle turns to see Matt eyeing the empty room, the fishing net hanging from the side wall and a small array of colorful buoys framing the doorway. "He's okay?" he asks.

"Seemed to be. But I didn't bring up that night with you."

"He deals with some crazy shit sometimes. Hey, how about a coffee?"

"No way, Kyle. I'm beat. This is my sleep time."

"That's pretty tough, sleeping with them banging hammers at your place."

"I close the door and tune it out." He stands and puts his hat back on. "Listen. I wanted to tell you good luck. Eva and I'll stop by for lunch one of these days."

Kyle swings his hand around to shake Matt's as the back

buzzer sounds. "That's my dairy delivery. I'll let you out that way." He walks Matt to the rear door while pressing his damp hand into the fabric of his pants, then turns back to stack the dairy order as the deliveryman wheels it in on a hand-truck. There is enough milk and eggs and cheese and butter to keep the place going for a couple of days. After lining it sequentially by date in the refrigerator, he goes to the office and pulls out a framed picture of his kids from the grocery bag and sets it beside the telephone. Perspiration trickles down his face and he glances at his damp hands before brushing them on his pants again. Everything needs to be laid out within easy reach. He opens his new planner to the right July week and lines it up in front of the telephone, laying a new pen diagonally across it. The calculator goes in the top desk drawer and will be used to tally the day's numbers.

"Jesus, breathe," he says, then gives the side window a good shove, pushing the sticking sash open and sucking in a deep breath of outside air. When he turns back to the bag, all that is left in it are five packages of black tees, each containing two shirts. He's been so nervous lately, he can shower twice a day. Sometimes three times. He sets the stack of packages on a top wall shelf, first ripping one of them opened and unfolding a new tee, holding it in his hand as he returns to the desk chair and clicks the keys at the computer.

A large photograph of The Dockside hangs near the window so that Jerry can look at it, then gaze outside and imagine it is his boat docked on the open waters. Kyle studies it, trying not to think that the shirt he put on at home is soaked through. It would be easy to blame it on stacking the milk and cheese, going in and out the back door into the summer morning.

But that isn't it, and he knows it. In one swift move, he pulls off his damp shirt and wipes it over his face and neck, then tosses it into the trash can and slips the new one on over his head before his staff arrives.

~

If illustrating fashion designs is creating an illusion of reality, Maris thinks she should be damn good at it then. Her whole life is apparently an illusion of reality. Sitting in the kitchen with a full pot of coffee, she considers the sketches spread around her on heavy-weight paper. Using markers to give a full-color reality, her hand fills in the sketched jeans and denim jackets with shades of blues and grays, using rough strokes to convey energy. The diagonal pattern she draws is evidence enough that the fabric here is denim. Just like the baby's birth records will be evidence enough, filed in some public records, of the obvious.

It is the stuff that's not obvious, the reasons and the mystery, that draw her. Her customers can get denim clothing anywhere. So she has to give them something more, something they need without even being aware of it. She's needed something too, without being aware of it, all her life. Her sister. Are there international directories on the Internet? Her hand rises to her necklace. Can she find the aunt who once sent her the star pendant?

Turning to her gel pens, she looks at the designs covering the countertops, the table, and even the floor, then adds the finishing gold stitches and rivets, finally establishing the need. Every denim piece in this line will feature a subtle constellation. A curve of stars running across a shoulder, or a few twinkling around a belt line. Constellations are stories in the stars, and don't women need stories, seeking to find themselves, seeking wishes when they look skyward? Ever more aware of the body beneath the clothes now, on one last bell bottom design she creates volumes of fabric from the bend of the knee to the top of the foot, with the bell falling in folds. Her gel pen dots silver stars rising from within them. Then she picks up her stylus and adds stars to the sketches on her digital design pad as well.

If it weren't for the knock at the door then, more designs would have spread into the living room next. She is surprised to see Jason outside, his back to the door as he waits.

"Jason?" she asks. Madison stands beside her, wildly wagging her tail. Maris opens the door and the dog squeezes past.

"Hey, Maris," Jason says, bending down and scratching the scruff of the dog's neck. "Okay, you too, Madison. I'm glad I caught you at home."

"Come on in." She pushes the screen door further open. "What's up? Can I get you anything?"

"No. This won't take long." Madison distracts him, pushing her muzzle into his hand and making him laugh. "I just need to ask you something."

She moves to a white wicker chair and motions to a matching chair beside hers. "Sure, sit down." Both chairs face the road outside, framed by the petunias spilling from her porch flower boxes. "Did you come from work?" she asks, noticing his suit pants and white button-down shirt.

"I delivered some preliminary designs this morning. Routine stuff." He loosens his tie. "And I want to make sure you're doing okay today."

"I am. Thanks for asking."

"You're sure?"

He looks at her like he doesn't really believe it and she hesitates, thinking of the manic designing she's accomplished in the last few hours. "I'm feeling better at least, let's put it that way."

"What happened here?" He reaches to her face and brushes his fingertips over her cheekbone.

"What's there?" Her own hand rises to her face.

"Looks like you got a sunburn."

"Oh, that. I was sitting outside earlier. Sketching." She stands then, opens one of the porch windows, and sits again. "So what's going on? You wanted to ask me something?"

"I do." He sits back and still considers her. "It's about your dog. I was wondering if you've found a home for her yet."

"No. Everyone wants a puppy. Why, do you know someone who will take her?"

He nods. "Me. I will. I'd love to have her."

"What?"

He holds up his hands, unwilling to argue. "She's a great dog, Maris. And once my studio is open here, I'll be home a lot, working in the barn. She'll be good company for me."

"That is very sweet, and she'd be so happy living at the beach. But are you sure?"

The dog lies near him watching him talk. "I am." Jason hitches his head toward her. "And I don't think she'll have a problem with it either."

Maris leans forward and sees the dog lying at his feet. "Are you kidding? She loves you." She watches the dog for a moment, then sits back fighting tears.

"What's wrong? I thought you'd be glad."

"I am. This is the best news, don't get me wrong. But I've had some other news, too, and yes, I would *love* for you to have Madison. But not yet."

141

"Wait. You're leaving tomorrow, right?"

"There's been a change of plans. I'll be here another two weeks at least."

"What's going on?"

Maris stands and moves near the windows facing the direction of the Sound. "I could tell you it's all about my father's house, that offers are coming in and so I've postponed leaving." She turns and faces him. "But you wouldn't buy that, would you?"

"Seeing you upset like this? Probably not."

"I didn't think so. But it's really personal. I'm sorry."

"Don't be sorry. Seems like it's floored you though."

"That would be putting it mildly." She sits again and turns to him. "So I'll be around for a little while longer."

"And not sounding too happy about it."

"I wish I could be. You know I love it here. But things happen sometimes that have a way of overshadowing everything else."

Jason reaches to a glass lamp on a small table between them and adjusts the shade. "Maris, I know a little something about shadows. Believe me. And sometimes you just have to let an old friend distract you for a while to get rid of them."

"What do you mean?" she asks, a slow smile spreading over her face.

"I mean I've got the perfect cure for your blues. Come on," he says, standing and heading to the door. "Let me take you out."

"What about your work?"

"It's my lunch hour. I've got time. Lock up, it'll be worth it."

Jason drives on roads past old farmhouses and red barns. There are green pastures and long stretches of crumbling stone walls until he gets on the highway and heads north.

"Give me a hint where we're going?"

"No hints." He wants it to be a surprise. When he'd touched her cheek earlier, it looked like it could only be one thing, that she'd been crying.

"Hm." She looks out at the scenery. "Taking me out for an ice cream in the country?"

"I could, afterward. But that's not it. And no more guessing."

"Okay then." She turns in her seat to face him, resting her head on the seat back. "So tell me about these preliminary drawings you've done."

He glances at her and describes the home at Grey Rock. "It's a really imposing cottage and wants a lot of attention." He describes the large open front porch and the walls of windows facing the sea. "I raised the ceiling on the first floor to fit taller windows, so the sunlight pours inside."

"Sounds beautiful."

"The dramatic elements are something else, but the shingles and the gambrel roof still give it that classic New England seaside look."

"Nice," Maris says as the traffic gets more congested. "And we definitely are not seaside anymore."

Jason glances over his shoulder to change lanes. "No, we're not. A good friend told me something recently about riding a particular horse to help her feel better."

"You're taking me horseback riding? In the city?"

Jason signals for his exit. "That's right."

"But we're not dressed for it." She checks out her skinny jeans, tank top and metallic leather sandals, then glances at his suit jacket hanging behind the seat. "You're in your work clothes."

"Don't worry." He pulls around a wide traffic circle and finds a space beside a park in the center of the city. Tall trees line brick walkways and a great pavilion stands like a huge barn. Strains of music reach them as they get out of the SUV. "Let's see if we can find Shadow," he says, taking her arm to walk her closer to the horses.

⌒〜

Maris stands alone in the shaded pavilion watching the carousel horses whirl past while Jason stops outside to call a client on his cell and reschedule their two o'clock appointment.

"My afternoon's clear," he says from behind her. She feels him standing close as they watch the horses. He touches her arm and points at a shiny black horse passing by, its head raised, large teeth exposed in a wide whinny. Yellow and gold cabbage roses line its arched neck and a horse-hair tail swishes behind it. "Shadow," he says, his voice near.

She cups her hand over his and glances back over her shoulder at him. "This is so amazing."

"What do you think? Do you want a Jumper or a Stander?"

"What's the difference?" she asks, turning back to the horses.

"The jumpers have all four feet off the ground. They remind me of your old horse running back home when he saw the barn."

"I like that black one you showed me."

"All right then. Let's go find him."

When the ride stops, he gives her a boost onto the large black horse and climbs onto the one beside it. Her horse's

144

head is tipped up, its ears pinned back, its neck arching gracefully. Cabbage roses extend from shoulder to shoulder across its chest on a wide blue and gold painted ribbon. And when the carousel starts moving, when the music begins to play, she rides her Shadow again, far away from home movies and baby sisters and family and sadness. Life is just her and her horse, flying free in the wind.

Jason touches her shoulder and points to the thousands of twinkling white lights circling the Wurlitzer band organ and climbing high into the ceiling before stretching out like rays of the sun in straight lines over each set of horses. With wide-eyed expressions and flared nostrils, horses leap around her and she leans back, laughing and watching the lights glitter and spin to the grand music. Her worries blur away on the back of her dancing black stallion swirling through speckled sunshine, galloping all the way home.

Jason pulls a handful of ride tickets from his shirt pocket when the ride slows. "We can stay on as long as you want."

"Yes!" When she looks out the pavilion windows, the world outside, the green lawn and trees in the park, the tall buildings beyond, the whole view undulates in green and gray, like a rolling wave of the sea.

⌒〜

"Let's try the chariot," Jason says when the ride stops again, taking her hand to help her climb down. They walk to one of the ornate seats and sit close together.

"I can't believe I'm on a carousel," Maris says, laughing.

He watches her, not saying that he loves the way she is smiling. He is still getting used to the idea himself. "Neil knew all about this one," he tells her instead. "Being a history buff and all. It's a Stein and Goldstein, made by

Russian immigrants." Maris leans against his shoulder, admiring the horses in front of their chariot seat. "They built it in Brooklyn in the early 1900s, and only three of their carousels are still around today. This is one of them. Those are the Kings, or the Leaders, that lead the chariot. They're generally Standers."

"Their feet are on the ground."

"See? You're a regular equestrian." He moves a strand of hair behind her ear as though it is all part of this moment, of him taking care of her and cheering her up. "And all because of Shadow."

"You know," Maris says as the carousel begins to move again, "this is one of the nicest things anyone has ever done for me."

Jason reaches his arm around her shoulder. "I'm glad." He glances up at the twinkling lights and not at her, keeping his gaze anywhere else until Maris touches his hand on her shoulder and he turns to her. "Does it help?" he asks.

"Very much."

The chariot ride isn't about Maris anymore, and he thinks they both know it. It's about rediscovering a summer friendship on a hot July afternoon, in the shade and breeze of a fantastic old carousel. It is about living and wondering. His arm around her shoulder draws her to him, his other hand gently touching her face as he leans down and kisses her. When he feels her face tip up toward his, he closes his eyes. And when her fingers light on his face, and touch his neck, his kiss lingers still.

~⌒~

The white flickering lights become stardust, just for a moment, just enough for her to notice. Maris knows, when his lips touch hers, that life can change in one magical moment. So much of the past two days have been about only feeling.

This is real. When she closes her eyes, there is only his touch, his embrace, his skin beneath her fingers, his kiss. As her fingers glance his face and touch his neck, their kiss deepens. But only for a moment, only until Jason pulls away with a long breath and takes her face in both his hands. He looks like he wants to say how glad he is that she isn't leaving tomorrow. He looks like he wants to take their kiss somewhere else, to a place with no intrusions, no history, no conflict.

The ride begins to slow, the scenery outside becomes clear.

"Shh." He puts a finger gently over her lips. "Don't say anything." His thumb strokes her cheek. "I'm sorry," he says, his face still close.

"Sorry?" His kiss had been the sweetest one she'd ever received.

He sits back. "You're dealing with something serious in your life, and you're involved with someone else." His hands drop to hers, his fingers lighting on the diamond. "I'm not being fair to you."

Maris takes his hands, wincing at the sight of her diamond. Beyond Jason's shoulder, the dancing horses come to a stop beneath the rays of twinkling lights. She looks up at him, at his face, seeing the faded scar there, wondering what just happened between them. When she starts to talk, he stops her.

"Don't." He shakes his head quickly. "Just let it go." He lifts her hands and presses his lips to them before standing and helping her out of the chariot. "It's okay," he says as she steps off the carousel.

Wait, she wants to insist. They'd kissed. *What happened?* her mind cries. But when they move out of the deep shade of the pavilion into the sunshine of the park, it all feels like a daydream. The fantasy of sitting close in an opulent chariot with the gentle breeze on a warm summer day is over. Walking across the green grass, past wooden benches set around a large flower garden, her heart breaks.

"Ready to head back?" He glances at her while fiddling with his keys.

As though nothing has happened. Maris nods and they walk side by side, not touching. She watches him slowly roll back his shirt sleeves in the heat. His gait seems tired, too, so his leg bothers him now.

"How about that ice cream?" she asks, trying to smooth over the unease. If they can just get back what they started their excursion with. Something about the afternoon, some hope, stayed behind with the horses and cabbage roses and music, fading further with each step.

thirteen

WHAT'S THE NAME OF THIS antique shop?" Eva asks when Maris exits the highway in Addison.

"Circa 1765. I noticed it last week and thought we could find something for your decorating. It's so pretty, and right near a covered bridge. I just have to stop at the jewelers first."

"The jewelers? Why?"

"I've gotten things there, growing up. Earrings and a gemstone ring."

"Ooh, you're buying something?"

"Not buying. Just sizing."

"Sizing? You're all a mystery today. Sizing what?"

Maris smiles and drives down along Old Main Street toward the cove, past historic ship captain homes with widow walk cupolas, past a landscape nursery overflowing with tiny shrubs and flats of impatiens and marigolds, past the Whole Latte Life coffee shop opposite The Green. Towering oak trees shade an ice cream parlor and a bridal boutique selling vintage and antique gowns, alongside a local jeweler. She parks the car at The Green, reaches into her purse and slips on the engagement ring from Scott,

149

extending her hand for Eva to see.

"You got a diamond?" Eva asks, taking Maris' hand in hers. "Whoa, this is gorgeous."

"Thanks."

"When did this happen?" Eva turns Maris' hand, studying the stone.

"A couple weeks ago. Scott actually surprised me by sending it with my laptop."

Eva looks up from the ring. "And you didn't tell me? Uh-oh. What's wrong?"

"Nothing, really." Maris pulls her hand back. "This is pretty big stuff, and I had to let it sink in. But I think I'm ready to wear it now. Really."

"Oh, I'm so happy for you! I know Scott missed your dad's funeral, but these things happen, Maris. It seems like he's really serious."

"He is." Maris thinks of the two-week window of time he gave her, two more weeks at the place she loves more and more each day. With a deep breath, she says, "We've waited a long time to do this, so I guess I'm finally engaged." She holds out her arm, looking at the diamond. "But the ring's too big and I want to get it sized at the jeweler here. And I didn't tell you because you'd get too excited."

"*Too* excited? It *is* exciting!"

"Yeah, but you'd have me walking out of that wedding shop there with a gown in hand if you had your way."

They get out of the car into the early Saturday morning sunlight. People walk with their coffees on The Green, past barrels of zinnias and geraniums around a stone wishing fountain sending shining silver droplets into a high plume of water. The water sparkles like starlight in the summer sun and Maris thinks they'll stop and make a wish afterward.

"Well," Eva says as they cross the street. "We can at least go in and look at the gowns, can't we? You might see something you like."

Maris eyes the bridal mannequins in the window, one wearing a deep-v gown with sheer lace bell sleeves. Another vintage dress, cream silk taffeta, is covered with silver beads and mother-of-pearl paillettes reminiscent of the star constellations she brought to her latest denim designs. That gown catches her eye, shimmering with celestial wonder and wishes both.

"Maybe after. Let me drop off the ring first."

She opens the door to the jeweler and they walk into the small, hushed shop. Green carpet with gold swirls spreads before them in a room lined with glass cases of treasures, each case edged with an old burnished brass trim. A crystal chandelier hangs from the center of the ceiling. And she thinks that it's not the gemstones and gold that are the treasures. It's what they signify that bring riches into our lives. The anniversary necklace hanging on a thin gold chain, a woman's eyes tear-filled as her husband clasps it; the sterling silver charm bracelets collecting happy memories with each little heart or seashell or flower charm; the birthstone earrings commemorating the month of one's arrival here on this earth; the wedding rings and graduation watches.

What charm, or jewel, would signify the precious and valuable images she found in that home movie? The loss it revealed is strong enough to drive her to search for even a hint of it. Yesterday she slid her hand over every single closet shelf and inside every cabinet drawer in her old family home, twice, turning up nothing except a few dusty knick-knacks. Until she knows more, she's hesitant to tell even Eva about the baby. Because there's also a what-if? What if she's wrong about the whole idea?

One of the jewelers asks to help them and Maris shows him the diamond ring.

"Well, congratulations! And when's the big day planned?"

"We haven't really set a date yet."

"But soon, soon," Eva adds.

"I'm still getting used to being engaged," Maris begins, "and I guess it would help if the ring fit better. I brought another ring that fits perfectly. Can we match that size?"

"Possibly. Which hand do you wear that ring on?" he asks of a citrine gemstone ring she shows him along with the diamond ring.

"My right."

"Each finger can be a different size," he explains. "So let's measure first." He thumbs through a set of steel gauge rings. "Then we'll measure the citrine on the mandrel to find the right match."

They agree on a comfortable fit and the jeweler wraps the ring and sets it in an envelope. "We'll call you when it's ready. It might take four or five days, is that okay?"

When she turns to leave, the crystal chandelier sparkles above her and all Maris suddenly sees are thousands of twinkling lights streaming out over carousel horses, seeming like stardust when Jason kissed her in the chariot. His arm folded her close as the kiss deepened, as the music played, as time and motion blended into one. *It's okay*, he'd said afterward, after apologizing for giving her that sweet summer kiss on a beautiful old carousel on a hot July afternoon. As she walks through the door to the summer day outside, she hesitates and glances back at the jeweler turning away with her ring.

⌒～

The orders keep coming. *Out of sight, out of mind,* Jerry told Kyle before he left. A glance at the clock tells him that Jerry would be in Maine right about now, way out of sight and too far away to help. He reaches for the next lunch slip clipped on the order rack. Rob works the other stove. He comes in during peak hours, the same way Kyle had over the years. Rob is second-in-command today. Now Kyle knows the difference between first and second. First is the host, these are his guests.

He opens his eyes wide and focuses on the order clipped in front of him, wiping his hands on the thick white apron as he reads the standard fare: grilled cheese with tomato, plain grilled cheese and a BL, no T, circled and underlined twice with a smiley face beside it. He backs up from the stove and scans the diner until he spots Lauren sitting in the middle booth at the window. He knew it. Hailey hates tomatoes on her sandwich. They stopped in on the way to the cottage, and the kids are coloring their placemats while they wait for the food.

Kyle shoves the order in his pants pocket. "Rob, I'll be right back, okay?"

"Yeah, I'm good here," Rob says from the other stove, dishes lined up on the warming tray in front of him.

Kyle goes into the back office, lifts the apron over his head and tosses it over the chair. From the shelf on the wall, he pulls a new tee from a package and takes a long, deep breath. It takes only one quick move to peel off his damp shirt, mop his face, slip the new shirt over his head and put his apron back on. He tosses the old shirt into the trash and goes back to the stove.

"How's this for service?" he asks when he carries out their plates. "The boss delivers."

"Daddy! Are you eating too?" Evan asks.

"I'll have a bite of yours." He slips into the seat with

Lauren. "You guys ready to hit the beach?"

"Mom says we can't swim today," Hailey says. "Because we have to unpack and clean the cottage first."

Kyle glances at Lauren beside him as she takes a bite of her grilled cheese. Faint shadows are visible beneath her eyes. "Mom's busy today. You two be sure to help her out," he orders very seriously. "Whatever she says, you listen."

"We will," they answer while chewing and picking at French fries, all while leaning half over the table, their feet scooted beneath them.

"You have to blow up our tubes," Evan says as he tries to uncap the ketchup bottle.

Kyle takes the bottle from him. "Okay, buddy. Leave them out for me tonight."

"I couldn't fit all the boxes in the car and left some in the garage," Lauren says. She dips a corner of her sandwich into the ketchup Kyle just poured onto her plate.

"I'll bring them down tonight." He watches her pull off a piece of crust.

"Are we going crabbing tomorrow?" Evan asks. "We need bait."

"We'll see." He has to be at the diner at the crack of dawn. "I'm spending the night for the kids' sake," he says under his breath. When he sees Lauren nod, he pours a maze of ketchup over Evan's fries. "I've got to get back to the kitchen. We're mobbed." He starts to stand, but sits again and touches her arm. "I'll help you unpack tonight," he says into her hair as he leans over and kisses the side of her head. "You look tired."

He slides out of the booth, but before walking away, stops at the end of the table, rests his open hands on it and leans over low. Grease from the big stove had spattered his chef apron.

"Hey," he says. His kids look at him for a long second, mid-chew. "Where's my kiss?" he finally asks.

They climb all over themselves, stretching up to plant greasy French fry kisses on his face.

"That's better."

~

Eva and Maris walk into the kitchen a couple hours later to see Matt leaning against the counter wearing a pair of cargo shorts, Yankees shirt and old work boots, loosely laced, his arms crossed in front of him.

"What's up?" Eva asks, setting her purse down. "I thought you were scraping paint with Jason."

"I was. But I got a call and had to leave."

"This doesn't sound good," Maris says. She and Eva both cautiously sit at the mahogany pedestal table Eva found in the shop in Westcreek.

"It's not. One of the beach guards called me. Nick. He caught Taylor and her friends vandalizing."

"What?" Eva asks. "She's at soccer with Alison."

Matt shakes his head no. "She lied, there's no soccer today. She and Alison were with a couple boys spray painting a fish or dragon or something on the big boulder up at Little Beach."

"Taylor was?" Maris asks.

"All of them guilty as charged," Matt answers, grabbing a red plum from the fridge.

"Oh, those little shits," Eva says. "Where is she?"

"Calm down," Matt tells her. "She's upstairs and knows damn well she's screwed."

"And so grounded," Eva adds.

"Evangeline." Matt looks long at her while polishing the

155

plum on his shirt. "Like we never horsed around on the beach?"

"Not really. At least not doing any harm to anything."

"What do you call stealing that boat?" Matt asks, sitting across from them at the table. "They're just being kids. So go easy on her, okay?"

"Wait," Maris interrupts. "What did you call her?"

Matt bites into the juicy plum. "Call who?"

"Eva."

"Evangeline," he says around a mouthful.

"That's my name," Eva says, standing and turning on the oven. "Ooh, I'm so mad at Tay."

"It's beautiful. I never knew that was your name."

"I used to hate it. Eva I liked, but Evangeline?" She sets a few eggplants on the counter and looks up at the ceiling toward Taylor's room. "I thought it sounded so old."

"Evangeline," Maris says under her breath.

"I'll deal with Taylor later," Eva says then. "We've got to get the eggplant parmigiana ready for Monday. And shoot. I just remembered I have to show a house today."

"What's Monday?" Matt asks.

"Girls' night out with my friend here, and Lauren too. Dinner and a little fun diversion."

"A diversion? Like what?" Maris asks.

"I listed a property yesterday. Foley's old place."

"You're kidding. You went inside? How'd it look?"

"Musty. No one's used it for a few summers." Eva pulls a bowl and large plate from the kitchen cabinet. "The back room looks exactly the same, stuck in another era. Well. Stuck in our era."

"Is the jukebox still there?" Matt asks.

"Sure is." She grabs a couple eggs from the fridge. "And that's our diversion. A girls' night out at Foley's."

Matt leans back and takes another bite of the plum, watching her closely. "Eva. Do you really think it's a good idea breaking in there? Talk about rebellious."

"I'm not breaking in. I have the lockbox combo," she says, washing the eggplant at the sink. "And the owners live in New York. They won't even know."

Matt looks from Maris to Eva and shakes his head. "It's not a good idea to be browsing in cottages you list. I don't like it."

"Oh, I just like to look around a little. No harm done, Officer."

"But it's not ethical, and some day you'll get caught."

"You're such a party pooper. We'll just stay a few minutes. Maybe listen to a couple tunes."

"Leave me out of this one." He stands with his plum and grabs a hardware store bag from the counter. "I'm headed back to Barlow's. He'll never get that barn done with the antiques he's using." He walks out through the front porch, calling back "I'll grab a grinder for dinner. Behave yourselves!"

Eva rolls her eyes. "Peeling paint's the best thing that's happened to Matt. It turns off the cop in him. Must be some kind of tool phenomenon."

"Well, Eva. Matt *is* right about snooping around in other people's cottages. You're oddly fascinated by places that aren't yours."

"Do you know what he told me the other day? That it's my subconscious way of still searching for my birth mother. Like it's in me, this need to dig and find answers."

"Maybe he's right. You're checking everywhere you possibly can to find anything."

"To find my mother, you mean."

"I guess. Or some hint of her, in some way."

"What a pair we are. I'm searching and you're running away."

"Running away?"

"It seems it, sometimes. From Scott." Eva gets a chunk of Parmesan from the refrigerator and sets it on the table for Maris to grate. "I mean, I know he gave you a diamond, but here you are a thousand miles away from him? Going out for clam dinners with Jason?"

"That was nothing, really. We just ran into each other and ended up getting something to eat. That's it. Well, kind of. Until the carousel happened."

"The what? When? A carousel? We so need to talk, with a dude like that interested in you and you denying it. But I've really got to deal with Taylor now." She stops and looks at her watch. "And I have to show a house at four-thirty. So after dinner Monday, when I'll have to unground Taylor so she and Alison can babysit Lauren's kids, we're definitely taking a walk to Foley's. A little girl talk and a little beach magic will work wonders to clear your thoughts. You know. Salt air, it cures what ails you."

fourteen

N OW THIS HOUSE HAS THE granite countertops you wanted," Eva says as she walks the couple through a family room that opens onto a large kitchen.

"The appliances are white, though. We really wanted stainless," Nancy says, sounding disappointed.

"Well there's good news and bad there. You can have stainless, which is good, because the current owners are taking these appliances with them to their new place. Which is bad, because you'll have to buy new appliances."

"But that's negotiable then, in the price of the house?" Russ asks.

"Everything's negotiable." Eva leans against the counter, enjoying the central air conditioning while the couple opens and closes cabinets and drawers. "We can work the price of appliances into the offer. And take a look out your kitchen window there. The marsh is right out back, so you've got gorgeous views. Why don't you go out and see the yard, talk about the house, and I'll write up any questions you have for the owners."

With the couple outdoors and the house quiet, Eva walks back into the family room, drawn to the built-in shelves on the side wall. All sorts of books spill from them, children's books and novels and memoirs. She thinks you can glimpse a family's life by the inscriptions in those books, and pulls out a couple of novels, opening the covers and skimming the pages before setting them precisely back in place. While turning away, a blue cover with gold print catches her eye, an old, illustrated *Alice's Adventures in Wonderland*. The pictures inside are pen and ink drawings done with fine detail, the Cheshire Cat and Queen of Hearts and Alice, too. She studies a picture of Alice holding aside a curtain to the rabbit hole door that opens to a garden far beyond, then flips to the inside cover and reads the inscription, running her fingers gently over the words: *To my daughter, Wishing you beautiful wonders this year. Happy Eighth Birthday! I love you ... Mom*

Suddenly Nancy and Russ are walking back inside the kitchen, excited to write up an offer on the house and submit it as soon as possible. "We want to get the kids settled in before the school year begins," Nancy tells her.

That's always the way. When clients are serious about buying, they make it happen fast. The couple walks through the house to the front door, Nancy already talking out her decorating ideas while Eva puts the key in the lockbox. "Why don't you follow me back to my place," Eva suggests. "I've got the contracts in my office, and we can fax over the offer to the listing agent."

"Perfect," Russ says. "But aren't you forgetting something?"

"I am?" Eva asks.

He points to the book she holds in the same hand as her purse. "You were reading that when we came inside. In the family room."

Eva looks down at the book. "Oh gosh, you're right! I

was so distracted with the thought of submitting your offer. Let me put this where it belongs." She turns around and opens up the lockbox and front door again. "Back in a flash!"

Inside, the house seems even quieter now. It doesn't help that her own heart races when she leans back against the closed front door. Her face perspires and her hands are shaking. All it will take is a minute or two for them to believe her, to think she walked through the house that is soon to be theirs and returned the book to its rightful place on the shelf. Instead she opens her large purse and tucks the book carefully inside, then goes back outdoors into the bright sunshine.

～

Jason decides to keep the barn's natural wood ceiling details. "Look, it's got that steep pitch, and you can see the beams in its structure, with those lower cross beams for support. I like it, but it might be a little too rustic."

"Hey," his brother answers. "Rustic works. It's got character, man."

The power sander Jason uses on the rear wall takes off the old paint, leaving exposed wood. The motor of the sander strains as he moves it over a rough patch, going over and over it in a circular motion to wear the finish smooth.

"It's dark, though," Jason says as he continues to sand. His goggles are coated with dust. "Tough light to work in. That's why I thought about sheetrocking over some of the walls."

"What? Are you crazy? Sheetrock?"

"Why not?" Jason pulls off his goggles and blows the dust off of them, taking a short walk back and forth to keep comfortable standing for so long.

"You'll cover the beauty of the place. There's history in those old beams. Come on," Neil insists. "You're going all wussie on me, white walls."

"Fuck you," Jason answers when he leans down and blasts the sander on a lower part of the wall. He works in the loft part of the barn, having hauled his sander and scrapers up the stairs to the rear wall. A long extension cord snakes through the railing down to an outlet below, and the noise from the commercial grade sander is enough to wear ear protection. But he thinks that might block out Neil, too, so he doesn't.

A few minutes pass, and nothing. No word from his brother. He keeps the sander moving in a circular motion and then hears Matt down below turn on the boom box radio that's sat on a shelf for the past ten years. Some classic rock anthem fills the space like they are in a concert arena.

"What? Did I offend you?" Jason asks. He stops and drags his hand through his dusty hair.

"Huh," Neil answers when Matt starts up his sander again. "Takes more than a two-bit cuss to scare me off."

The scream of a random guitar riff competes with the scream of the power sanders, so much so that Jason can't tell one from the other.

"You need light," Neil suggests.

"What?"

"Light, man. Clean up this wood to brighten it and get lots of light."

Jason uses both hands to work on the wall near the corner. "Like hanging lamps, from the beams?"

"You've gone dense, bro."

He stops his sander and the dj on the radio rattles on about some summer concert series at a pavilion the next town over. His voice echoes in the vast emptiness of the barn.

"See that wall there?"

Jason squints through his goggles. "Where Matt's working? It's got all my good shelves on it."

"No, guy. The other one. The one with all the vines growing up it on the outside. Which, I'm just saying, ain't looking too sweet."

"Hey, Neil. I only have two hands. And one leg for God's sake. Give me a break. So what, you want illumination on the wall?"

"Like shit I do. I want windows. Floor to ceiling, right to left. Make it a wall of freakin' glass. You'll have all the light you'll ever need."

Jason walks over to the loft railing and looks out over the barn, studying the wall from top to bottom. It isn't a bad idea. An old hooked rug hangs over the railing, and below, a metal file cabinet and ancient table saw sit in the middle of the room, waiting to be tossed. Scrap pieces of wood and a stack of grimy bricks accumulate near the door, a junk pile he and Matt built as they moved through the barn. He opens the beer he'd brought along and takes a long swallow, then wipes his arm across his forehead and glances up at the ceiling. "I've got an idea." He downs his beer while thinking about it, then picks up his sander and finishes the far wall. Dust floats everywhere, paint and wood particles dancing in the bit of sunlight coming in, glinting like gold dust.

"Let's have it," Neil says, waiting. "You're the boss."

"Skylights. Two big ones." He keeps the sander whirring in a large circular motion and pictures the sun streaming in through the ceiling, rays of it moving across the space with the passing hours of the day. "It'll be perfect."

"What?"

"It'll be great, give the place a different look, you know?" he shouts over the sander motor.

"You all right, Barlow?"

Jason spins around to see Matt standing near the top of the stairs to the loft, the enormous stuffed and mounted moose head balancing on the top step. "Yeah, why?" He sets down the sander and wipes off his face with a dirty rag.

"I asked you what you wanted to do with this moose and you say it'll be great? The dust up here must be getting to you."

"Shit," Jason answers without saying that he can't believe Matt heard him talking to his dead brother. "I heard you wrong, man. But you know, that thing does have a certain rustic charm. Remember when we all swiped it from Foley's, after it closed down?"

"I remember. And if you think this ratty thing's rustic, you need some ventilation up here," Matt says, turning and sitting on the step then, surmising the barn interior. "And what about your leg? All this dust and mess can't be good for it."

Jason pushes his goggles up on his head and leans on the railing. "It's not. After I screwed it up hauling Kyle out of the water, I invested in a few good leg covers. *After* my prosthetist fixed up the damage. I didn't need the salt water ruining any of the components, and that night really did a number on it." He shows Matt the black cover protecting the limb from the dust. "But I'm good to go now."

"That was a crazy night, definitely. Too bad you had to mess around with your leg."

"No shit."

"All right, then. Is this moose good to go, too?"

"No, I'm not sure yet. Don't throw it out."

Matt picks up the moose head and hauls it back down the stairs. "You're the boss," he says.

～

Late that night, the clear chime of the doorbell wakes Maris. She sits up in the dark and listens. The clock on the bedside table glows 3:30 when she reaches over and switches on the lamp. Something is wrong.

It can only be Eva and Matt; there must be some sort of emergency. Surely Scott hasn't travelled here from Chicago. So she moves quickly, wrapping her robe around her. The yellow light from the bedroom throws a faint cloud of illumination down the stairs to the foyer. Madison shifts position on the cool kitchen floor and Maris' heart leaps at the sound. She doesn't turn on the front hall light, not wanting to light up the house before she knows who might be standing outside.

But something feels off and she stops. Outside, there are no car engines running, no voices talking, no movements detected. Her hand skims along the wall near the porch door until it comes upon the switch for the outside light. She snaps it on and that is when she remembers the house doesn't *have* a doorbell. It is a summer cottage with a brass lighthouse doorknocker and casual screen door. At these beach places, friends just call out for you through the screen, wanting to take a walk or share a cup of coffee on the porch.

Looking out at the night, it would be easy to be spooked by it all. Because as real as it sounded, no doorbell rang. No one stands there, outside. There is only a curtain of black, laced with the silver fog of early morning.

But somehow, she isn't spooked. Instead, she thinks of

165

her mother and steps outside barefoot, standing in the damp grass. The idea of her mother feels like the wisps of fog floating over the dewy grass. Gentle, safe, reassuring. She finds her mother in her life this way. Because who's to say some essence of her doesn't linger at the place she loved so much? That's another reason Maris lingers here at the sea.

After a few quiet moments, she returns to the dark porch, sits in a painted, straight chair near the door and wraps her arms around herself. A stand of decorative wooden herons seems to gaze sidelong at her, waiting with her. Waiting to know some truth. The doorbell sounded so real. That happens sometimes, memories and sounds and images come to her crystal clear. The problem is, she doesn't know where they come from.

fifteen

LAUREN KNOWS WHAT IT FEELS like to have a wave wash over her. The force of the swell stays with her, becomes a part of her even. Because she learns from it instantly. She learns not to resist it and face its force, but instead to move with it, to become a part of its motion until it eventually releases her. There's really no beating it, no escaping it, once she's caught in that wave's path anyway. She's not fast enough, or soon enough, or strong enough, to do so. Once the wave is upon her, that's it. She goes with it, and becomes a part of it.

When she waded into the sea water earlier today, standing only ankle deep, the tug was there, pulling at her feet, luring her closer, leading her to step deeper, then deeper until she stood waist high in the salt water, the ever-present undertow pulling more at her body the deeper she went. But the thing about an undertow is that it begins with those waves, which have rolled ashore and broken on the beach. The wave comes first, then the undertow returns the water back to the sea, beneath the surface of the successive waves. Always. It never stops.

So sometimes she stops it her own way, at least for a

while. She pulls one bottle of gin and one of tonic water from her straw beach tote and sets it on the old table at Foley's.

"What the hell?" Eva asks. "What are you, the designated bartender?"

"Drink up," Lauren answers, reaching back in that tote for three plastic glasses stacked inside each other along with a zipped bag filled with sliced lime. She knew before she even came in here, she knew when Eva called her and told her their plan to revisit the past at Foley's. That wave would take her down, left to its own devices. So she brought along her coping device. Because that darn wave of emotion rises up every time she thinks of the night Neil grabbed her arm and led her up the stairs to this funky old beach joint. It was the middle of summer and the place had been neglected and closed up all season, but Neil yanked the screen door open and jimmied the lock into Foley's. Or his fury did, fury at her continued wedding plans with Kyle. Fury insisting she break it off with Kyle before the wedding got any closer. The wave that night, it held her against the wall just inside the doorway, his arms locking her in place, his hands taking her face in them before he kissed her and she went with the wave, completely. There was no fighting it. And diving into that wave, letting it carry her along, she agreed that when she saw Kyle next, she'd tell him.

Eva sits beside her now in the old restaurant booth. "Maris, shut off that ceiling light, would you?"

And Maris does, but not before plugging in the old jukebox and dropping a quarter in, choosing a familiar Creedence song. The glow of the jukebox illuminates the dark room like misty moonbeams.

"Great, between the liquor now, and Eva breaking and entering, we're screwed if someone sees us." Maris slides into the booth seat across from them.

"I'm telling you it's not breaking and entering, Maris," Eva insists. "You're considering making an offer on this place."

"I am?"

"Yes. I even brought a contract in my purse. Just in case. Okay guys? That's the story."

"It's no skin off my back." Lauren adds more gin to her own glass. "I'm just the bartender. That's what happens when you're married to a cook. You're always thinking food and drink."

"Well hey, that's a nice fringe benefit to having a cook around. You'll never worry about entertaining."

"Oh yeah, great benefit. Goes right along with finding the money to put the food on the table."

"Things will turn around for you and Kyle. Just hang in there," Eva says.

"You know," Lauren answers, "I get so sick of hearing that. Especially from people like you."

"Like me? What's that supposed to mean?" Eva drops a lime in her drink and takes a sip.

"Like both of you. We've got Maris the fashionista sitting here all gussied up in her latest denim board shorts, looking hot with her hair cut just so, wearing just the right sandals, the perfect beaded cuff on her wrist. And you," she says, turning to Eva beside her. "Miss Life-At-The-Beach. Oh poor me, I'm having a tough time selling million dollar waterfront beach properties, browsing through exclusive homes, all prettied up to fit the title, wearing big old fancy amethyst stud earrings and all. Just where do you get off telling me to hang in there? I've been hanging in there for years now."

"Amethyst studs?" Maris asks, reaching over the table

and lifting Eva's hair to take a look. "Whoa. Those look a little familiar, Eva. Did you actually take them from that cottage?"

"Maris, first of all, they're from my mom, okay? Amethyst is my birthstone? February? And second, Miss Lauren. You're right, I get to tour some fabulous beach homes. But have you seen mine lately? It's about as far from fab as it can get, and I've got years of work ahead of me to fab it up. I'll need lots and lots of commission checks to pay for it. As for Maris, she practically gave up her whole personal life building her amazing design career. Fashion is no easy industry to conquer. Okay? So back off and let her be stylin' in peace."

"Wait," Maris says. "Wait, wait. What's going on here?"

"What's going on?" Eva asks. "Lauren thinks we're some hoity-toity bitches, and then you insinuate that I stole these earrings! Maybe coming here was a bad idea."

"I'm sorry, Eva," Lauren says. "I didn't mean that the way it sounded. Sometimes things at home, and with Kyle, just get to me and quite honestly, your lives look pretty damn glam."

"Glam? Try watching me search online for my birth mother, getting sucked into that endless void with tears dripping down my pathetic face. Or try helping Maris clean out the family home by herself when her father just died. Glam my ass."

"Just stop it now. Lauren," Maris says, "how about a refill on the gin and tonics instead? And go light on the tonic this time. And you, Eva. Quit being a drama queen. I'm putting a few quarters in that jukebox and I swear, the first one to whine again has to take the stage, karaoke style. And I mean it, you two!"

The *Closed* sign hangs in the diner window, so Jason looks in through the glass door. Every chair is pushed in snug, every napkin dispenser jam-packed, every table wiped to a dull shine, every salt and pepper shaker filled. More than running a tight ship, the order leans toward manic. It is a diner, after all. He pulls on the door, surprised to find it unlocked. Inside, there is more of the same. Pink and white sugar packets are neatly sorted in the curl of their silver stands. Silverware settings are placed evenly across the counter for the breakfast crowd. Even the fishing net falls in perfect folds over the wall.

He takes a seat on a counter stool and waits, his hands clasped beneath his chin, his thumb finding the scar there. Minutes pass in such silence he doubts that Kyle is even here, somewhere, hidden away in the back. So he hooks two fingers in his mouth and gives a quick whistle.

"That you, Barlow?" Kyle calls out from his office.

"Who do you think it is? Either you better be cooking me up something good for dinner, or let's get a move on out of here."

"Cooking's done, man," Kyle says as he comes in from the back, pulling off his white apron. He loops it over his arm, presses out a crease and grabs the keys from the counter. "I've had it."

"Again?"

"What's that?" Kyle asks, straightening a stack of menus and switching off the main ceiling lights.

"Never mind. What's wrong with your pickup?"

"Battery's dead." They walk out the front door and Kyle locks up, pulling on the doors twice, and then again, after locking them.

"Where's Lauren?" Jason asks.

"I don't know. Couldn't reach her at the cottage.

Couldn't get Matt either. He must be working. So thanks for the ride, guy. Appreciate it."

"No problem." Jason puts the key in the ignition. "Where do you want to go, your house or the cottage?"

"Take me to the beach, okay? I'll need to take Lauren's car in the morning."

Jason pulls out into the traffic. He glances over at Kyle, who is reaching for a pack of cigarettes on the dashboard. "Buckle up."

Kyle taps out a cigarette, then clips his seatbelt. "Hey listen, about that night on the boardwalk."

"Forget about it. We all have our days."

"Yeah, well. You've got some lousy shit to deal with, and I didn't mean to screw you up like that."

As easy as that, one grateful sentence from a friend, and all the shit can come rushing back, washing over everything else. Jason is tired of it and doesn't want to go there today. "You working things out? You and Lauren?"

"Not yet. But you know, thanks." Kyle slips the cigarette back into the pack and sets it on the console between them. "You saved my life that night. Seriously."

Kyle might have been dead, if it weren't for him. It's no easy thought for either of them. But still, something about the whole thing is really about Neil. Insinuating its way into the truck now. "What's up with the smokes?" Jason asks. "Either you want one or you don't. Quit dicking around with everything, Kyle."

"What are you talking about?"

"The cigarette, your job, your wife. That night on the boardwalk. Jesus, that was some serious stunt you pulled. What the hell. Make a decision for once."

Kyle picks up the cigarettes again and lights one, taking a long drag and opening his window. A mile passes in silence. "How's your leg in this heat?"

"It's okay." Jason glances at him again. "The humidity's a bitch though. I have to wipe it off sometimes. You know. The perspiration's tough." He turns under the railroad trestle into Stony Point. It is just after nine o'clock and pale moonlight falls on the beach streets. It's that kind of slow summer night when it'd be easy to while away the hours on a front porch with a cold drink. "Lauren know you're coming?"

"No." Kyle points for him to take the next left and Jason pulls into the driveway alongside the cottage. "Come on in and have a beer," he says as he opens the door.

"You're busy." Jason noticed the bag of paperwork Kyle brought from the diner.

"Nah. Just menu planning. Come on, we'll put the Yankees game on. A drink for my life, okay?"

"Jesus, let it go, man." He opens the door and checks his watch. "One brew, then we're even."

"All right, Barlow. You've got a deal."

sixteen

THE UNDERTOW SNEAKS UP ON her, she doesn't realize it at first, until its insistence keeps at her. Then she pays attention. Lauren makes it through the wave of memory, through picturing Neil pinning her to the very wall in this very room, demanding they stop keeping what they had a secret. It was time, he'd argued. She finishes her second gin and tonic and pours the next.

"Did you bring your paints to the cottage?"

Lauren looks at Eva beside her. Her paints. She could name all the beautiful pieces of driftwood she painted years ago. Seagulls on gray piers, a stormy sea beyond. The boardwalk reaching across the morning sand. A sailboat docked just offshore. The blue cottage on the beach, facing the sea. The rowboat painting, her first, that Eva has now.

"No," she finally answers. "They're up in my closet at home. I thought about it when I saw the rowboat painting at your place." She felt so happy that day thinking she might paint again. So many of the images she painted held memories of her and Neil. Then the washing machine broke, weeds choked the lawn, the employment agency called with an assignment. "Things just got too uptight with me and Kyle."

"Maybe in the fall," Eva suggests. "When the kids are in school, you could paint and sell them online. I'll sell them from my office, too. People love buying souvenirs like that."

"Now that's a great idea," Maris says. "Selling a little piece of Stony Point, captured by the hands of a local artist."

"You make it sound so easy. And it used to be, but not anymore."

"Used to be?" Eva asks.

Lauren looks from Eva beside her to Maris across the table. "I could've had the life you guys have. Creative, fun. Living your passion. I was this close to having it." She holds up her hand, her thumb and finger spaced just so. "With Neil."

"You mean Kyle," Eva says.

"No. Neil."

Maris chokes on her drink and presses a paper napkin to her mouth. "Neil? You had a thing with Neil?"

Lauren takes in a long breath, going with the pull, letting the undertow take her out now. She sips her drink. "I did."

"When?" Eva and Maris ask at the same time.

"When I was engaged to Kyle."

"No way! How? Where?" Maris asks.

"Right here. He saw me painting on the beach one time and we got to talking and stuff and, I don't know. Then he'd come looking for me painting, and the next thing, we were together. But nobody knew."

"Holy shit. You were two-timing Kyle?"

"I was about to break up with Kyle, Maris. Okay? I was so, so close to having a really different life with Neil."

"Wait. Wait," Eva says. "You mean, you two were like, together? Like, serious? In a relationship? How could I not know this?"

"Hey. You were busy with those glam lives, like I said. Maris, God only knows where you were living at the time, climbing that elite fashion ladder. And Eva, your hands were full raising your love child. Taylor. She was just a kid."

Maris reaches into her purse and slides a quarter across the table. "Now you've got to stop doing that, Lauren."

"Stop what?"

"That sounded like more whining to me, and I thought we weren't going there anymore. It's not our fault, or our *glam* lives, that caused your dilemma. Pick a song. It's karaoke time."

"Fine." Lauren swipes the quarter from the table and walks across the shadowy space to the illuminated jukebox. After working on her third drink, there is a definite wave swaying her with each step, pulling at her as she stands in the warm room. The jukebox becomes a time machine, each song a memory. "See if I tell you the rest of the story," she calls over her shoulder.

"Tell us in song," Eva calls back. "Pick a good one!"

Waves are most often formed by distant winds, sometimes from far, far away. While the wind is blowing, they move over the surface of the sea, varying in size. But once the wind stops, the waves continue to roll and change from a wave, into a swell. They keep travelling across great distances before they come to a beach to break on. In intervals, one swell after the other will continue rolling in. Grief, for Lauren, comes in swells. The distance she travelled with Neil—from painting a piece of driftwood, to agreeing to leave Kyle—gave their affair time, lots of time, to grow into swells of grief once his death hit her.

Lauren considers the record selection. And while looking, she braces herself, leaning her hands on the jukebox, head bent down, studying the songs. The swell is coming straight at her, lifting her right off reality as she drops in the quarter. No one but Janis Joplin will do, will capture her feelings.

So in this musty room, with the soft light of only the jukebox seeming like hazy moonlight of another time, catching dust particles in its glow, particles that have lingered from past nights with Neil, bringing those nights back to life, breathing life into her memories, and into her grief, she pleads with him to just take her heart, pieces of it over and over again in such a way that at first Maris and Eva are silenced by her performance, by her, standing on the small wooden floor, swaying in front of the old jukebox, pleading for him to tear apart her heart, please, because she'd rather have the pain of that than nothing.

And in her insistence, in her honesty, Eva and Maris have to believe her. When she sings about Neil holding her, when she pleads with everything she has, orders him to rip apart her heart again, they do too, and she is no longer alone in that desire. They sing with her, tormenting her with the awareness that he took pieces of her heart with him when he died, somehow, as she bends over and twirls around and sways in such a way that she doesn't realize when her friends go suddenly silent, though the song on the jukebox continues as she closes her eyes, throws her head back and feels his arms gently come around her waist. And Lauren leans into those sweet, strong arms, into the moment the song brings her, and she feels him sway with her, leaning down, his face pressing into the side of hers, and she knows she's gotten Neil back tonight, because in his arms, once again, her heart's there too.

⌒⌣

177

"She doesn't even know," Maris says to Eva. "Holy shit, she's wasted."

"And screwed." They had watched Kyle pull open the screen door and walk into Foley's right as Lauren was lost in that song, and he stood still for a few moments before moving behind her and slipping his arms around her waist.

Just as the song ends, Lauren turns and gasps, jumping back. "Whoa, whoa! Kyle."

He looks long at her in one of the most uncomfortable pauses Maris has ever seen, then asks in the silence, "Who'd you think it would be?"

She stands there, catching her breath, her hand to her neck, and Kyle looks past her into the shadowed room, toward the old booth, a couple dusty tables, the pinball machine in the corner. When Lauren takes a step and stumbles, he catches her arm and leads her back to the booth where she slides in beside Eva.

It isn't until then that Maris notices Jason standing in the doorway too, taking it all in. She gives Eva a swift kick beneath the table and Eva spins around to see him. That's when she starts gathering the cups, but not before Lauren grabs hers and takes a long sip. Kyle leans over and reaches for the gin, holding up the bottle to see how much they've drunk already, before letting out a low whistle.

"Really," Eva begins. "We should go now, guys."

Kyle swings a folding chair around and sits at the end of the booth. "I'm not going anywhere until I hear what's going on."

"It's nothing, Kyle." Eva extends her hand for the gin bottle.

"Nothing? After that performance we just walked in on?"

Maris looks over to Jason and motions for him to join

them as she slides over in the booth to make room.

"Listen," Eva explains. "The place is for sale and we just stopped in to take a peek before we never get to see it again. And then, well, we just got to reminiscing."

"Looks more like partying to me." Kyle takes Lauren's cup, adds a splash of gin and takes a long drink.

"How'd you find us here?" Lauren asks.

"Barlow gave me a ride to the cottage so I can use your car tomorrow. My truck battery died." He looks at Eva then and raises an eyebrow. "Taylor and Alison said you might be here."

"And now we're leaving," Eva insists, reaching for Kyle's cup.

But Kyle is quicker and leans back with it. "Oh no. Not yet, we're not."

Jason sits beside Maris. "Well. This is something. You ladies doing a little time travelling tonight?"

Lauren divvies up what is left of the gin between the three glasses, finishing off the tonic water, too. Maris wonders now if she's ever stopped living in that other time.

"We were just having some fun," Eva says, "and one thing led to another when Lauren snuck in the booze. I'll definitely lose my license if anyone sees us. Really, we have to go."

"Hang on, Eva," Kyle says. "Let me just soak some of this in."

"If anyone asks," Eva says, "Maris is thinking of buying this place. She's our out."

"Considering staying on, are you?" Jason asks, nudging her arm.

"Don't fight it, Maris," Kyle adds. "Chicago can't hold a candle to this place."

And in that moment, seeing them all here again, seeing

Lauren missing the life she lost, seeing Kyle reach out for her, seeing Jason without his sidekick brother and seeing Eva ever searching for the mother she never knew, Maris wonders which is true. Is Stony Point the place they forever return to for comfort, or is it the source of all their troubles?

"Come on," Kyle says to Lauren.

"Where?"

"Let's dance." He takes her hand and stands up, giving a tug so that she'll follow him to the jukebox, where they choose a slow song.

Maris watches as Lauren leans into Kyle even though he seems uncertain, his arms stiff around her. "Hey," she says quietly to Jason. "Did Lauren have a thing with your brother, back in the day?"

"Why do you ask?"

"Because that's what she told us, right before you and Kyle got here."

He watches Lauren dance with Kyle, her eyes closed, her face on his shoulder. "She did. I guess they were pretty serious."

"Shit," Eva says. "So she wasn't kidding. Did Kyle ever know about it?"

"I don't know," Jason says, talking quietly. "Sometimes I wonder. But I do know that Neil was crazy about her. He told me she was going to break it off with Kyle. That was right before the accident."

"Wow," Maris says. "I never even knew."

"Yeah. Honestly? When I got out of the hospital, I was surprised Kyle and her were still together. I don't know why Lauren stayed with him, after all that."

"Who knows what the heck goes on in people's lives?" Eva asks.

"No kidding. I have a hard enough time keeping up with my own. And right now I do know what's going on in mine. That music needs to be kicked up a serious notch." He looks at Maris beside him. "Dance with me?"

Okay, so it is this place. It is Stony Point, the candle flame drawing them all to it. Where else would Maris ever get to hang out in an old beach joint, pick some rocking tune from a vintage jukebox and dance with an old friend on a hot summer night? Chicago? Never.

And now, tossing a look over her shoulder to Eva as she and Jason choose a song, as he turns her to the dance floor and as his hand strokes her arm before pulling her in closer, she wonders if Eva's curious interest can see through the dance to every moment of hers and Jason's time together during the last week. Oh, she and Eva go way back and can read each other in a glance. So will Eva's eagle eyes see through the way he touches her, the way he holds her, the way he watches her, to their time at the carousel, to the moment he kissed her on the chariot?

But Springsteen gets them going with the mention of the glory days gone by, with the idea of getting together and talking about those old days much like they do tonight, and instead of feeling sad about the past, they think about their good times, and it makes Maris want to celebrate the ones that passed even more, to relive some part of them, because, really, why not?

And Kyle must have the same thought as he repeats the song one more time, and during the second go around, Jason turns her away from the booth, his back blocking Eva's watchful eye when his lips brush her forehead, pressing them there for a long second, until Kyle taps Jason on the shoulder and they switch dance partners, before the four of them, Lauren, Kyle, Jason and herself just get down with the song all together. Kyle sings every line, Lauren, oh yes, Maris sees it, Lauren wipes away a tear too many times, craving, missing, longing for stories to tell of her and Neil. And in some way, they all hope those glory days aren't over, but if they are, can't they bring them back to life, for a night even, a song, a look? Can't they bring the past back, somehow, tonight?

"Let's go, guys," Eva calls out at the song's end, finding a rag to wipe off the table. But instead, Kyle opens a couple cabinets, seeing what is left of their past here.

"Let me just catch my breath," Maris says, laughing still from the last dance. "That felt so good, didn't it?"

Jason sits in the seat beside her. "You bet."

"I haven't danced like that in …" Lauren pauses, catching Jason's eye. "Well. In years, I guess."

And so Maris knows. It was with Neil. She is saying something to his brother, tonight, as they relive their glory days. And if time can stop, doesn't it at that moment when Kyle taps out a rhythm with the drumsticks he finds in a back cabinet. It is the soundtrack to so many of their old nights here, Neil drumming along with the jukebox, counting down the summers of their lives, keeping the beat on the table, a chair back, his own lap.

"Hey, man," Kyle says to Jason. "These are yours now. Really. Don't leave them here."

Jason takes his brother's old drumsticks and shifts them in his hand.

"Do you still have his drum kit?" Kyle asks.

"No. Got rid of it a long time ago." He sets the drumsticks on the table and rubs his open palms on his legs.

"Hey," Maris says. "You okay?" Her hand reaches for Jason's arm, her fingers brushing his skin.

"Yeah." He picks up the sticks, shaking his head. "Just a little spooked."

Maris leans forward to see his face, wondering about cues and their ability to invoke flashbacks, when the screen door opens and distracts Jason. She follows his gaze as Matt walks in from the deck, his uniform boots heavy on the floor. He squints at Eva first with a glare as she stacks the empty glasses, before motioning to Maris.

"You've got a visitor," he says.

"Me?" It is either the dark of the room, still lit only by the glow of the jukebox, or it is just the time that has passed, but it takes a moment for Maris to recognize the tall shadow filling the doorway behind Matt. He wears jeans, a black shirt and brown leather running shoes. The heavy watch on his wrist was a gift, from her. She stands then, to get past Jason, and he slides out of the booth but not before taking hold of her arm.

"Maris?"

She glances back, hoping he sees her quick smile of regret. Would they have walked on the beach later? Talked beneath the stars? "It's okay," she tells him. "Really."

He lets go of her arm and Maris feels the pure silence hanging in the room, right before she puts an end to any lingering music, any lingering memories, and brings them all abruptly to the absolute present, to Eva ever searching out her mother, to Lauren longing for a different life, to Jason still talking to his dead brother, to Matt annoyed with everyone. She does it all with her next, single word. "Scott?"

~

"Wow," Eva says under her breath once the introductions were made, after Scott declined her invitation for a bite to eat at her cottage, after turning down Kyle's offer of a beer, when Maris and Scott finally move outside the door, out on the deck.

"Wow is right," Lauren agrees. "That's her Chicago guy?"

"I guess so," Eva answers.

"They serious?" Kyle asks.

"They're talking marriage, so yeah. I can't believe he flew all the way here."

Lauren straightens the last of the napkins, folding them in half and stuffing them in her bag. "How'd you find him, Matt?"

"I was at the Guard Shack, talking to Nick. He had a radio with the game on, and we were bullshitting when this dude pulls under the trestle in a silver beemer, looking for Maris. Or for her cottage address."

"She didn't know he was coming?" Jason asks.

"No way," Eva answers. "She'd have told me."

"We got to talking a little, and first I brought him by our place," Matt explains, turning to Eva. "When you weren't there, I remembered you said you were dropping by Foley's. So I thought, no harm done to stop here. Never expected a God damn party going on."

"Shit." Jason looks toward the door. "He's not going to be too happy about it."

"I wouldn't either," Kyle agrees. "Already seemed a little uptight. What's he do in the city?"

"Some type of corporate attorney who's apparently getting impatient to have Maris back." Eva stands, grabs her handbag first, then a deck of cards from the shelf and drops them on the table. "We can't very well leave with them standing out there. Get a Set Back game going and let them have a few minutes together. We came in through the front door, so I'm going back in to lock up."

As she walks out of the room, through the hallway headed for the front of the cottage, she hears Kyle. "Your call, Barlow." After locking the front door, she passes through the kitchen and in one almost imperceptible motion, reaches over the counter for the spoon rest shaped like a colorful beach umbrella and drops it into her purse.

seventeen

M̲ARIS, WAIT." SCOTT TAKES HER arm and pulls her into the shadows on the deck. Flashes of sheet lightning move across the distant sky over Long Island Sound. "What's wrong?" he asks as he tucks a strand of hair behind her ear.

"Why don't we walk on the beach? We can't really talk here." She starts to turn but he pulls her back.

"Where you running to?"

"What?" she asks.

He backs up against the wall, watching her. "Apparently I interrupted something in that room."

"You did," she finally agrees after a pause. "But it's not important."

"I get the feeling it is. What's going on?"

Maris glances over her shoulder toward the room inside, then moves beside Scott, facing the little room tacked onto the cottage. "It's called Foley's, this place. Years ago, it was the hangout for the beach kids. It's on the market, so we just got together one last time tonight, before it sells. You know. We played the jukebox and talked about old times."

Scott takes her hands in his. "You're sure that's it?

Because I'm wondering what's shook you up. I've never seen you so rattled."

"You shook me up. I mean, not you. But you told me last week you had to be in court tomorrow. You know I hate surprises."

"I thought this would be a good surprise. And I moved a few mountains to change my schedule to get here."

Maris takes a long breath. "Why didn't you call first?"

"A month without you is why. I missed you, Maris." He studies her closely, his hand caressing hers and stopping on her ring finger. "No ring at this beach party?"

She looks quickly down at her hand. "The ring. It's at the jewelers, being sized. Really, Scott. We've got so much to talk about, including getting married."

"I know, that's why I'm here. And if we can't finish tonight, you'll come home with me? Tomorrow, or the day after? For a few days anyway?"

Maris knows now exactly why he came here. To break the Stony Point hold, to untie the ropes, to unlock her heart. He lifts his hands to her shoulders and stares at her, waiting.

The others are talking and laughing on the other side of the wall. She hears a voice inside, recognizing the satisfaction of someone trumping someone else's Set Back hand.

Scott leans in and tips her chin up, kissing her, and it is like walking a high wire, faltering in two directions until he takes her shoulders and pulls her closer. Reality is in front of her, his touch being the undeniable evidence. He's been in her life and still wants to be, his kiss a reminder of that life, of her Chicago townhouse, of her career. It all returns as clear as his presence.

Behind her seems vague suddenly. The past month has

been filled with home movies and memories, carousels and summer kisses, stargazing and walks on the beach. It passed like a misty dream. It shapes her life here, but is it reality? Scott would brush it off with a look, a dismissive gesture. His hand reaches behind her head and his fingers tangle in her hair.

But it *is* reality. It has to be. It just takes time to bring the visions into focus, to understand the past, to fit it all somehow onto a thirty-year-old 8mm reel of film. She reaches her hands to his face, deepening her kiss while she also pulls back. This is her own card game and he is forcing her hand.

The realization also comes that there is no bluffing with him. She pulls away with a quick breath. "Scott." She pushes her hair back and collects herself. "Why don't we take that walk on the beach now, where we can really talk? Would that be all right?"

It only takes an instant, the flash of an expression. It moves across his face and she isn't sure what to name it. Regret maybe? Impatience? He raises her left hand and touches the empty spot where his diamond ring should be, then moves past her to the stairs.

"Wait." She follows close behind him. "Scott, I can't just leave. I've got to tell them goodnight. Come in with me."

Scott turns back at the top of the stairs. "I don't need to go in again. I'll wait down there." He motions to the parking area below the deck. "Don't be long."

The card game folds when Maris steps back inside the room. She sees the change even as the screen door creaks closed behind her. All eyes rise to hers.

"You all right, hon?" Eva asks.

She nods, standing just inside the door. "Scott's waiting outside. I just wanted to say goodnight, okay?"

"He had a long trip. I can make sandwiches and coffee?" Eva asks.

"No, Eva. But thank you anyway."

"Well you better call me tomorrow," Eva insists.

"I will. Thanks everybody. I had a great time tonight."

"You're sure he doesn't want to join us?" Kyle asks.

"Another time, maybe."

"Have a good night then," Kyle says with a glance outside to where Scott is waiting.

Kyle wants only one thing, to fix his marriage with Lauren. And Maris knows that he would do the same as Scott, would fly across the country for Lauren at a moment's notice.

"All right. So I'll talk to you guys later." Her eyes stop on Jason and she walks quickly to him. "You," she says softly. "Thanks for the dance." She leaves a breath of a kiss on his cheek but before she can turn away, he catches her hand. Maris looks back at him.

Dance? Matt mouthes to Eva.

"Take care of yourself now," Jason tells her before letting go. He speaks softly, but she hears what she needs to. It is all there, the caring, the kiss, the beach walks, the carousel, the dance. She feels herself in his arms again beside the glow of the jukebox. It all follows her out of the room and has her glance back at the door once she walks down the staircase.

◦‿◦

"Damn you, Neil," Jason says as he steps onto his porch and flings his brother's drumsticks across the room. "Damn it all to hell." There have been other bad nights over the years, times when the pain in his leg competes for all his attention.

189

He goes into the bathroom, opens the faucet and throws handfuls of water on his face. While standing there, his leg aches enough to elicit a groan. When the phantom pain comes on suddenly like this, it is excruciating. He runs the hot water until it scalds, then shoves a towel in the steaming stream. Sometimes the burning heat of the towel, wrapped around his limb, alleviates the pain. But he drops the towel in the sink instead and bends at the waist, rubbing his leg from the thigh down to the knee, kneading and pressing in a desperate effort to massage the pain away. When he finally stands straight, he drags his hands through his damp hair, unsure of what to do. What is the point of living here, of restoring summer homes, of restoring his and Neil's lifelong dreams, if it means doing it alone?

What, really, is the point?

Leaving his beach home behind, he drives to The Sand Bar. It will be dark inside, and hours pass easier over liquor. He can sit and nurse one long drink, or let the liquor wash down his throat, depending. By the time he returns to Stony Point later, sleep will take him over then.

Parked outside the bar, Jason folds his arms over the steering wheel. It's been a long time since he's let himself be physically touched, since a woman's skin touched his. Since he has touched anyone. It always has to be Neil's touch, his impact, he last remembers.

But Maris gives him permission to feel good somehow. He danced tonight.

That is the point.

He takes a good, long look at The Sand Bar before shifting his truck into reverse and heading back toward Long Island Sound. The tides, the waves reaching on the beach beneath the pull of the moon, they are always there. She would want him to do *this*. To go and walk on that beach. To try and strike a deal beneath the stars, walking along the high tide line with Neil and his memories and his cues.

By the time he pulls into the long driveway of his home, the cottage sitting high on a ledge with the Sound beyond, moonglow dapples the trees in the yard. He steps out into the misty darkness covering the land; waves break on the rocks. Maybe he's misread things over time. Maybe everything feels like pain, but it really isn't. The one pain is so great, it takes over all other sensations and he has to distinguish it. Because if he has to name it now, it feels more like fear. Fear keeps him standing there, unable to go inside the house and be alone. Loving someone who isn't there, Maris, Neil, is familiar enough.

The fear comes in knowing that loving someone at all means leaving Neil behind, once and for all. Means letting him go. He isn't sure he knows how to live without his brother.

In the backyard, the barn stands in the shadows. New sliding doors have been installed, with a large multi-paned arched window above them. He goes inside and turns on the bright work lamps, their light stark in the night. An interior, non-load bearing wall still needs to come down. A heavy pry bar leans against it. Jason lifts the bar, inserts the tip beneath a plywood panel and begins ripping down the beams.

⌒⌣

Reinvention is an inherent part of fashion design. It keeps styles in vogue. Her design sketches find new ways to create with denim, new ways to see bell bottoms, new ways to cut a blazer. After all these years, Maris has become a master at reinvention. And isn't that what her future calls for now? So she looks at what her life is, how it fits her, where it works and where it doesn't. Then she does what any credible fashion designer would do next and looks to future trends.

In the dim candlelight of The Sand Bar, stories unfold around her. Some are sad, some sweet. After all these years designing, she has become a good judge of situations and body language, always having an eye on how fashion fits people's lives. And Scott's body language gives her an indication of her future trends when he sits back defensively. He'll resist change. Her hands, usually designing with graphite pencils, or ink, or paint, reach for his hands across the table as she tries to design their future. Her spoken words become the sketch lines of her life. Their weight varies, with bold lines of her time at the beach leading to the delicate lines of the 8mm home movie, because bold to delicate invites the viewer to follow along, to move with the sketch.

If a garment has lots of detail, Maris keeps her sketched poses simple to accentuate only the garment's features. Her future is intricately detailed, with an engagement waiting for her, while a lost sibling draws her eye, and a family home needs to be sold, all at the same time that a design career keeps moving, regardless. So she keeps her present word sketch simple, outlined with the dusty carton she found in her father's house and shaded with the few mementoes inside it. An empty gift box from an Italian jeweler colors it gold; a tiny baby blanket softens it; an 8mm film deepens it with the Christening scene in her long-ago home.

She sketches the story simply, leaving out evening walks beneath the sea's stars that leave her feeling more connected than ever to her mother. Leaving out the best design work she's ever done that happens while sitting on a cottage front porch, the salt air influencing her vision. Leaving out beach friends and their casually poignant history here. Simple, simple. She sketches only what matters most, wanting to find the future trend of her days so that she can foresee what her life might come to look like.

Scott takes in her designs, then brushes them off as though long ago and far away are not part of the future. "You've lived your life so far unaware of any secrets, any mysteries, all while building a significant career," he says, pausing to sip his drink. "And we've been happy. Until now, it seems. Until you found this past of yours. But when only today mattered, there were no problems. So I don't get why you won't let it go."

And so her lines get bolder. The past influences everything she does, especially her fashion designs, she insists. Her denim specialty connects her completely to her summers spent at this very beach, and to her mother's love of the shoreline, to the breeziness of the whole beach essence that has long been a part of her life.

As she speaks, she employs one of her trademark design techniques, leaving off lines in the sketch. It is an effective way to engage the viewer in the process, having them fill in the lines with their own vision. Engaging Scott in his own take on the possibility of a long lost sibling lets him be a part of the process, a part of her future.

But sitting in the dark bar, a glass of wine in front of her, a glass of Scotch in front of him, she can never move her future past a preliminary sketch. He won't help her choose the fabric of a future design, won't put together a prototype of chance, won't allow her to try on the possibility of different lifestyles. Retro doesn't work for him.

So though Saybrooks' next fall line of denim design sketches spill from every nook and cranny in her little rented cottage, capturing all the time she's spent at Stony Point, drawing on the love of her mother, and her mother's love of the beach, tying it all together with a constellation of stars that began with one 14 karat gold star from a faraway aunt, that is the extent of her designing. On paper only. No graphite penciled words, no watercolor nor gel pen phrases, no blank white future, no varying emotional lines and no home movie shapes hinting at a silhouette of family history, could come together in a sketch of what would happen in her life even tomorrow, never mind a year from now.

eighteen

MARIS WANTS HER LIFE BACK.

Last night, Scott stood in the doorway of her front porch, looking out into the darkness. Sea air cooled the cottage. Crickets chirped. Maris sat on the porch. She had lit a small hurricane lamp and jumped when he finally spoke.

"I'm going to leave." Neither of them moved. "You have unfinished business here that's between you and your past and I'm not going to stand in your way, Maris. Just fix it, and then we'll talk, okay? I'll get a room at the airport and call you tomorrow. Find your answers so that you don't have a reason to stay away from me."

He walked out of the cottage and she sat without moving for an hour afterward, trying to understand who was right. Did a baby born thirty years ago matter now? Or had she caused the most important man in her life to walk away, evading commitment once again?

She looks up at the sky over The Green in Addison now. Maybe today is the day she'll find everything out. Wisps of white clouds streak across that blue sky while she stands in front of this converted colonial home, shaded by an old maple tree. Somewhere, a jet rises to that same sky and carries Scott on a flight back to O'Hare at this very moment, the moment before pushing open the door to her father's attorney's office.

The reception area is hushed, with thick carpeting, with taupe and burgundy window treatments and wallpaper, with framed artwork reassuring the eye of the importance, of the seriousness, of your business. An antique mahogany chest of drawers sits against a side wall.

The receptionist looks up from her computer screen. "May I help you?" she asks.

"Yes." Maris approaches the half wall surrounding the workstation. "I need to see Attorney Riley. I don't have an appointment, but I can wait. It's about my father's estate. Louis Carrington."

"I'm sorry, but Tom is on vacation and won't be back for two weeks. Is there something I can help you with?"

"Vacation?" She looks away with a long breath. "Can he be reached? Or could I get a message to him? If I could just talk to him on the phone."

"I can have the covering attorney get in touch with you."

Maris has gotten to the point where her life hinges on minutes. Scott wants her back today, she knows it, sometime in the next one thousand four hundred and forty minutes. Her job at Saybrooks will be held open for only so long, a few weeks' worth, maybe a month of minutes. And the clock ticks down on a job offer from a Manhattan design house. Then there is the minute of 8mm film.

But there are other minutes, too. *You can stay with us as long as you need to.* Eternal minutes. *I'll keep your secrets. Pinky swear.* She thinks of the overnight bag she packed earlier, preparing to fly to Chicago today with her answers, and then she remembers the brief minute spilling with possibility. *Considering staying on, are you?* How have the minutes of her life spun out of control with summer kisses and walks on the beach and hands touching over a glass of wine, a cup of coffee, a conch shell?

Maris reaches into her shoulder bag for one of her business cards. It will take only minutes to scan birth and death certificates of her family. A few minutes of the attorney's time will set her life straight. She jots down her Stony Point and cell numbers. "Please, if Attorney Riley checks in, will you have him call me?" Her hand shakes as she gives over the card. "I'll be staying on here for a while longer before getting back to Chicago."

"Ms. Carrington," the receptionist says. "As a rule, Attorney Riley does not check in while he vacations with his family. The best I can do is schedule an appointment for his first day back. He likes to leave that day open to catch up, but I'm sure he'll understand."

How will she get through the next two weeks waiting for answers? *We'll drown your sorrows in seafood.* Scott wants her back now, forcing the question of her family to take on a life of its own. *Let's see if we can find Shadow.* Maris glances up from the appointment card. *Dance with me?* "Thank you," she says as she turns to leave and head back to Stony Point. *Chicago can't hold a candle to this place.*

⌒⌒

Wearing their bathing suits, Eva and Taylor move out thigh-deep into Long Island Sound and walk across the width of the roped-off swimming area. Their fingers dip into the salt water and occasionally Eva dribbles a stream of cool water over her shoulders. Some mornings their talks are light, or spent laughing as they dodge a random crab or jellyfish. Schools of minnows pass them by, then reverse direction and approach again, as though listening in on their voices.

Taylor has been acting vulnerable and clingy lately, not to mention crying out for Eva's attention with the spray painting incident. It seems to Eva that maybe her daughter is worrying, afraid that Eva will love her less if she finds more family.

"But I thought you weren't going to do that anymore," Taylor says in the water, their bare feet skimming the sandbar as they walk and talk about Eva's online search for her birth mother.

Eva wonders if Taylor knows, if she can sense from another room in their beach home, if she tips her head up from a magazine article or song on the radio, her gaze vague, when Eva grows too quiet for too long in her office. "I limit myself and only check my own search page every now and then. Like once a day."

"So you log on to see, and if there's no email, you log off?"

"Usually. Sometimes I search a little and find a few birth parents curious about the child they gave up."

"Just in case they're your parents?" Taylor asks, sweeping her fingertips through the sea as they walk.

Eva nods. "And it would be nice to not have to wonder anymore. So when Grandma and Grandpa come over for lunch today, I'm going to ask them more about the adoption."

"You don't think they'll get mad?"

"No, honey. They understand my curiosity."

"Huh." Taylor pulls her sun visor down lower. "We should probably get going then. Maybe today's the day you'll find everything out."

"Let's walk one more lap," Eva says. "And hang out with the fishes."

Taylor points to a shadow in the water. "Uh-oh. Crab alert." Eva jumps and they evade the shadow with quick, high steps.

"False alarm! It's only seaweed," Eva says, laughing with relief.

～～

Eva sets out cloth placemats. The antique mahogany table looks more beautiful with each ray of sun that reaches in the window, with each bouquet of flowers spilling from her wide crystal vase.

"Can I help?" Theresa asks from the kitchen doorway.

"Set the plates for me?" Eva puts the flat pan of bacon beside the stove as the oven heats. "Where's Dad?"

"On the porch, reading the paper with Taylor." She sets the dishes in place while Eva shreds the head of iceberg lettuce.

"Would you slice the tomatoes, Mom? The knife's in the drawer."

Theresa rinses a few tomatoes and picks a sharp knife from the silverware drawer before sitting with it all at the table. "Jason's doing a great job redesigning the front of the house."

"He is. Once the wallpaper's up, I can finish decorating my office. Hopefully Maris won't leave too soon, she has some really good ideas." Eva puts the shredded lettuce in a shallow bowl edged in gold and sets it on the table before taking a seat across from Theresa. She watches her slice and neatly stack tomato slices in an angular pattern around the dish.

"Mom."

Theresa keeps slicing. She wears navy shorts and a short-sleeve cotton top. A gold necklace hangs around her neck and she has on small diamond stud earrings. Her hands look younger than their years with her nails nicely manicured. Eva is aware of every small detail about Theresa as she watches her closely for a reaction.

"Matt and I were in the attic bringing down these old chairs and we found the wall mirror there. The pretty one, with etched scrollwork on the corners?"

Theresa wipes the knife edge on a paper napkin and sets it on the edge of the dish. "Mirror?"

"Come on, Mom. How many mirrors do you suppose you left behind in the attic when you moved? And how many cherry mantel clocks, which I also found. And picture frames?"

"Okay, okay. So I think it's safe to say that those things are from your other family. They gave it all to us so you'd have a sense of belonging, of a history with them, too. But we always thought that, growing up, you'd be more comfortable without reminders of your adoption. After all, *we* were your family now. That's why we put it all away in the attic."

"But how did you even get this stuff? You must have known the family then?" Eva pulls her chair in closer, wanting to sit close, to hear every word of this.

"Oh, I see what this lunch is about," Theresa says. "You want to talk about your adoption, maybe get some answers now." She moves the tomato plate over to the side.

"So? Is there something wrong with that?"

"Well no. But it would've been nice if I'd known ahead of time."

"How do you think I feel then? It would be nice if I

200

knew, too. Because let's face it, I'm not a kid anymore and you can take *everything* out of the attic now, so to speak."

"It's more complicated than you'd think, Eva."

Eva takes a long breath. "Listen. You know that necklace Maris has?"

"With the star on it?"

"Yes, and her name is inscribed on the back in a beautiful cursive. She wears it all the time."

"Yes. Yes, I've seen it. It's very striking."

"It's from her mother's sister, who lived in Italy. She had it made special for her. The star is to remind Maris how her mother loved walking along the beach, watching the stars over the sea. The aunt hoped Maris would think of her mother when she wore the necklace, and of her aunt too, across the ocean. They'd all be connected that way." She pauses, touching her neck where a pendant might hang, "I'd love to have a connection like that, too."

"Don't you have it with me? I mean, we all know you're adopted, but don't you feel more than just that?"

"Knowing I'm adopted is a fact. It defines me, and it leaves me with lots of questions and feelings."

"That's true." Theresa stands then and walks to the sink, turning back and staring at Eva. "Adoption *does* define you. It makes you *my* daughter."

Eva stands too and puts the bacon in the oven, then sets a plate of cold sliced cantaloupe on the table. "While the bacon's cooking, I want to show you something." She leads Theresa to her office and clicks to the adoption registry on her computer. "*This* is what adoption makes me. It makes me crazy. I'm on this site all the time, looking, looking, looking, and I can't take it anymore." She wheels back her chair and lets her mother see the screen.

Date of Birth: February 11
I was nearly one year old at adoption. Adopted family relocated from Mystic Connecticut to Stony Point Connecticut. I have auburn hair. Eva is searching.

"That's you?"

"Yes. Who else would it be?"

"But how does this work?"

"If someone sees this and recognizes some fact that identifies me, or them, they'll send me an email. Which would be an initial contact. It could be a parent, a sibling, anyone."

"Eva," Theresa says. "You shouldn't get your hopes up like this."

Eva turns and looks at her through tears. "You don't get it, do you? *This* is me. This takes over my life." She stands then and points for her mother to sit in the chair, then leans over and changes screens to parents searching in the year of her birth.

Date of Birth: March 3
Worcester, Massachusetts
Catholic Charities. Birthname Baby Girl Tyler.
I signed papers when you were two days old and the tears have never really stopped. Birthmother Audrey Tyler is still searching.

"Look at that one, Mom. Look, really look," Eva says, crying now.

Date of Birth: August 4
Springfield, Massachusetts
Baby Girl Chappel. Birthmother Susan Chappel.

"It's the only posting and she has nothing. Nothing! No baby name, no memory, no evidence, no tears. Just a date?" She kneels beside Theresa. "She's had this posted for years. What if it's me she's searching for?"

"Oh, Eva," Theresa says, starting to stand.

"No!" Eva blocks her from standing. "No, Mom. This is my world. You have to stop pretending that this emptiness I feel doesn't exist. *This* is what I live. *This*. Wondering if I should respond to that poor woman."

"No," Theresa answers, reaching for Eva and tucking a strand of hair behind her ear. "No, you shouldn't, dear. That's not your mother."

"But how do you know for sure?"

"Well, I just do. I *adopted* you. And I was about to tell you everything. The whole story of your first family. I swear I was, years ago, right when you graduated high school. But then you came to me one rainy day and told me you were pregnant and that took over our lives. I just couldn't burden you with the rest when you were dealing with a baby so young."

Eva reaches over and logs off the site. "Well it's time now. I can't go on wondering and dealing with this awful obsession anymore. Please, Mom."

"Okay, of course." The oven timer sounds and they go back to the kitchen. "Just let me get a few things ready, okay Eva? There's more to the story than you'd think, and I have to talk to Dad, too. I want to do it right, I want you to be okay with it all. We'll take you all out to dinner somewhere nice, I promise. And I'll tell you your story."

"But not today?" Eva asks.

Theresa shakes her head no. "Soon, I promise. We'll tell you about the mirror today, and the mantel clock you found. About how when you were a baby, before you came with us, those things were special to you and your birth mother. How she'd sing *Bom Bom Bom* along with the clock chiming, and you'd mimic her too, as a baby, whenever you heard the chime. And, well." She takes the paper towel Eva holds out to her and presses it against her eyes. "We'll start today, okay? With a few stories?"

Eva turns away, pulls the bacon from the oven and sets it on the stovetop, then slams the oven door. "Well fine, if that's how you have to do it. But I'm warning you, really. Taylor and Matt can't stand seeing me like this much longer, either. It's best for all of us to just know."

~

Maris' eyes open, and she lies still in the dark. For a moment she thinks she is still at her father's house in Addison. She drove there when she left the attorney's office, parked in the driveway and studied the colonial, trying to remember anything that might help her put the pieces of that home movie together. Then she walked through it, glancing into the empty rooms, sitting on the sofa left behind, watching the neighborhood through the living room window.

Now the sea air drifts in the window above her head and her eyes adjust to the night sky, its constellations linking planets and universes together. She is back at Stony Point.

She walks through the living room, past the overflowing bookcases, past the cherry writing desk, past the brocade furniture. There is a panic to her rushing through the colonial house as she heads up the stairs. Wait. Colonial house? Or cottage? The hallway seems longer and longer now as she walks through it, looking. It goes on and on, the doors to the side coming one after the other after the other, the hall extending further again with each step she takes. She looks to one side, then the other, struggling to reach the end.

Her pace quickens to a run, to her own room where she finally throws herself on the bed, hiding her eyes, blocking what she saw out the window when she'd stood on her toes and moved the straight curtain aside. The morning sun had made her squint. A blanket of white snow carpeted the grass beneath the dogwood, and the stroller leaned against boxes set in the driveway as her father put the baby in the car.

"Angie?" she had called out. "Bye, Angie." There was nothing left. No matter how many times she went down the hall and looked in that bedroom doorway for all the years to come, all the familiar baby stuff, the crib, the changing table, the mobile and music box and toys that must have filled it, they were all gone. But soon that is gone, too, that memory, and all she has is a vague sense of something missing. She'd been afraid to ever go in that room again.

With a gasp, she sits up in her bed, perspiring, and quickly reaches for the lamp, turning on the light to be sure of exactly where she is. Then she goes downstairs and walks through all the rooms in the cottage, leaving a light on in each and every one, illuminating the vase of spiky cattails, the hurricane lamps on the mantel, the stand of wooden herons, the wicker baskets hanging from ceiling beams, the white painted kitchen shutters. Everything, everything has to be seen and visible to assure her it was all a dream just now, only a dream.

nineteen

THE NICE THING ABOUT BEING on vacation is getting out of bed in the morning and putting on your bathing suit, having nowhere to go except the beach. Nothing to do but sit in the sun. No plans to make except deciding when to walk down the length of the beach, the sea at your feet, the sun at your back.

And Lauren does all of this, every day. But the days following the Foley's reunion test her after Kyle spent the night. Her walks on the beach trailing behind her children grow slower. Her time beneath the umbrella passes differently. This is Kyle's last week working at the diner. Then he will be here, and so Lauren wonders about their night together last week, and if it was even about Kyle or more about missing Neil. It's just that Kyle is always there, stepping into Neil's place. So is that what her marriage is about? Kyle is there, Neil isn't.

On the front porch now, with her thoughts mingling with the early morning birdsong, Hailey's coloring books and crayons lay spread all over the floor. She knows why her daughter spends hours absorbed in the pictures, her little arm moving back and forth, fingers pausing over the selection of colors. It takes her out of the moment, somehow, concealing the fissure in their family as she talks to the puppies and trees and clouds she colors. Lauren crouches down and places the crayons in the box, pressing them into neat, even rows. When she stands, the bottom of the box slips open and the crayons all slide out, plinking to the floor, a few of them breaking in the fall. And so she crouches and picks them up again, her hand cupping the bottom of the box, stopping after every third or fourth crayon to wipe a tear from her face.

It isn't the crayons and she knows it. It is that there is a fissure. It is that Kyle always makes so much out of nothing, and she has to go see him now. He'll revisit last week in a look. Lauren tells herself that the gin eased her into bed with him after Foley's. She didn't resist him, moving easily beneath his touch. And it felt good.

Damn good, she thinks, wondering if it was the thoughts of Neil earlier that night that made it so good. Or maybe it was only a little bit of easy sex on a warm summer night. The next morning Kyle drove her car to his temporary job at The Dockside, his pickup truck landed in the shop and she was left stranded at the beach. Real life stared down any leftover hopes from the night before.

Not for Kyle, though. He arm-wrestled real life, and very early the next morning, before he had gone to work, he touched her and she still eased into his arms. "Feel nice?" he whispered after making love to her again. She nodded against his chest. "Better, even," he said, "than last night."

"Maybe," Lauren answered.

Kyle sat up, propping the pillow behind him, his fingers playing with her hair. "See? It's proof, Lauren. All because of fate. I read in the Sunday paper that fate gives richness to life. That we find deep meaning in questions about destiny, or whatever you want to call it. If my battery didn't die, I never would have found you last night, and would I be here right now?"

Lauren didn't believe in fate. Destiny didn't bring them together. Real life did. "Let me answer your question. It wasn't fate. It was the alcohol and the dancing, Kyle."

"No," he argued, dragging his finger along the line of fate on her open palm. "See? We still have a chance." She watched him stroke her palm. "If you didn't love me, I doubt you'd be lying here like this."

Lauren closed her eyes, picturing herself like he saw her, stretched out naked beneath the sheet. She turned on her side. "The gin did it, Kyle. That's all."

"So you're still under its influence now? Is that what you're saying?"

"No. You know what I mean."

They stayed there for a long time, neither one talking. Because whenever they started to talk, they seemed to lose something else. By the end of that day, by the time he had worked a full shift in the diner cooking and cleaning and managing and locking up, by the time she'd spent hours on the beach with the kids, swimming and sandcastle building and reading, and then returned to the cottage to shower and cook dinner, by the time Kyle brought her car back, Lauren's worry came true. He wanted to spend the night again.

She drove him to the garage to get his truck with its new battery and clean oil and a hefty charge to pay. "We had a deal," she said in the parking lot before he got out of the car. She worried that he'd get into his pickup and drive to the cottage. He sat in the passenger seat wearing his work clothes, the black pants and a black tee. His face needed a shave at the end of the day and he looked tired. "The first two weeks apart, to think about things. And don't you have to plan the week's menus anyway? And log the receipts?"

"I've been going in early to do paperwork before the diner opens. And come on, Ell. What about last night? And this morning?"

"Don't make something out of nothing," she said.

"Nothing? Is that what you call it?" He glanced away as he inhaled deeply. "Is that what everything with me is? Nothing much? I'm just a substitute for the real thing?"

"Kyle, give it a rest."

"A rest? Neil's dead, Lauren. That's who you were singing to in Foley's, weren't you? Neil. And that's who you wished you were with last night. You were drunk, Lauren, good and drunk and missing a ghost." He pressed his arm to his sweating forehead.

"I didn't want this, Kyle," Lauren answered, her voice flat.

"This?" he asked, motioning his hand between them. "But you did. We were engaged when you started screwing around. It was just a stupid fling you had."

"No. It wasn't."

"Then why didn't you cut me loose back then? After he died." He stared at her, his look daring her to answer, before getting out of the car and walking away. Kyle didn't come back to the cottage that night. In fact, she hasn't seen him since then, not even over the weekend.

Now she has to. She is running low on cash and Kyle won't be at the cottage until the weekend coming up. Maybe. If they are even still together. The kids are at swim lessons and she signed them up for a nature walk along the beach afterward, so if she leaves now, there is time to drive to the diner. Kyle will have cash on him. Or she can borrow from Eva or Maris. She hates to do that, though, so decides on the lesser of two evils and pulls on a pair of denim shorts over her swimsuit. In this heat, no one will even look twice.

On the way to The Dockside, someone is hammering a sign onto a front lawn. It is two towns over from Eastfield, and she makes a mental note of the street's location. If the crayons hadn't fallen from the box, fate would have had her pass the street minutes before the sign went up. Destiny. She shakes the thought from her mind.

All morning long, eggs, hash browns, bacon and sausage cooked simultaneously. The breakfast orders on the carousel in front of him never let up. He adjusts the flame beneath the hash browns, slowing the cooking down. The other burners look good, each a different heat from the next, depending on the food. He watches and lifts and flips, making sure the food will be done all at the same time. The sense of control, the coordination of cooking, comes naturally to him. He grabs a pre-warmed plate and fills another order. The good thing about being so busy is that the constant stream of beach tourists keeps him from wondering if Lauren might ever drop in. So when he places the plate on the high shelf for the waitress, he is surprised to see her sitting at the counter with a cup of coffee, watching him. He turns away, then looks again. A sunny-side up egg begins to sizzle. After doling the remaining food onto three more plates, he asks Rob to take over. On his way out front, he stops in the office, puts his hands on his knees and takes a long breath. Even so, it doesn't help to get enough air to reach his lungs.

But still, Kyle takes any sign from Lauren as a positive

one, one that signifies the beginning of the end of their troubles rather than the end of their marriage. He finally comes out from the kitchen wiping his hands on a damp towel. Even his hands sweat now.

"Hey, Ell," he says as she sips her coffee. She is tanned after spending more than a week at the beach and the sun has lightened her blonde hair. "I've only got a minute." He never takes his eyes off of her, though, standing behind the counter and waiting.

"Kyle, how's it going?"

He nods, not breaking his gaze.

"Listen," she begins, speaking quietly. "I'm a little short on cash. Do you have anything on you or should I run to the bank?"

He looks up at the ceiling, taking another long, deep breath.

"What?" she asks.

"Nothing." He pulls his wallet from his back pocket and thumbs through the bills. "How's eighty for now?"

"Good. That'll hold me over for a couple of days." She takes the money and slips it into her handbag. "Thanks."

"Is that enough?"

"I'll pick up my check from the employment agency at the end of the week."

He studies her, trying to read her for a clue, an answer, some sort of invitation between the lines. Anything. A quick smile, a nervous gaze, a blush even. "Kids okay?"

"They're fine. They're having a good time." She tips back her mug, catching the last few drops of coffee. "You better get back. Sorry to bother you."

"Bother me?" He slips his fingers around his shirt neckline and drops his head, trying to loosen the shirt or relieve tension in his neck. Something has to give.

"Kyle? What's wrong?"

He leans forward, elbows on the counter, and stops inches from her face. "Us," he says in a low voice. "I don't eat. I don't sleep. I miss you and the kids so much I can't even breathe."

"Kyle." She glances around and whispers back, "Seriously? We're talking about this here?"

"Listen, Ell." He stands straight and when he stretches his neck, catches the eye of the couple sitting further down the counter. All the booths at the windows are full. A moment passes and his chest rises with a deep breath. He leans very close to Lauren again, his elbows on the counter between them, their faces nearly touching. "How can I say this?" He bows his head, thinking. "Don't say that to me. You don't *bother* me." When he looks up at Lauren's pretty grey eyes, at her sun-freckled skin, it all feels so close, but he can't reach her. She lets everything else, which is Neil, get in their way. "Just remember that, okay? You never bother me."

She slings her straw handbag over her shoulder, shifts on the stool and stares at him. When he nods at her and steps back, she turns and walks out the door. He watches her go out into the heat, leaving behind only a mirage that fades as she pulls her car out of the parking lot and merges with the morning traffic.

～

"I thought we'd have some time to talk. Mondays are usually slow." Eva hangs up the phone. "Let me jot this down, a leaky hot water heater in one cottage and a dead refrigerator in another."

"People so don't want those problems on their vacations."

"No kidding. Now where were we?" Eva asks as she sits at her kitchen table while writing down names and appliances. The telephone rings again and Eva's face drops. "Oy," she says, standing to answer the call. She talks to a client who wants to see two new listings, at the same time glancing to Maris sitting in the window seat, waiting with a steaming mug of coffee in her hands.

"There goes our good, long cup of coffee," Eva says when she hangs up, sits and grabs a quick sip from her mug.

"It's okay," Maris tells her. "You've got a full plate today. Business emergencies, job pressure, and all the while wondering if you're pregnant?"

"I know, do you believe it? And while trying to plan my dinner for you two."

"Forget the dinner, Eva. Your house is like a war zone right now, it's too much."

"To put it mildly." The kitchen is a mess of knick-knacks and framed photographs moved out of the way of the wallpaper crew working in the living room. Freshly sanded walls leave a blanket of dust over everything not covered with a drop cloth. "So how about if we take you out to dinner instead? Would you mind?"

"Mind? That'd be awesome."

"Good. Because you and Jason did so much for us this summer and we really want to thank you both. I never would've picked that sand dollar wallpaper without you."

"Is Wednesday still good?"

Eva nods. "Definitely. After Scott showed up, I was afraid you might leave for Chicago right away."

"I'd never do that to you, take off without notice. But now you'd better take off and meet that refrigerator delivery."

Eva stands and moves beside Maris on the window seat.

Sunshine comes in behind them along with the scent of the sea. "Hey. Everyone can wait ten minutes," she says, lacing fingers with her best friend. "You had so much to tell me, and not only about Scott. Something about your family?"

"It's a long story, we'll talk later. It's okay."

"Well tell me about Scott anyway?"

"I don't know if we'll ever be able to repair this, Eva. Not after he flew back to Chicago the next morning."

"Of all nights for him to show up, it probably didn't help to find you in Foley's sitting with Jason."

"Probably not."

"And what about the engagement? I'm not seeing the ring. Did you get it from the jewelers yet?"

"I did. But nothing's definite right now. It may happen, it may not."

"Have you talked to Scott since?"

"Two nights ago. He's worried now. He wants us to stay together and said he'll wait me out."

"You mean while your dad's house sells?"

"Partly."

"There's more? What's going on?"

"When you have time. But Scott did say that if he flies out again, it'll be only to see me. There's no pressure to hurry back until I'm ready."

"Well at least you have that." Eva checks her watch before turning her apologetic eyes on Maris. "And I've got to reschedule the rest. I'm really sorry. Rain check?" She slips out of the seat.

"Anytime. I'll let myself out. Go take care of your business."

"Okay. And I'll call you about dinner." Eva rushes upstairs to her bedroom where she stops and runs her hands over her flat stomach. The coffee leaves her feeling woozy. Or the heat does. She stops in the bathroom to put on lipstick, wondering if it could be more than the heat bothering her today.

~

Lauren counts the side streets following the traffic light, watching for the third street on the right. When she turns the corner, she sees the sign halfway down. It has bright red letters on a black background, reading *For Rent*.

Doing this now, it feels like the divorce has formally begun. She parks on the street in front of the blue colonial duplex, taking a look at the place from the car. The lawn and bushes are trimmed, the house vinyl sided and the yard fenced in. The street seems quiet, which will be good for the kids.

Before getting out of the car, Lauren slips her wedding band off her finger and puts it in her shorts pocket. There are two front doors and she hesitates before knocking on one. An older woman opens it with one hand, a wet paintbrush in the other.

"It's available the first of September," she tells Lauren through the screen door. "We're painting now, changing the locks. The usual."

Lauren nods as though she knows. As though the divorce has already happened. "I have two children. How many bedrooms are there?"

"Three, dear. One's very small, though. And if your husband's handy, we can negotiate the rent in exchange for mowing, fixing up, that sort of thing."

"Oh, I must not have been clear. I'm recently divorced." She tries the words out, seeing if they fit. Is this what she wants to be telling people? "Can I see the place?"

The woman's glance drops in a quick questioning once-over. *Can she swing the rent? Would she have men over?* She unlatches the screen door lock and holds the door opened for Lauren to walk through, all the while giving her the necessary details. "The rent is nine hundred a month, with no utilities. And we need a two-month security deposit."

"That's fine," Lauren lies. Her hand is clutched in a tight fist around her handbag shoulder strap as she enters the empty duplex. "I could have that for you when I sign the lease."

For the next half hour, a potential life opens before her. She has to consider certain possibilities. And why not? Kyle does. He keeps tabs on jobs down south without talking it over with her. He bookmarks employment trends online. He reads about career planning. If she plans to divorce him, she'll have to know at least this much. What harm can come from testing water faucets, opening kitchen cabinets and glancing into tiny bedroom closets? She just wants to look.

It takes only that half hour to realize how close they've come to permanently screwing up their lives. Upon close inspection, the house looks dingy around the edges. It can't compare to the small home they work so hard to maintain back in Eastfield. Their little Cape Cod shines with the dedication she and Kyle put into it, one part money, three parts elbow grease.

And when she considers being a single, working mother trying to raise two children and support this place on an inadequate income, she imagines that her life, too, will be dingy around the edges. It will be shabby and tired, just like the carpeting and baseboard molding in the duplex. No, this is not the life she wants. There has to be another way. What has she done now? She pictures Kyle standing at the big stove and understands what she saw earlier when she watched him unnoticed at the diner. He wasn't whistling. He wasn't talking to Rob about what he'd read in the newspaper or heard on a talk show. He'd been too quiet, only worrying.

"Thank you," Lauren tells the landlady. "But I don't think it will work for me."

"If you change your mind, let me know."

Lauren hurries to her car, shoves her hand into her pocket and finds her wedding ring. Heading back to the diner, she glides through stop signs and toots at slow cars, feeling like she is late for something. The diner is still mobbed, and she pushes open the door, walks past the crowded counter and pokes her head into the kitchen. Kyle's back is to her and she notices again the horrible bruise on his arm. It's faded to a yellow-green now.

"Kyle," she says.

He glances over his shoulder and sets down the spatula, wiping his hands on his apron. "Lauren, what's the matter?"

"Nothing." This is not about running into his arms. This is about seeing what they really have. There are circles under his eyes and he perspires. He looks a wreck and she wants to help get him through the week. "It's Evan," she says, making up something on the spot. "I forgot to tell you before, but he wants to go crabbing this weekend." She moves closer, pushing her sunglasses on top of her head, at a loss for words. "Can you bring the bait when you come? Maybe some chicken, or day-old hot dogs?"

"Yeah." He turns up his hands. "That's it?"

It is. He knows they'll be waiting for him now. "That's it. Okay?"

He nods, never taking his eyes from hers.

Lauren watches him for a long moment, then reaches

her fingers to touch the fading bruise above his elbow. "You're busy. We'll see you Saturday then."

On the drive back to Stony Point, to her kids and her modest vacation, she knows that their lives are far from tired and shabby. Kyle never wanted much. Just the house, a yard and garden. His castle, he calls it.

Her parents have been married for thirty-five years now. Lauren wonders if all those thirty-five years were happy ones or if they had scraped through times too, when the only answer seemed to be escape. To climb out a window when no one was looking, and go! Maybe they first sank to the floor, close to that window, wrapped their arms around their knees and dropped their head and cried. Then, well then they stood and walked back to the marriage.

⌒

Appliances have been replaced, hot water heaters repaired. Eva also wrote an offer with a deposit on a large ranch home. She waits for Matt to come upstairs with his hammer.

"You sure you want to hang it here?" he asks as he measures the empty hallway wall outside their bedroom.

Eva stands at the mirror set on the floor and runs her fingers over the etchings, the same way she did all those years ago when she was a baby, according to Theresa. It was a gift from her birth family, and the story is that when she'd fuss as a baby, Theresa walked her back and forth in front of the mirror and she'd reach out and touch the etchings. "Oh yes. I want to walk past this mirror every day of my life." They measure and together lift the mirror into place.

"Good?" Matt asks.

"Perfect." Eva gazes at it at eye level now. "It's so beautiful. I forgot to show it to Maris this morning. Wait till she sees this."

Matt sits sideways on the top step watching her. "How're you feeling?"

Eva sits on the floor beside him. "Fine. Just a little queasy sometimes. But it could be the heat."

"Why don't you buy one of those home pregnancy tests?"

"I will, as soon as I get a chance." She feels something, then. Maybe she doesn't want to know. Maybe a baby now isn't what she thought a baby a year or two ago might be. "Did you make the reservations for Wednesday?"

"Seven o'clock. The Clam Shack."

"The Clam Shack? They don't take reservations. And I thought we were going to The Sea View."

"Too boring. We'll get some good take-out, then hit the mini-golf course there."

"Huh. That does sound fun." It sits right on the bay, too, facing the harbor, which is always nice. She twists a strand of hair, noticing its true auburn color. "I'll let Maris know so she dresses casual."

"Okay."

"Jason doesn't have a girlfriend, does he?"

"Don't even start. Leave those two alone. She's the small town girl who got away. That's how Barlow put it. He won't interfere so long as Scott's in the picture."

"More like the small town girl trying to find her way back," Eva argues. "Maybe Jason's wrong."

"Maybe. Maybe not. But for Scott to fly out here from Chicago, he must care a heck of a lot about her." Matt reaches over for his hammer and tape measure. "Maris has to work this one out on her own."

219

Eva watches Matt walk down the stairs rather than get involved with her fixation on Maris and Jason. She stands then, considering the mirror again. Her family's image once filled the reflection and if she looks hard enough, it's like there are some kind of ghosts hovering there. "Mirror, mirror on the wall," she whispers. Touching the etched scrolls on the mirror's corner, this is the closest she's ever come to her past.

twenty

A DRAWING BOARD AND CASE instruments are spread over the table on the front porch. Jason spends hours considering the cottage's front elevation, flipping through one of Neil's scrapbooks and going through sheets of drawing paper without success. The cottage he is working on sits high on a hill, its small windows allowing in a distant view of Long Island Sound. He thinks of knocking out the front wall and installing glass doors to a deck, extending the room outside. It doesn't seem enough, though. It isn't a masterpiece.

He finally grabs his sweatshirt and takes a walk along the beach, studying the sea view the cottage might have. It is a still night, the waves breaking lazy on the shore. His gaze rises to the sky. Thousands of stars give depth to its blackness.

"Don't forget the sky," Neil always reminded him. "It's the most important part of the landscape. It changes all the time." *That* is the masterpiece.

He considers his design impasse, moving along the high tide line slowly. At the end of the beach, he turns to the night horizon, where the black sky imperceptibly meets the dark sea. "Are you out there?" he asks before scooping up a handful of small stones. One by one, he throws them into the water. Moonlight catches the silver ripples. "Tell me what to do." Minutes pass as the ripples widen and thin. When Jason returns to his drawing board to complete the cottage design, still nothing works.

Since the accident, there have been times when he's called his sister late at night. Usually when the house felt really still, like the hands of the clock have just stopped, or on nights when he decides not to go out for a drink. He still can't get through certain moments alone.

"It's not about drawing, or architecture," she says now.

Jason drags a hand through his hair. "But I can't get this one right."

"Get what right?"

"The design. It's like the answer is just out of my reach. I think I have it, and when I look again, it doesn't work." He turns back to the table as he talks on the cordless, sits down and picks up his pencil.

"You already know how to finish that design. You do them without even thinking. It's something else."

Jason switches on the desk lamp and sketches on a blank sheet of paper. "No, you're wrong. I just got back from walking on the beach, trying to see it from that angle."

"And we know what you're doing when you walk on the beach like that."

"And that would be?"

"You're talking to Neil, looking at *something* from all angles. So what's your problem with him now?"

"I'm telling you—"

"It's late, Jason. What are you really trying to *get right?* Maris?"

Jason's hand stops sketching for a second before

continuing with the design. "Maybe. Matt and Eva are taking us out to dinner tomorrow night."

"Okay. So that's what this is about. What's happening that you're *not* telling me?"

Jason continues sketching. "I'm not sure what to do."

"About what?"

"I guess I don't want her to leave."

"So you want to start seeing her?"

He sketches a tall gable into the roofline. "Maybe. I worry about her. A lot's going on in her life right now." He continues to sketch, the scratching sound of his pencil dragging back and forth on the paper.

"So you were on the beach talking to Neil, and now you're calling me. What are you looking for? Permission?" Paige asks. "Just go for it. You know Mom would give you hers. She wants you to be happy."

"Dad wouldn't." Their father had changed, after that day. They all did. But their father seemed to fade, somehow. "He thought it was my fault."

"He did not. Dad never stopped mourning Neil and mourning what *your* life would be without a leg and all. He died of a broken heart for both of you."

There comes a long pause then, one filled with the sound of the waves breaking outside on the rocks, and voices, and the sea breeze. "You didn't die." He strains to hear the voice over the surf. "You've paid your debt. Even though there was never even a debt to pay, it was an accident."

"Jason? I said, is she seeing anyone?"

"Someone back in Chicago. Scott. I'm not sure how tight they are, though."

"Well that's easy to find out. When you see her, ask questions. Talk to her, Jason. Touch her hand. Look at her eyes. If there's someone else, she'll tell you."

"I don't know. Then I just think about Neil and what he could never have. You know, like why should I have a good life? Why me and not him?"

"Would you stop it already?"

"Stop what?"

"Stop punishing yourself. Your guilt's crippling you way more than your leg. Unless you get yourself past it, you'll never lose the phantom pain, the flashbacks, everything."

"I'm serious, Paige."

"That's the problem. You're too serious. Why don't you just bring Maris home some night so you're not alone, if you know what I mean. Neil's gone, but you're not."

Jason sits back in the chair. He lifts the sketch and sees what came without thought. He knocked out most of the front wall, added a gable to the roof to raise the ceiling in the front, drew a wall of windows and topped them with an amazing arched grouping of windows facing the sky over Long Island Sound. He drops the picture, stands and looks outside from the porch. *Don't forget the sky*. It's how he keeps Neil here.

The next day, Paige's words stay with him as he completes the final elevations of the cottage design; as he showers and shaves and drives to The Clam Shack. They stay with him as he leans on the railing he stood at recently with Maris, looking out over the water, waiting for the others to arrive.

More than anyone else, he waits for Maris. He looks out at the harbor knowing damn well that she could have easily returned to Chicago last week. Everything would have been nicely arranged for her. That was Scott's reason for being here. To bring her back.

He glances over at the sound of car doors closing. Maris

gets out with Eva and Matt. He notices her cropped jeans and long tee, topped with a short denim cardigan. He notices her gold necklace, the wedge sandals, the big leather bag. Her brown hair is down and brushed back off her face in a way that deepens her brown eyes. He notices it all.

～

"Hey," Maris says. "I wanted yellow."

"Too late." Jason tosses the ball in the air and catches it. "You snooze, you lose."

"Fine." She looks over the rack of clubs and balls at the stand next door to the restaurant and chooses a red ball and miniature golf club to match. "I'm so going to win anyway. And I'm teeing off first."

"You're seriously striking out," Jason says. "Eva's at the big fish already."

Maris looks over to the first hole of the miniature golf course where Eva is taking aim at the large, opened fish mouth. Her ball does a loop-de-loop through the fish to the green on the other side. "Hey," Maris calls out when Jason walks past her and gets in line behind Matt.

Jason turns around and hands her the score card and pencil stub. "They get to go first because they bought dinner. And last in line has to keep score. No fudging the numbers."

Maris snatches the paper and writes in their names while Matt and Jason take their first swings at the fish mouth.

"How's Paige doing?" Eva is asking Jason when Maris meets up with them on the other side of the giant fish. Eva taps her ball into the hole. "Two," she tells Maris.

"She'll be here Sunday with Vinny and the kids," Jason says, taking aim.

"They'll be on the beach all day?" Eva asks.

"Pretty much. She's coming for Neil's anniversary mass in the morning, then they'll spend the day here." He turns to Maris. "Three."

"Do you have a mass said every year?" Maris asks.

Jason nods. "She schedules one every summer, then spends all afternoon on the beach thinking of the old times. The whole day's kind of a memorial to Neil. Did you get my three?"

"Oh, no." She pulls the pencil from behind her ear and jots down the numbers. "Sorry."

"Hurry up," Jason tells her. "They're past the windmill already." He walks over to the next green, throwing her a sidelong glance when she scoops up her ball without putting.

"Loser's buying a round of drinks afterward," Matt calls back at them. "Two, Maris."

"Sheesh, I can't even focus with the way you guys are speeding through. Slow down." She swings at her ball, which proceeds to head directly into one of the windmill paddles and ricochet straight back at her.

"Nice shot," Jason says, walking to the other side of the windmill. "Try again."

By the time she finishes at the windmill, the others are waiting for her at the smiling dolphin. "The best thing I ever did was start ripping that barn apart, moose head and all," Jason is saying. "I've got a lot of memories of my brother in there, and let me tell you, sometimes the mind plays strange games with them. But it's still good. Good to be back here."

Maris knows that Eva is glad he is back, too, for Matt's sake. Matt needs to hang out with someone not on the force, someone he can let his guard down with. Jason helps him out of some dark places, too, when they swing those hammers and crowbars together. "What'd I miss?" she asks.

"Two for Eva, three for me," Matt says. "Your turn, Barlow."

"I was thinking of fixing up the old home too," Jason says as he sets down his ball. "Maybe have you list my condo for sale, Eva."

"Wow, you'd make that move? Are you sure?" she asks.

"I think so. But hell, let's have fate decide. Right now. A hole in one through the dolphin and it's definite." He adjusts his stance a couple of times, tries a few practice swings through the air then takes aim at the ball. They watch it spin through the dolphin, out the other end, followed by a couple seconds of silence before the rolling ball clinks into the metal cup on the green.

"Huh," Maris says. "I guess you're staying."

He looks at her for a long second and oh, she knows that look. *The water's fine, jump in,* it says. *Take a chance on the dolphin, why don't you? Chicago, or Stony Point? No contest, really.*

"Hole in one, Barlow," Matt calls out after retrieving the yellow ball and high-fiving Jason. "Welcome back to Stony Point. Maybe you'll hang the moose in the house now?"

"No way. It's got a place of honor in my studio." Jason turns to Maris behind him. "Your turn." He waits a second, then asks, "Do you need some help with your aim?"

Maris glares at him and hands him the scorecard and pencil. "What would help is if someone else kept score. And really, now. A moose head? What's up with that?"

"Maybe someday I'll tell you the story."

Maris looks up at him, then back down at her club, adjusting her stance, gauging her swing, then looking back at Jason. "What?"

"Trouble concentrating?"

"You wish." She stands at the tee-off, lines up her club precisely and taps the ball through the dolphin before taking a low bow. "I'm just warming up."

～

The last hole of the course involves hitting the balls over a fifteen-foot rock waterfall, the cascading water flowing over the drop as the golfers swing. Jason listens as he stands, last in line, aiming his final shot. *Go for it*, he hears through the splash of the water and looks off to his right, past the falls. Sometimes the voice is so familiar, it feels like his brother is talking right over his shoulder.

He tallies up the scores. "Drinks are on me, at The Sand Bar," he says. "I'm in last place, way over par."

"What?" Maris asks. "There's no way I didn't lose. Let me see that card."

Jason winks at her and puts it in his back pocket.

"It's getting late, and Taylor's home alone," Eva says. "How about we finish this another time?"

"No problem." Jason turns to Maris. "What about you? You game for a drink with me?" And he knows, right away from her eyes, that she is. Ever since Neil died, he is more tuned in to body language, to looks and gestures, sometimes more so than words. Maybe it is because the last he knew of Neil, alive, was a certain pressure of his brother's body hitting his. And what you remember is what you had last. So he looks and pays attention now to more than what someone says.

Maris' eyes give it away in the bar too, a glass of wine in front of her, when she tells him about Scott's proposal and her reluctance to commit to him.

"Is that what was on your mind the other night when I found you here?"

"Part of it. There's a job offer on the table, too, from a New York design house. Director of Women's Denim, with my aesthetics shaping the line and bringing my vision to Italian counterparts. It's a huge opportunity and means a big move, with the option of my own studio. And then there's ..." She hesitates while Jason motions *no* as the waitress approaches again.

He looks back at Maris. "And then there's what? Tell me, and maybe I can convince you to stay longer."

"Maybe. Maybe you can."

And so he watches, and looks, and sees the gold hoop earrings, and the denim cardigan she designed herself, and the long hair tucked behind her ear so that it frames her silhouette. He sees it all, more in her expression than in her words about everything from the long-ago loss of her mother to the gold pendant hanging from her neck. Her words are fluid, once they begin, moving her right along with them.

Not one single detail passes without his notice and he wonders if they needed this decade between them to get back to Foley's deck all those years ago. She tells him about the day he found her here alone, about the lost home movie, and about an empty jewelry box and baby blanket she found in an attic box, about a second child and about her empty heart.

What he sees, too, that she isn't even aware of, is the way her fingers occasionally touch her empty ring finger before moving to the gold chain around her neck. She fusses with the necklace as she tells him about the appointment scheduled with Tom Riley, her father's attorney.

And he can't take his eyes off of her. "Jesus, Maris," he finally says. "You might have a sister out there somewhere."

She nods. "That's what I'm thinking, too."

"And what did Scott say to all of this?"

"He told me to leave it alone. That long ago and faraway doesn't matter," Maris says quietly. "Does it?"

Jason's gaze holds Maris' across from him. What the hell is wrong with that guy? You can't leave the past alone, she had to know, and so he reaches across the table and cups both her hands in his. "Do you know what happens if you leave the past alone?" He strokes her skin with his thumb as he considers how to put it into words. "I can tell you, from experience. It'll chase you down, Maris. Remember what that night on the boardwalk did to me? With Kyle?"

"Do I ever."

"That's what the past does if you turn your back on it. It hides behind corners, all the time. And when you catch sight of it, it scares the hell out of you." He pulls back then and finishes his drink. "Don't leave it alone."

"You scare me, the way you say that."

"Believe me, I know, sweetheart. Try to take care of it, for your own sake."

Maris doesn't say anything then.

"Think about it, at least." He stands to leave and extends his hand to hers, noticing that she doesn't let go as they walk through the bar and he opens the door to the outside night.

Jason knows. Walking alone on the beach later, he knows his future will slip through his fingers if he doesn't visit the past. He needs to settle an old debt, a personal one he owes only to himself. Neil's voice comes in on the wind as he walks along the packed sand near the water. It weaves in the sound of the waves, in the sea breeze rippling the night.

But he heard his own voice tonight, too, with Maris'. Seven years is long enough. He needs to set Neil free, to let the tides release him beneath the pull of the moon. Maybe the same way Neil holds him back, maybe he holds Neil's spirit back as well.

Standing at the water's edge, he rolls his brother's drumsticks between his hands, looking far out into the black sky. Then without any more thought, he reaches his arm back and for all he is worth, putting his whole body into it, he flings the sticks out to sea.

twenty-one

IT WAS A SUMMER THAT haunts her still. She noticed him hanging back all those years ago, wandering from one nearby craft tent to another while she finished up with a customer. "I've got the perfect place for this," the woman was saying. She had bought one of the larger pieces Lauren recently completed. An expanse of boardwalk reached across the painted driftwood, the sea stretching out beyond the beach. Curls of white paint topped the waves, giving them a sense of motion, of rolling in. "Right on the mantel, where we'll always see it. My husband will love it," the customer said, so happy with such a small thing. That intrigued Lauren, the way paint dabbed on an old piece of weathered wood had such power to evoke feeling. She carefully wrapped it in tissue paper, glancing up at Kyle as she did. The sun was strong and warm that day, and his face perspired as he lingered, browsing the refurbished antique kitchenware at the tent beside hers.

Another customer walked up as Lauren put the wrapped driftwood into a bag. "Aren't these interesting?" He picked up a piece shaped like a lighthouse, upon which she'd painted another lighthouse, waves breaking on the rocks below it. And she was glad for the distraction. Glad for a minute or two to wonder what Kyle could possibly want now. They were done; she'd broken up with him in no uncertain terms. At least on her part. The wedding was off. But he made everything about the talk doubtful, arguing it all. *You can't be serious,* he'd said when she told him it was Neil. *He's just playing you, Ell. He likes a good time.* And she shrugged off his words. Of course he'd slam Neil; Neil won.

"Do you have any with a cottage painted on it? A little white bungalow maybe?" the man asked. "I'm looking for a housewarming gift."

Lauren scanned her few shelves. She used a tiny tent at these weekend craft shows and filled in the empty spaces between the driftwood with large seashells and a few hurricane lanterns. There were about twenty painted pieces on display, seagulls and beach umbrellas and sandcastles, but none with a cottage. "I can custom paint one for you. Do you have something specific in mind?"

"I do, but how about if I get you a photo to copy?" The man took her card and said he'd call when he had the picture. Still he looked at her other paintings, the stormy sea in particular. "How long would it take to paint?"

"When I see the photograph, I'd have a better idea. Call me and we'll take it from there."

She saw, all the while, Kyle moving closer. He looked impatient, the way he paced, and walked up to her before the other customer was even gone.

"Kyle." She was still surprised to see him right there, his presence familiar and unexpected at the same time. She never thought he'd follow her around, looking for a way back.

"Ell," he said, with a smile, she'd thought at first. But it

233

wasn't really. It was more of an ironic look, because he was shaking his head, too. "Hey," he added. "How are you?"

"Well. I'm the same, I guess." Two days had passed since he'd picked her up to go out to dinner, when they never made it further than sitting in his car parked at the curb of her parents' house. Since she said she thought it better that he hear it right away, instead of having to drive her back home from somewhere when they'd be so upset. Two days since she told him she couldn't marry him, that there was someone else. That there was Neil. Since she left her engagement ring on Kyle's dashboard and walked away from his car back toward her house.

He stared at her for a long moment now, looked away, then back at her. "So you haven't heard anything?"

"Heard what?" Lauren asked.

Two women approached, sisters or best friends, Lauren thought. She was getting better at reading her potential customers. "Sara Beth, look at this one," one of the women said, picking up a smaller piece and admiring the sailboat scene painted on it. Kyle looked past them and caught her eye, motioning for her to move them along, he wanted to talk. She shrugged back at him and turned her attention to the women.

"Sorry, ladies," he said, reaching over and taking the driftwood from their hands. "We've got an emergency going on, can you come back later?"

"Kyle," Lauren interrupted. "Stop that."

"Oh, it's no problem," one of the women said. "We're just window shopping."

When they moved on, Lauren glared at Kyle.

"Close up," he said. "I have to talk to you. Now."

"There's nothing more to say," Lauren argued. "And I'm trying to sell my work, if you don't mind."

"Your work can wait. I'm serious, Ell. Close up shop."

And she knew, from the shaking breath he took to the sheen on his face to the way he didn't look away this time, that he wouldn't back down. She closed up her tent, grabbed her purse and followed him to the outskirts of the craft fair. This one was set up on a town green in Addison, forty miles from home, with lots of old maple trees shading the tents. He led her to a bench in a quiet spot and waited for her to sit.

"Kyle, really. You can't keep stalking me like this. I am not going to change my mind about us. The wedding's off."

He just looked at her and shook his head. "I'm not stalking you. There's been an accident, Ell."

"What do you mean, an accident?"

"No one called you? Eva? Your mom?"

"No. What kind of accident?"

He hadn't sat beside her, she noticed. Hadn't really stopped pacing until now, standing right in front of her, his shirt damp with perspiration, the sun making him squint. And in that moment, she heard the hum of noise around them. Cars, and people's voices. A few tents had radios playing, and a horse and buggy ride clip-clopped around The Green.

"Barlows," he said. "They were in an accident."

"What are you talking about? I just talked to Neil."

"When?"

"This morning."

"They were in an accident, Ell. Him and his brother."

"Jason, too?"

"They were on Neil's bike, it's bad." He dragged a hand through his hair. "Jesus, it's bad, Ell. Someone hit them, I guess."

"No. No, no."

Kyle nodded. "Matt called me. Jason's hurt pretty serious. He might lose his leg, from what they can tell."

"Oh my God. No way. And Neil? Kyle? What about Neil?"

He leaned forward and touched her leg, right above the knee. He just touched her, and she knew. That arm lifting, the hand reaching out, his fingers skimming her leg just for a second before he had to look away, then back at her. But it wasn't the looking away that told her; it was the touch.

She looked past him then and saw the white tents dotting The Green filled with colorful paintings and dolls and framed photographs and knit sweaters and handmade jewelry, the people dressed in their summer clothes and sandals. She smelled cooking sausage and steaks from the food vendors and heard the horses, again, clopping past behind her, the buggy wheels turning gritty on the pavement. Life, life, life all around her. Its color and sound and scent. She was as alive now, in this moment, as she'd ever be.

But when she looked up at Kyle, it all stopped. She saw nothing beyond his expression, heard nothing at all. She only felt, on the small area of skin above her knee, the sensation of his touch bringing her the news. It could only come from him, of course, bringing him back to her somehow. The life all around her that faded from view with his touch, faded from existence, only slowly, slowly returned, a color at a time, a word at a time, a decision at a time, over the time of hours and days and years to come. Over a wake and funeral that Neil's own brother was too much a physical wreck to attend, a wake where no one, no one at all knew, except Kyle, of the minutes she'd spent with the departed, minutes that led to hours, hours that led her deeper into her painting, led her to knowing her self and to leaving another man she'd loved.

That man, Kyle, stood beside her at that funeral, the man who never believed what she said she found with Neil, who never reduced what he had with her no matter what words she sent his way in the front seat of a car parked at the curb one Thursday evening while a neighbor mowed a lawn, while a woman jogged past. And though time had stopped with Neil's death, didn't the hands of time move again when Kyle managed to get her diamond back on her finger somehow, and they lived through the death that they thought they'd move past, but instead it became a part of them, the way it brought them back together.

Now, seven years later, it is all there, every bit of it returning to her. After Kyle's day of standing behind the hot diner stoves, after Lauren's hours on the beach with her children, after her waiting for him to show up for dinner at the cottage, after putting Evan and Hailey to bed without Kyle being there yet, after worrying that he'd gotten into an accident, after repeatedly calling the diner and getting no answer, then calling Taylor to babysit, after driving by their home looking for him, and passing The Sand Bar, after checking with Matt, after walking down the dark beach then, unsure where to turn next, after sitting in the sand, watching the moon rise, remembering Neil this first summer that she's returned to Stony Point since his death, dealing with the feelings her memories bring back, the past seven years catch up. And the end of those seven years comes with Kyle finding her on the beach, explaining that he'd fallen asleep in the diner office, sat down on the small sofa for a minute and was gone, and with her asking him one simple question, asking "How can we get us back?" Seven years of recovering that started with his touch on her knee led to this night, this hour, this moment.

Kyle stands and wades barefoot ankle-deep into the water. She watches him bend and scoop up a dripping handful of salt water, burying his face in it before running his wet fingers back through his hair. When he splashes another handful of water on his neck and chest, she stands and walks into the water behind him. Kyle turns to her, leans forward and touches her arm, right above the wrist. He just touches her while she watches. That arm lifting, the hand reaching out, his fingers skimming her skin just for a second before he has to look away, then back at her. But it isn't the looking away that tells her, or his words saying "All you had to do is ask, Ell." It is the touch.

She watches him standing there, breathing. One deep breath after the other. And when he puts his finger beneath her chin and lifts her face to kiss her, she tastes the salt water on his face, feels his mouth, his rough cheek grazing hers, hears the waves lapping at their knees, smells the sea, sees a distant lighthouse beam sweep over the black water, feels the tears burn her eyes, listens to the engine of a boat far out at sea, feels the breeze lift off the water, moving a strand of hair, sees the boardwalk illuminated back on the beach behind them, hears his voice and feels his hands holding her face. Life, life, life all around her. Its color and sound and scent.

twenty-two

KYLE SEES THE DAWN SUNLIGHT streaming through the windows, the sand pails and minnow nets set near the door, and realizes he spent the night on the front porch. The sea air smells sweet. The last thing he remembers is Lauren leaving to drive Taylor home from babysitting. He'd sat on the wicker lounge chair, all his worry lifted and he fell immediately asleep. Lauren must have draped a light blanket over him and he slept soundly for the first time in months.

But as he stretches the kinks out now, anxiety creeps right back. Today is his last day working at the diner. After that, a big empty nothing stretches before him. No job, no money. He takes a quick shower in the outside cabana, then looks in at the kids and Lauren sleeping upstairs. When he bends to kiss Lauren goodbye, he knows it wasn't a dream. Last night on the beach really happened. She wraps her arms around his neck and meets his mouth with a long, lazy kiss. But he can't be late for Jerry. "Have a good day," Lauren tells him as he backs away, holding her hand until it slips from his.

With a coffee-to-go on the seat, he drives in to work.

Jerry, tanned and relaxed, scrambles eggs and fries sausages alongside him all morning. The radio is tuned to a local talk show and the waitresses keep the orders coming. It is too busy to talk shop until Jerry closes up early, placing the red *Closed* sign in the door right after one o'clock.

"Owners can do things like that," he tells Kyle.

"Are you sure? We can talk later, after the lunch crowd."

"It's my first day back. I'm tired. What I want to do is review what happened here while I was gone." He pours them each a cup of fresh coffee. "And I want to tell you about my vacation."

Kyle sits on a stool. At least he'll get back to the cottage early and get a head start on his vacation, such as it will be. It is warm in the diner and his shirt clings to the center of his back. His fingers toy with the bent corner of a black binder on the counter. The binder holds the bills and supply orders he processed during the past weeks, clipped and sorted by date and category. He flattens the binder corner and tries to press out the crease.

"I really don't need to see those." Jerry sits on the stool beside Kyle and moves the binder back to him. "Not if you accept my offer." He slides a legal sized manila folder in front of Kyle.

Kyle looks up from the folder to Jerry's face.

"Open it." Jerry nods toward the folder.

Kyle doesn't believe the words he reads until Jerry explains.

"Twenty-five years in the business is long enough, Kyle. This vacation, not to mention my wife, convinced me that it's time to retire."

"Retire?" Kyle tears his eyes from the sales contract bearing his name and squints at Jerry.

"From owning the business. My family planned my

vacation as an enticement to slow down. The kids even pitched in and bought me that used boat I've always dreamed about. Imagine that? My boat. Nothing big, just enough to tool around out in the Sound, do a little fishing. But I'll need some part-time work to keep me out of trouble, too. Do you think you could use me here?"

"Wow." The shock of it moves Kyle right off the stool in a frantic walk around the diner. His hands light on different objects in the room. A booth back, a stack of menus, a chair that needs straightening. He can't stop touching pieces of the diner. "Do you realize what this means?"

"Of course I do. No one else will keep this ship afloat the way you will." Jerry watches him with a knowing nod. "I'm leaving her in good hands, Captain."

Kyle walks to the door and looks out at the parking lot. *His* parking lot. He turns back and sees the fishing net Jerry had hung on the side wall years ago. And the anchors and buoys placed here and there. *A big, shiny silver ship*, Kyle once said to him.

"Now get out of here," Jerry tells him after they discussed the financial details for an hour, "and talk it over with your wife and your attorney. Enjoy your vacation and take that time to really think about buying this place before you give me an answer." He stands and closes the folder.

"You're kidding, right?" Kyle asks. He grabs Jerry in a long hug, slapping him on the back. "There's nothing to think about. I'm in."

"I know, kid, I know." Jerry walks him to the door and they shake hands. "Talk to your wife anyway. I'll see you in a week, okay?"

Kyle doesn't even remember the drive back to Stony Point. Only one thought fuels his trip there. The Dockside.

Its every visual detail runs through his mind: the chrome stools, the red padded booths, the beautiful stoves, the boat décor. When he passes the Gallaghers' home, he pulls into the driveway, jumps out of the pickup nearly before it stops moving and walks right into the house with a quick knock at the door. He walks through the porch, through the newly papered living room, heading to the kitchen unable to contain himself. "Gallagher?" he calls out.

Matt, reading the paper at the kitchen table, looks up to see Kyle standing there, jangling his keys. "Kyle. I thought you were Eva. Make yourself at home, why don't you?"

"Thanks." Kyle swings a painted chair around backward at the mahogany table and sits down, leaning his arms over the top. "You are never going to believe this. Shit, I can't believe it."

"What's going on?" Matt asks. He moves the newspaper aside.

Kyle jumps up and grabs two cold cans of beer from the refrigerator, setting one in front of Matt. "Cheers, guy, to The Dockside. We have to christen my new boat."

"What? The diner?" Matt opens his can and takes a swallow of the beer.

"It's like I won the friggin' lottery. It's too damn good to be true." After a long drink, Kyle keeps talking, all the while walking around the room. "I was glad that Lauren and I were working things out, you know? That was enough. And then, shit, Jerry put this on the table." He looks up at the ceiling, laughing. "I know that place inside out, Matt. It's my second home. I can't believe it. I mean, I thought his kids would take over, but they're not interested." He runs his hand over the new granite countertop. "Never have been, according to Jerry. They've got big careers and are glad to see the diner go to me. Imagine?"

"What a break. Congratulations." Matt holds up his can in a toast. "You'll do right by that old diner. What did Lauren say?"

Kyle sits down again and takes a breath. "Okay, here's the thing. She doesn't know yet. I want to surprise her. Can I leave my truck here for a while?"

"Sure, why? What's up?"

Kyle shakes his head. He doesn't want to tell. "Does Eva have any shopping bags around? Big ones, like from a department store?"

Matt searches the broom closet off the kitchen. "I don't know, how's this?" He holds up a big square bag with heavy looped twine handles.

"Perfect. Everything's perfect, man." Kyle finishes his beer before spinning his chair back in place. "Thanks, guy. When you see Eva, tell her *do not* tell Lauren. I want to surprise her. And listen, I'll be back for my truck in an hour or so." Kyle walks out of the house, the bag folded in a neat square under his arm as he walks toward the far end of the beach.

～

"I still can't believe you're doing this," Taylor says. "Are you sure?"

Eva flashes a grin. "Do you want to try, too?"

"No way." Taylor drops into a seat and reaches for a magazine, all the while keeping an eye on her mother.

When Eva sits in the salon chair, her damp hair toweled dry, she touches its length distractedly.

"Okay, Eva," her hairdresser says. "So you're taking the plunge. How short do you want to go?"

"To my shoulders. With lots of layers. To about right

here." She motions with her hand up along the side of her head, at the same time searching for the reflection she saw this morning when Matt stood behind her and pulled her hair back. She really noticed her cheekbones then, and her eyes. Women say there comes a time when they look into the mirror and see that they've actually become their mother. Does she look like hers? "It has to all be off my face, and I want these colored ends cut off." She needs to find her mother this way, too. To know she is seeing something of her in the reflection. The hairdresser runs her fingers over the ends still holding on to the ash blonde dye. Eva wants that feeling back now, that spark of recognition that she did get when Matt pressed her hair back and said how it was funny that more than anyone, she looked a little like Maris around the eyes.

~

Maris spends the afternoon on the beach, hidden beneath a straw cowboy hat, watching the families around her. Young or old, it is the mothers and sisters who draw her eye with the way they speak to each other. The way they sit together. The way they touch. She had all that for only the briefest time, which makes her miss it all the more right now, sitting among it. So instead she pulls a novel from her beach tote, but the words swim out of focus until she shuts the book and sets it aside.

She reclines in her sand chair at the water's edge, her own saga opening in her mind; there is no need to read one on the page or watch those around her. With her cowboy hat pulled low and Attorney Riley's appointment only days away, the questions keep coming. Did a baby die in the car accident that took her mother? What family motive kept

244

her existence from Maris? And then there is the empty Italian jewelry box she found in the carton with the 8mm home movie. Is there another pendant meant for a sister? Did her aunt in Italy know the secret then, too? Is the box from her? And where is Elsa? Where are the answers?

By late afternoon when the sun's shadows fall long, she packs her lotion and book and comb into her canvas bag. The rays are weaker now and she tips her chair back and closes her eyes behind her sunglasses.

"A dinner for your thoughts?"

She sits up to see Jason standing there wearing an old concert tee, wrinkled cargo shorts, a paint scraper still in one pocket, his face unshaven. Even needing a shave, she notices the scar slightly raised above his jawline. "Hey, Jason. That sounds an awful lot like an invitation?"

"It is." He leans an arm on the side of her chair, balancing as he crouches. "So you free for dinner? Maybe a mini-golf rematch after?"

"Oh, am I ever. Being alone with your thoughts is so overrated." She stands and picks up her tote. "I'm ready to head back. Let me change and feed the dog first."

"Okay. We'll keep it easy, maybe go out for a pizza."

They walk back to Maris' cottage together, but Jason continues on. Maris has just enough time to shower and slip on a denim skirt and black tank with leather flip-flops before he picks her up for dinner.

Now a hot chicken and eggplant pizza cools on a raised silver platter between them. More than a decade has passed since she's been at Ronni's Pizza, but nothing's changed. It is one of those pure time-machine places, always a full house of people and noise, of wooden chairs scraping about, of pizza trays sliding from the big ovens, of the telephone ringing with take-out orders, and of talk.

"This is the best seat in the house." Maris slides a pizza slice onto her dish. "I used to come here with Eva twenty years ago and it was always a contest to spot the train first." She turns to the large window at their table. Across the street, behind patches of scrubby grass, the railroad tracks run by. Beyond those are East Bay, then Long Island Sound further out. Train tracks and water extend for as far as the eye can see.

"Neil and I did the same thing when we were kids."

"I remember being able to *feel* it first," Maris says.

Jason nods as though he knows exactly what she means. His hand skirts along the low windowsill now. "You can come in here and just sit and lose a whole decade, easy."

A decade ago, his brother was alive. He is seeing the restaurant through those eyes, Maris knows, dealing with triggers and memory and longing. She sips her soda and gazes out the window. Her eyes search Long Island Sound at the horizon. Jason is lifting a piece of pizza onto his dish when she feels it. Before she can even speak, she points to the window first, because, heck, winning means everything at Ronni's. "Train!"

It is a subtle change in the air, a hum from deep below. Looking at Jason, she can feel, at their table, the immense, palpable speed and power of the approaching train before it even comes into view. It is like the calm before a storm, you feel it and brace for something else. A few seconds later, the Amtrak blows by the front window on its way to Boston and everyone in the restaurant stops eating, stops talking, for only moments, until its whistle carries back to them after the train passes out of sight.

Kyle should be here by now. Lauren looks out the window, checking the street for his pickup before reaching for her comb. When she's nearly done French braiding her hair, he pulls in the driveway. She glances out in time to see him reaching across the front seat for a large shopping bag.

"Hey you," he says when he walks into the living room. He touches the side of her face. "Where are the kids?"

"They're at Alison's. She and Taylor are taking them to the movie on the beach later."

"Good." He studies her, touching her hair. "What do you want for dinner?"

"Want to go out? Maybe for fish and chips?"

Kyle heads into the kitchen. "Sounds good. I'm starved."

Lauren follows him and leans against the kitchen counter, watching him grab a peach from the bowl on the table. The bruise on his arm has nearly faded away. When she reaches out to touch it, Kyle turns and pulls out a chair for her.

"Sit. I want to ask you something." He bites into the peach. "What do you think if I take some business management courses? Just a night class or two."

"Business?"

"To help me set up the books on a new computer system. I read that there's some new software to keep the latest business tax records in order."

"Tax records? What are you talking about?" When Kyle slides Jerry's offer to her, she scans it quickly. "He's selling you the diner? Is this for real?"

"Yes it is," he says around a mouthful of peach.

"Really?" She looks up at Kyle's face. Maybe part of life, the good in it, comes from how you look at stuff. Stuff like ten years of sweating out part-time, temporary work behind a hot stove in a diner. Ten long years grow into this.

"It's ours, Ell."

"This can't be true." She rereads the contract, slower this time. "But there's a lot of cash involved. How can we ever manage to buy it?"

"We never touched that severance money from my lay-off, and hell, I'll beg, borrow and steal the rest. I just really have to come up with the down payment." He finishes the peach while pointing out different figures on the contract. "Jerry's holding the mortgage, kind of like a retirement plan for himself, and he's giving us a low interest rate. And he'll stay on for a few months till I get the hang of things."

"No way. What if he changes his mind?"

Kyle points out Jerry's signature. "Don't worry. And I was thinking, maybe I could give it more of a bistro feel. You know, keep the boat theme, but update it. Make it kind of a café type of place. The Coffee Pier, The Driftwood Café, something like that."

Lauren sits back in her chair, motionless. "I can't believe this."

"Wait, there's more. Wait right there." He pushes back his chair, tosses the peach pit in the trash and rushes through the cottage. "And close your eyes!" he calls out from the porch.

Lauren squeezes her eyes tight and sits on her hands to keep them off the contract. Not seeing brings the evening birdsong to her: a lone robin settling down, a distant blue jay. She knows this is good, that days like this come few and far between. Something tells her, in her heart, to remember every moment, every touch, every word. This gets you through the rest.

~

Kyle checks that her eyes are closed, sits and sets the bag down behind him. He scrapes his chair over beside hers, takes her hands in his and holds them to his lips for a long moment. "You'll be really busy with the kids getting back to school in a few weeks, and the business will be crazy at first. But not forever."

Lauren opens her eyes and watches him closely.

Kyle catches her tear with his thumb. "Things will quiet down. They always do. And then, well I think you'll be needing this." He reaches behind his chair and sets the shopping bag on the table. Driftwood swells from the bag in every weathered shade of gray and brown that he could find along the beach. They came from the seaweed line, from along the rocks, and from Little Beach, past the patch of woods, where her love of painting began. He stuffed in as many pieces as he could, all sizes and shapes, in every which way. In a smaller bag he packed her paints from the back shelf in her closet at home.

"Woo-hoo," Lauren laughs. "Yes!" She stands and shifts around the driftwood, pulling out random pieces like they are precious jewels. "Now I get it. The Driftwood Café?"

Kyle moves behind her and when his arms wrap around her waist, pulling her close, she leans back easy against him. He bends down, brushing his face against her hair. "I did good, didn't I?"

She whispers something that he misses, and so he turns her around. "What did you say?" he asks.

She leans back against the refrigerator and his arms hold her there, the refrigerator behind her as he leans close, stroking her hair, touching her ear, watching her, waiting to hear the words.

And when she starts to talk, to say the words he'd missed, he stops her, slips his arm under her legs and scoops her up. "Wait, Ell. You can tell me upstairs."

twenty-three

Maris spreads her sketches on the dining room table as the coffee brews Sunday morning. Up with the sun, the day awaits fresh and open to possibilities, inspiring her to pick up her graphite pencils, to play with light and shadow, to add texture to her designs. While the rest of the world still sleeps beneath cool, cotton sheets, or tangled in summer nightshirts, she intends to immerse herself in the fall denim line taking shape in her cottage. A constellation continues to connect the pieces, the stars travelling from one style to another, from cuffed jeans to a cropped blazer to a pair of slim denim gloves.

She walks first to the front porch doorway, sipping her coffee. Except for an early jogger passing by, the street outside looks still, yet liquid somehow, like a watercolor painting. Shadows and light softly blend in the greens of the maple trees, the blues of the sky. Summer quiet follows behind the jogger's footsteps, touching upon the porch and its comfortable old white wicker furniture. Above the windows, a high shelf holding brass hurricane lanterns and starfish and pale pink conch shells reaches around the room. Spiky cattails rise from the large clay floor vase in the corner, standing against the crisp white paneling. Outside, scarlet red geraniums and pretty petunias spill from the flower boxes Maris filled weeks ago.

But seashells and white wicker and summer flowers can't keep complications away. She sits in a chair on the porch, cupping her coffee. This complication is a new one. No man has ever kept her from her work before. Her career had become a shell, curving around her like the intricate whorls of the conch, shielding her, until now.

Until Jason Barlow suggested they hang on the beach when he drove her home last night. *Summer will be over before you know it,* he said. And so they took a lazy walk on the sandy boardwalk, talking easily as twilight closed in.

Until he took hold of her hand, steering her off the boardwalk toward the water's edge. They walked slowly, and she noticed he kept to the firm, packed sand as they followed the high tide line before them.

"Sometimes," Maris said when they stopped at the end of the beach, "it feels like I left behind a shadow of myself here a long time ago. And on nights like this, maybe I came back to connect with it." They were standing near the rocky outcropping, watching the waves break on the ledge. Jason didn't answer. Instead he took her hand again and they walked back down the beach.

All Maris knows about his shadow comes from what Eva told her earlier in the summer. Seven years ago, Neil and Jason rode together on Neil's motorcycle, a Harley Davidson he'd bought. They'd been involved in some horrific crash that ended up taking Neil's life. She pictures the two of them, Neil driving, Jason hitched behind him on a hot summer day, two brothers about to meet their fate.

"Good God," Maris says to herself on the porch, imagining what might have followed. It isn't the beautiful day or family distractions that keep her from working this morning, from focusing on design. From adding diagonal texture with a white pencil, before drawing the gold stitching with a gel pen. Illustrations give the illusion of reality, but some realities are too authentic to ignore.

~

Saint Bernard's cedar shingles are weathered driftwood gray by Long Island Sound's damp and salty air. The bottom third of the stained glass windows tilt open so that the sea breeze might visit upon the warm Sunday masses. Maris arrives as the entrance hymn begins, choosing an empty seat in the center aisle, several rows down. Holding the opened missal, she scans the church for Jason and Paige. The pews are full, and Matt, Eva and Taylor stand near the front. A light tap on her arm startles her and she turns to see Paige slipping in beside her.

"Where's your brother?" Maris whispers.

"I thought he'd be with you."

"With me?" Maris looks from Paige to the altar. They bless themselves as an elderly priest leads the parish. His deep old voice moves slowly.

"In the name of the Father, and of the Son, and of the Holy Spirit."

"Amen."

"He never showed up at the house," Paige says quietly. "It's a good thing I had my old set of house keys. Vinny and the kids are there now."

"May the peace of our Lord, Jesus Christ, be with you all."

Maris turns back toward the altar. Rays of morning sunlight shine through a stained glass window above it. A bank of flickering candles glimmers to the right. Ceiling fans paddle the warm air and the simple wooden pews feel cool to the touch. The scent of the sea comes through the opened windows.

"Jason does this sometimes."

Maris tips her head closer to Paige to hear her hushed words as they sit for the Readings. "Does what?"

"Disappears. Most years he shows up, but others he vanishes. He must be having a hard time this year." Paige glances at her, then scans the church before shrugging and turning to face the front.

Maris thinks that at this sad mass, on this sad day, Paige looks accepting. The loss of Neil has become a part of their family. Her hair is brushed back and she wears a blue sundress. She sits straight, her hands folded in her lap, and her face wears the calm, knowing expression that comes only with motherhood. Her children aren't with her, though. She came here strictly for her two brothers, dead and alive.

"Coffee later?" Maris asks, leaning close. When Paige nods yes, Maris gives herself over to the mass, to its words and music, to the Gospel and the prayers, to the reality of why she is here.

"For all of our departed brothers and sisters who have gone to their rest in the hope of rising again, especially today for Neil Barlow, for whom this mass is offered, we pray to the Lord."

Neil Barlow. Two words that make the death real. Hearing them spoken by a priest at the altar, she understands how the reality of that very sound might keep Jason away.

But memories never die. On the August day of Matt and Eva's wedding, Maris hugged Eva for a long moment before she and Matt left for their Cape Cod honeymoon, and before their car pulled away, Matt had to hit the brakes. Maris trotted along close beside the car, and when Eva rolled down the window, she leaned inside and hugged her again, holding Eva's hand in hers and saying how much she would miss her. No one ever left her again without a goodbye after her mother died.

Late August endured its own partings. Its autumn-tinged air bid farewell to the tired beach cottages closing up for the season; reluctant families retreated to their work-a-day lives; summer itself relaxed its hold. That year, late August became the roll of credits at the end of a long, wonderful summer about two friends coming-of-age. Even Maris would stay only for the weekend before leaving for campus Sunday night.

That evening after the wedding, the tide was low and she walked alone, barefoot in cuffed jeans, along the cool, packed sand just below the ragged line of seaweed at the water's edge. Neil apparently had the same pensive idea.

"Walking the driftline?" he asked as they crossed paths.

"The what?" The word sounded dangerous, like she walked a fine line drifting between danger and safety.

"The driftline."

Maris looked at Neil, thinking he would never leave Stony Point. He seemed so beach bum. His hair was wavy in the late day sea dampness and he still wore the formal, now wrinkled, wedding shirt from earlier in the day, over a pair of jeans. He stopped and pointed down the beach toward the rock jetty. "See it?"

The low setting sun had swirled a soft pink light on the expanse of sand before her. What Maris saw was the dark, tangled line of seaweed meandering the length of the beach.

"The seaweed?"

"That's the driftline. Kyle told me he read it in a book on beach life." They walked alongside the seaweed then, weaving right along with it. "But it's not only seaweed," he said. "It's all the other stuff the tide brings in with it, too."

He stopped and crouched down. With a stick of driftwood, Neil lifted the damp seaweed, exposing pieces of pastel sea glass and one perfect, white clamshell. A hermit crab in a periwinkle snail shell scurried for cover.

"See?" Neil asked. He looked up at her. "Everything's connected."

Maybe it took this long to see it. Maybe she really didn't get it back then. Because aren't they all connected here, in some sort of driftline of their own, drifting in and out of each others' lives? When she thinks of Eva and Matt and Jason and Lauren and Kyle, and Neil, always Neil too, isn't it the same?

The feeling has her glance around the church and when she looks over her shoulder, she spots Jason in the far back corner. While others sit, he kneels, his elbows on the pew in front of him, his head bent low. He wears a navy suit, perfectly tailored, with a pale yellow shirt and silk tie knotted just so. Only the very best, Maris sees, for his brother.

Maris turns back and starts to stand. "Jason's here," she whispers to Paige, carefully passing in front of her and walking up the aisle to the back of the church. Jason still kneels as she hurries behind the rear pews and walks down the side aisle, then quietly kneels beside him.

Jason looks up at her. His face is clear, there are no tears. But you can see when someone is straining to hear; she's done it herself, listening, listening in the wind, at the water's

255

edge, in a song, to hear her mother's voice. He'd been talking, in thought, to Neil.

"Pray brethren, that our sacrifice may be acceptable to God, the Almighty Father."

When they stand in response, Maris takes his hand. Comfort sometimes comes from the slightest gesture. He stands so very still beside her, she notices the calm, the steadiness of his stance, the slow rhythm of his breathing. When it's time to offer peace to one another, she takes his shoulders in an embrace, pulling close. "Are you okay?"

She feels his hand rise to her head as he bends low near her ear. "I'm all right, sweetheart," he assures her, then backs up a step as his hand briefly touches her face.

And that is the last she hears from him. Returning from the communion procession, when Maris steps back into her pew it takes several moments to realize that he hasn't followed behind her. At first she thinks that maybe other parishioners moved in front of him until she finally realizes he has left, has received communion and walked right out of the church without saying a word.

～

An hour later, Maris sits in her kitchen surrounded by country baskets and dried flower arrangements, blue china plates displayed on the pine wall shelf behind her.

"This kitchen is divine." Paige sits at a breakfast stool. Sunlight streams in through the white window shutters. Dried flower bunches hang from the painted ceiling beams. "You must be loving your summer here."

"I am, in a way," Maris begins, holding the coffee decanter aloft to fill their mugs. "This beach just gets more beautiful with age."

"You sound like my brother." Paige adds cream to her coffee. "He was never happy being away from here."

"Neil?"

"No." Paige shakes her head. "Jason."

Maris sips her coffee. "I thought it was Neil who adored this place. He obsessed over every detail, studying the old cottages, the landscape."

"Only because his big brother did. That's such a misconception people have about Neil. More than anything, he was *Jason's* biggest fan. He copied everything about Jason."

"Tell me about him."

Paige considers Maris. "In the past seven years, you ended up being the best medicine for him."

"What do you mean?"

"He's really had a difficult time since that wreck. It's taken everything out of him just to put himself back together. First there was depression, and later he was practically dependent on pain medication. I mean, it really got out of hand. But he's clean now, has been for a couple of years."

"No way. I can't even imagine it."

"That's what I'm saying. He really wasn't easy to be with, so you're like this beautiful breath of fresh air in all of our lives. But mostly his. He started to come around after he got his second prosthesis, but I think you're his magical cure."

"Wait. A second prosthesis?"

"The first one wasn't a good fit. It didn't have the technology this one has either, and its limitations were such a reminder of the accident. Once he got his natural gait back, the best he could, he reached for all the other pieces of his life, especially architecture. Barlow Architecture is his real strength now."

"He mentioned he tried corporate work, right after the accident?"

"He did. It's only been two years that he's back to the cottage designs. Before that, he worked with large firms in Hartford, which didn't really suit him. But his head was still messed up too, so it served a purpose, giving him time until he could get back to where he and Neil had left off. They were quite a team."

"Only now he's flying solo."

"Not really. Neil's influence is in all his designs, so on some level, they're still together. I think that's what brought him back here, that connection."

"A good sign?" Maris asks. "He's facing things?" She pulls warm cinnamon rolls from the oven and sets them on a blue china plate between them.

"I thought so, until he pulled that disappearing act this morning. Even though I'm sure it meant the world to him that you were at the church." She reaches for a swirled roll. "Yes, I really think you're his reason for coming back to life this summer."

"I don't know about that."

Paige runs her tongue over her teeth, collecting a sweet bit of the roll's curlicue of icing. "Listen, for the past seven years, he completely indulged his guilt. And he never thought he'd meet someone who could get him past that, until he saw you again."

"I really can't take that credit. I'm not sure you're right."

Paige plucks her sticky fingers from her mouth before wiping them on the napkin. "Oh, I am. I've heard all about things. The carousel? Mini-golf? The Sand Bar?"

Maris tips her head. "He told you about all that?"

"In passing. The thing is, you haven't seen how self-absorbed he's been all these years. His world shrank to his injury and Neil's death. Period. You mean a lot to him."

She looks at Paige, then turns away, uncertain. Her eye catches a glimpse of the sketches she'd set out earlier in the dining room, one of a leather jacket with denim details at the collar, in the side inserts, in the lining. It still needs work, the final layer. Leather sketches have to be rendered in layers to see the dimension of the material. White paper comes first, showing through the initial color to give it highlights, then darker tones to illustrate the nap, followed by an extremely soft layer of black pencil over the whole thing, to pull all the colors together. It is a beautiful sketch, and almost done. She thinks it one of the best pieces in her new line and had been anxious to finish it this morning. How easy it would be to turn her back on all of Stony Point, on the quirks and accidents and friends and familiarity and happiness and problems and just sink into her designing, sink so deep she couldn't find her way back. To have an important meeting to get to, one where trend reports would be reviewed. To get on a plane for the summer textiles trade show, where she'd lose herself even more in the fabric samples needed for this line, awash in deep sea blue denims. To return to Chicago to oversee the final prototypes of her fall styles, and see them fitted on models so she can make final adjustments. Or to settle in Manhattan. After all, the design firm there wants to talk to her soon about their brand aesthetics and conceptual development and international travel balanced with telecommuting as they entice her with their job offer. Where else could she work from home *and* travel abroad?

"You know, that accident took *Jason's* life, too, for a long time," Paige is saying when she turns back. "And I'm not sure if he'll ever get over the guilt." She stands and straightens her dress. "Please, give him a chance Maris, before you go back to Chicago. Just a chance."

"Wait. Guilt? Why is he guilty?"

Paige offers a sympathetic smile. "I've said too much, because that's really his story. I'm sorry, but he's got to tell you himself." She reaches for her handbag from the counter. "And I've got to get back. The kids'll be anxious to get on the beach."

"Maybe Jason's there at the cottage?"

"I doubt it. But if he is, I'm kicking him out and sending him straight here." She walks through to the porch, pulling her sunglasses from her purse and setting them on her face. "We'll save a chair for you on the beach, if you decide to come."

~

Before getting back to her sketches, Maris brings her laptop onto the front porch to check her email and a few design sites. She opens an email Scott sent this morning, asking her to come home for only a weekend, to talk with him in their old familiar places, the tiny restaurant they love, the gazebo in the park. She reads the email again wondering if maybe she should, then opens the attachment he included, smiling at the photographs he took of the gazebo beside the flower gardens, of her empty seat at their kitchen table. They'd been together for a long time now, and he'd proposed, after all. Maybe a visit would give her definitive answers. Her hands hover over the keyboard, ready to hit Reply, when she notices her empty ring finger and so goes up to her bedroom and puts on the refitted ring. Returning to the porch, she turns her hand, watching the diamond catch the light and getting an idea to incorporate a star stud on the leather jacket she is designing. She sets the open laptop on the porch table and goes in to the dining room, to her sketches laid out.

Inspiration comes like that, suddenly, from something as seemingly irrelevant as a sparkle from a diamond. But in that sparkle she sees starlight. After pouring a glass of wine, she begins sketching various gold studs with star cutouts that can be incorporated into the leather jacket. She tries a few variations, on the denim, on the leather, unsure of just how to showcase this particular star feature.

And all the while, she knows. She knows what Scott wants with her in Chicago. It is a nice life, actually, that anyone in their right mind would find hard to leave. They live in a lovely townhouse, she's climbed to the top of her career, and Scott is a good man who wants her back. Chicago is safe: financially, professionally, emotionally.

Yet she is having a hard time extricating herself from Stony Point where she lives essentially unemployed, homeless and single. And a part of a certain, struggling driftline.

Picking up a bronze color gel pen, she varies the color of the stud to better show the diamond cutout, when she hears the slow, crunching sound of tires on the gravel driveway. *Give him a chance, before you go back.* She sets the sketches aside and stands on the porch, watching as Jason parks and gets out of his SUV. When he steps down onto the gravel, he favors his prosthetic leg, though she wouldn't have noticed the falter if she didn't know him. He still wears the morning's suit, but the tie has been loosened, the top shirt button undone and the jacket hangs casually open now.

Madison's tail swings like a slow pendulum as she stands at the screen door. Jason laughs a little when he turns to see them both looking at him. "Maris," he says through the screen.

"It's open." Her fingers lace around the wine glass she holds. He comes inside and gives Madison a good scratching on her neck. "Are you okay?" she asks, thinking he looks tired now.

"I will be. If you're not busy this afternoon."

She sets the wine glass on the table alongside the laptop. "No, I'm not. What's up?"

"Take a ride with me?" A bead of perspiration clings to his temple.

"Right now?"

He nods.

"Let me get my bag and lock up the back door."

She goes upstairs and changes into faded denim skinnies and a camisole with a light jacket. When she adds a touch of makeup, she catches a glimpse out the window of Jason in the front yard with Madison. He smokes a cigarette and is talking with the dog standing at perfect German shepherd attention near his feet.

Maris grabs her purse knowing the twists and turns of this day are about to bring her into his world. At the top of the stairs, she turns and runs back to her bedroom to take off the diamond ring, then grabs her leather sandals. Downstairs, she sits on the porch to slip them on, noticing that Jason had finished off her glass of wine.

twenty-four

I WANT TO EXPLAIN MYSELF to you." Jason's attention stays focused on the highway, though he seems very much aware of her, adjusting the air conditioning and glancing at her every move. "When I saw you at the mass this morning," he continues, "I knew I had to explain things before you left here." He passes a slower car in front of them, then opens his window a little. "But I'm not really sure how to do this."

"I'm listening."

"I'm sorry about this morning, at the church. I wasn't walking out on you, or on Paige. Jesus, Paige stood by me all the way to hell and back. I just needed to compose myself." He pauses while checking the rearview mirror, then glances at her again. "I want you to stay, Maris. In Connecticut. In my life. But you have to know my story first, and the best way to tell it is to bring you there."

"And where would that be?"

"The scene of the accident. There's more to it than you're aware of. More than anyone's aware of, except my sister. You have to understand my leg, and my face, and what I see when I look at the scars. There are others, too.

Road burns did a good job of ripping up my back."

As they drive inland, the highway hugs the Connecticut River on the east. Pleasure boats drift about and the river's ripples sparkle silver beneath the afternoon sun. The road curves along with the river while to the west, the towns grow more congested.

"Paige has arranged an anniversary mass for Neil every year since he died." Jason drives at a steady pace, using his signal and passing cars infrequently. As he nears his destination, though, she notices the vehicle slows up. "And every year, it takes more and more out of me."

~

The town of Addison lies on the outskirts of Hartford. Developers have filled the old farmland with tracts of colonials, sprawling ranches and contemporaries in the south end of town. The central and north end hold the older real estate, the large homes set back off the streets under the umbrella of stately oaks and maples.

Maris grew up, after her mother's death, in Olde Addison in the historic district near the cove. The presence of water always soothed her, even here. The cove forms a little inlet, a thick comma off the Connecticut River that local residents use as a boat ramp and as a permanent summer docking for larger pleasure boats. It is a pretty little area, surrounded by woods on two sides with a large old barn and colonial homes gracing its entranceway. Patches of green grass spread out around weathered picnic tables. It's a nice place to have a sandwich and watch the boats docked on the silver expanse of water.

Under different circumstances, Maris would have mentioned all of this to Jason. She would have suggested that they sit at a table and look at the boats for a while.

Now he drives west out of Olde Addison on streets nearly deserted and quiet in the summer heat, except for the occasional drone of a lawn mower. They pass older Federals and English Tudors with deep lawns, then a newer, close development, until they turn onto the Turnpike. There are no trees there, no summer lawns to soothe the eye with cool colors, only warehouse stores and fast-food restaurants and simmering parking lots. Less than a mile before Hartford, the vehicle slows as Jason pulls into the breakdown lane, then carefully off onto the shoulder of the road. A traffic light hangs ahead of them, with the city line a few blocks further. He opens both windows and kills the engine before sitting back with an uneasy sigh. To their left, a large cemetery covers a sloping hill, and to their right, on the other side of a swath of roadside brush, beyond an immense parking lot, a strip mall houses a grocery store, discount store and other small shops.

Jason sets his sunglasses on the dash. "This is where my brother died."

"Here?" Maris had lived away since high school and had no idea the accident occurred just outside her hometown. "Right here?"

"Past the light there." Jason looks at the road beyond the traffic signal. "Not in a hospital bed, or even on an ambulance stretcher where someone could have helped him, or comforted him at the end. No one wiped his face or told him it would be okay. He died alone on the street." He unknots his loosened tie and pulls it slowly from his collar. Even on this scrubby patch of turnpike, birdsong comes in the windows. Maris takes the tie from him and neatly folds it while he looks outside. She turns and sets it on the back seat.

"We were on his bike that day. A Harley Neil bought a couple years earlier. He didn't even ride it much, just a little bit in the warm weather. It was more a conversation piece than anything else."

A few cars approach, and he waits till they drive past and the quiet returns before continuing. "Neil needed a part from the bike shop further back on the Turnpike. It was one of those hot days when nothing's doing, so I went along for the ride. We drove up on the back roads from the beach." He checks his mirrors and glances out at the pavement. "The back roads were cooler than the highway. Lots of shade. Less traffic."

Jason leans forward then, resting his arms over the top of the steering wheel. Maris thinks that his small details are his way of painting the picture of the whole day instead of just a picture of death. It seems the only way to get through that day, today, right now, or he might never get out of it.

"We were at the bike shop for about an hour and decided to go to The Elm Café for a grinder, maybe a beer. You know, hang out awhile, shoot the shit. It's in the south end." He turns to Maris. "Have you ever been there, The Elm Café?"

"A few times."

He nods, as though satisfied that she is following his journey to the accident. "We figured we'd drive down the Turnpike," he continues, his voice low, "and turn off up ahead there." He points to a further intersection where the Turnpike comes to an end at the Hartford line.

"The thing is, when we left the bike shop, Neil tossed me the keys. Just turned around and said *You drive*. I never forget that, the way I grabbed them right from the air. I see them, I hear them jangling like it happened yesterday. It's funny how you remember random things like that."

The occasional car that passes them now seems out of place. Jason is taking her somewhere inaccessible to anyone else, where their lives pause while the rest of the world goes on normally around them. For him, that has been a long reality. He'd paused right here on this strip of road for seven years now.

"So I drove his Harley down this road and we stopped at that light there." He nods toward the traffic light in front of them, his hands still resting on the top of the steering wheel. "The light was red and we were waiting for it to turn green. There were no cars in front of us, no one behind us. It was quiet, with just the bike idling." He pauses. "We sat there for a single minute like that. But that minute, Jesus. It was the last minute of his life."

His eyes squint then and Maris sees how easily it happens. How that day lives inside him, just waiting for any cue to begin again and again and again. Watching him tell it is the same as standing on the side of that dry, scrubby pavement seven years ago, the heat beating down on the blacktop, the sun mercilessly blinding, the air warm and heavy. Everything about the day, relentless still.

⌒⌣

He wore a black tee, dusty Levi's, construction boots on his legs straddling the bike, keeping balance, dark sunglasses in the bright sunlight as he waited for the light to change, glancing down at the bike gauges. Neil sat hitched behind him wearing sunglasses, his hair a mess.

Jay. Neil's arm reached forward, pointing to the mirror. *Hey Jay.*

He saw it then, coming up behind them. He'd never seen a car move that fast, so fast that it took a second to register that the growing shape was, in fact, a car.

A whirlpool of roaring grew louder and rose up, overtaking and spinning around them, deafening their ears to anything else. And he knew, he just knew, that engine headed straight at them was fully opened. Every bit of breathing, of pulse, of strength, went into heaving five hundred pounds of bike a few feet over. Every molecule and atom re-formed to drench every bit of his skin while burning every muscle. Time grew greedy, taking all of it and giving it to the terror behind them, leaving them not even one second to ditch the bike and run for cover.

The sunlight turned white then, pure glaring white as Jason took the force of his brother's weight fully on his back, the impact bending him over enough that Neil's body flowed like a wave over his head and shoulders, and without him there to bear his brother's weight, without his resistance, the body was airborne. But that pressure on his back, it stayed, as though Neil were holding on. It was still there as the world went suddenly silent, all sound muted, unable to keep up with the motion that would not stop, that spun the bike incessantly, Jason feeling his jeans hooked onto something twisting up his leg, keeping him attached to the machine. Afterward, he would always know that sight and sound ceased working in the heat of violence. Because a soundless ripping burned through his leg, a flame of pain with no direction to take so it took it all, before that bike released his leg and flung him across the pavement off to meet the brush growing wild on the side of the road. Then, nothing.

～～

"And I wake up," Jason is saying as Maris listens to the story. "Now. In the middle of the night sometimes, because

I hear that same absolute quiet in my sleep and I'm on this road again."

She shakes her head no.

"See, my only escape is sleep," he continues, "but then I *can't* sleep because I think over all the choices I made that day." His voice grows nearly inaudible. "And I wonder if there wasn't a moment when I could have changed it, so I wouldn't have killed my brother."

Maris closes her eyes. "No, no, no," she whispers. "It wasn't your fault."

"No? Neil let me drive and I didn't even see the car coming. What the hell was I doing? He saw it before I did." His open hand hits the steering wheel hard. "When I think that he *died* because we were short a few seconds, it makes me sick. If I'd been watching my mirrors, my brother could still be here. Everything changed in twenty seconds."

"No, it was a freak accident." She looks from the road to him. "Why are you punishing yourself? You did the best you could under a horrifying circumstance." She pauses, not knowing if she should say what else she thinks, not knowing how he will take it. How angry he will get. But he has to know it means something, means everything, to her. She reaches for him, turning his head to face her. "And you survived," she insists.

"That's right. I did." He fights the grief then, she hears it. "And my brother died right there on the blacktop. He didn't deserve that, nobody does. He looked up to me and I didn't come through for him. And you ask why I'm punishing myself? I don't know. Why was I driving? Why did Neil give me the keys? What made it him instead of me that day?" He sits back and drags his hand over his eyes. "He needed me. Oh Christ, it's just too much, Maris."

"Listen. Listen, you've got to stop blaming yourself. You've got to let that go."

"But if I let go, he's gone."

There it is. His fear is of losing Neil completely. This is how he keeps him alive. "Jason, Neil will always be a part of you. In your memories, in your heart. Come on, he's in all your designs. And as sad as it all is, everything happens for a reason. So something came out of that accident that you're not seeing and can put it all to rest for you."

Jason looks out the window at the road. "I don't think so."

"Stop it," she says, her voice rising. "Just stop it and don't you give up. Listen, you're here where Neil died, looking for answers still."

He turns and watches her and she sees his defiance, the look that says she can't change this. "So let's say Neil drove the bike that day. Neil was in control."

Jason nods almost imperceptibly.

"Okay. Okay, so see? He would drive down the Turnpike the same way you did, but there would be little differences. Maybe he'd arrive here a few seconds later than you did. And the bike would be positioned differently than when you drove it. And with that car coming out of nowhere," she pauses for a moment, "maybe you'd *both* be dead today."

"Would it really make a difference?"

Her eyes sting with quick tears and she turns and reaches for the door handle, struggling with it for a second before pushing the door open and nearly spilling out. Just as quickly, Jason lunges toward her and grabs her arm.

"Maris, please."

"No, no *you please. You please!*" Tears streak her face and she turns to get out of the SUV. She'll walk home if she has to, she is so angry. Why doesn't he see it? She struggles, but he holds tighter, his other arm reaching around her and turning her back to him. "God Jason," she cries. "*Would it make a difference?* Those beautiful beach cottages would never be restored. Your sister's children would've lost *both* uncles. Your beach house would be sold, your father's *barn* torn down. Your parents ..." She smiles sadly. "I would never have ridden the carousel."

"Okay," he says, then reaches past her and closes her door. "Okay."

"And you wouldn't be in my life this summer." She waits then as a few cars pass them, the radio blaring in one. "Don't you see how your life moves with others? We're all connected, you know? Didn't Neil ever explain that to you?"

"Explain what?"

"The driftline. On the beach?"

He looks at her and shakes his head.

"Sometimes you have to be on the outside looking in to see things clearly," Maris goes on, quieter now. "I am on the outside, and the answer you're looking for is right in front of you." She turns in her seat, facing him, reaching her hand to the side of his face for just a moment. "Your brother loved you so much. And if he saw how you've come down on yourself, loading your head up with guilt and conscience and *whatever*, wasting your life, he'd be really pissed off. And he'd let you know it, too." She leans close, grabbing his arm with a small shake. "He's gone, but he wants you to live. Don't you see it?"

"No, I don't."

She studies his still face, his eyes. "The keys, Jason. The keys. You know how sometimes you get a sense of something that is about to happen, just for a flash of a second? Maybe that the phone will ring, or the car break down. Well when he tossed you the keys, which was *not*

271

random, he must have known in some way. He handed you your *life*." Tears streak her face again. "He knew. You're *alive* because *of* Neil," she insists. "Alive. So let your brother go, and live, Jason. That's what he would want. You know he would."

Maris is surprised at how her chest fills, how her lungs drag in breaths. The bike might as well lay twisted on the road in front of her. Sirens might as well be screaming, blood might as well be staining the pavement. She is with Jason completely, comforting him at the crash. "Just live," she pleads.

～

Jason looks long at Maris before slipping out of his suit jacket with agitation, pushing open the door and stepping outside, standing motionless, not sure what to do, where to go. The air shimmers with heat; dry grass snaps beneath his shoes in the slow steps to the edge of the road. Standing at the hot, black pavement, he crouches down, his arms resting on his knees, his hands clasped in front of him. He becomes unusually aware of his prosthesis in this position and though he wears a special sock where it attaches to his leg, the skin there is soaked with perspiration.

Warm minutes tick by on the roadside and every emotion pumps through his heart. Anger. Loneliness. Grief. He came to his brother's deathbed looking for answers, for some way to let go, and it is happening because there is something else now. Someone else.

Still crouching, Jason bows his head and closes his eyes with this goodbye. In time, how much he doesn't know, her hand rests on his shoulder. He reaches his own hand up and presses it over hers. She gives him a small smile when he rises to his feet, his shirt wet with perspiration, his face wet with emotion.

"Come here." When he reaches for Maris, she steps close and he holds her face with his hands and presses his lips to her forehead. She is the here and now and he will not let go, not of today, not of tomorrow.

She pulls back and looks at him, her fingers touching his face, lighting on his scar. "You okay?" she asks.

Jason nods and slips his arm around her, walking her through the dry grass back to the SUV. "Let's get out of here."

"Are you sure?"

"I am. I'm tired, and have to sit down somewhere quiet."

He closes the door for her as she settles back into her seat, then walks around to the driver's side, wiping his face and giving a salute to the road before opening his door. Maris reaches for his hand as he pulls into traffic and drives away.

twenty-five

IN HARTFORD'S LITTLE ITALY, THEY walk a few blocks past brick-front bakeries, pizzerias and clothing boutiques with racks of boho clothes set up outdoors. Tables spill from cafés under the shade of sloping canopies. Local markets sell fresh produce, peppers and spinach pies. Three-story tenements, their small lawns manicured, shrubs trimmed just so, line the side streets. Finally they turn into Bella's, into its dim interior, its aroma of lasagna and fresh baked bread, its quiet.

"Hungry?" Jason asks. A crystal vase holds a small bouquet of silk flowers and a candle's flame flickers low inside a red glass globe between them.

"Starved."

He asks for a carafe of wine and after their meals are ordered, fills each of their goblets.

"Welcome back," Maris says as she cups her glass in front of her. He had put on his suit jacket before coming into the restaurant, attempted to straighten back his disheveled hair and his face shows a shadow of whiskers. What she sees now, behind the evidence of the difficult day, are glimpses of the old Jason.

"Welcome back?"

"To life, Jason." She reaches for his hand and holds tight.

He touches his glass to hers in a silent toast. "Every now and then it all comes to me in a flashback. Like that night on the boardwalk with Kyle. I needed you to know, Maris, in case it happens again. Hysterical amnesia is funny that way."

"I'm glad you told me."

"Paige is the only one who knows I was driving the bike."

"You never told your parents?"

He shakes his head. "The first week in the hospital, I was in rough shape. The whole business with my leg, and well, it was bad. The doctors didn't know how I survived the crash. So by the time I was coherent, the police reports had been filed. Somehow they got it that Neil was driving. Whether they misunderstood me in their questioning when I was pretty much out of it, or if a witness said something, I don't know. But I didn't have the strength to even move, never mind go through it all again. So I let it be."

"Except with your sister."

"With Paige," he says, nodding. "The details of that day came back slowly. Little things, like Neil pointing to the side mirror, I didn't remember for years. But I knew that I was driving as soon as I woke up. So one night, Paige stayed late at the hospital watching some television show in my room. Never mind that I lay there with no leg and partial memory, she knew something *else* was eating me up. And it seriously was. So I told her." He pauses and sips his wine.

Maris knows that even in his pause, in this small silence, a part of his story is being told to her. There's an aloneness to it, and that's the place he'd been in until he told his sister.

"She never blamed me. You know my sister. Once I told her, she did everything she could to help me get my shit together. The phone calls and letters and home cooked meals never stopped. Never. Through the physical therapy, head therapy, medical therapy, she didn't give up on me."

"You're close."

"Very."

"You weren't involved with anyone who could help you? No girlfriend?"

He sits back and sets his hands flat on the table. "Maureen. One look at my missing leg, physical therapy schedule and mostly at my loss of income and she split."

Maris considers a *life* rich, his in architecture, walks on the beach, family, the past. "And no one since, in all these years?"

"No one steady. Not until today."

She tips her glass to his. "And what about the car that hit you, was it a kid? Joyriding?"

He hesitates, as though still not believing it. "It was an older man. Late sixties. He had a heart attack at the wheel with his foot on the gas. I doubt he even knew what hit him. Or what he hit, either."

"Did he survive?"

"He did. He pulled through." He lifts his glass, sips the wine. "So what was it all for? That was God's plan? To just pluck Neil off the earth that day?"

"I don't know," Maris says under her breath, picturing the day's sad carnage. "How did *you* survive, afterward?"

The waitress places a basket of warm bread and a plate of foil-wrapped butter tabs on their table.

"It's been a long trip, let me tell you," he answers. "Fueled by a dose of liquor and medication along the way."

"Your way of losing yourself?"

"To put it mildly."

"Sometimes I think that's why I eventually moved to Chicago," she says. "To lose myself. You had your medications of choice. Mine was the big city. Chicago felt like a really good tranquilizer."

"How so?" He leans forward, taking both her hands in his.

Maris thinks back on her whirlwind city life. "It's simple, actually. Between my hectic career, Scott and the crazy social calendar we kept, I had no time to look over my shoulder. Chicago kept me very busy, and *that* was the drug, leaving no time for questions. An aunt in Europe? A missing sister? Family secrets? I was cushioned from it there."

"You're not going back?" Jason asks, his eyes never leaving hers. "I saw the email on your porch today."

"Scott wants me to fly back next weekend. To talk about things. He doesn't think it's over between us."

"Is it?"

Maris watches the man seated with her, his dark brown eyes glancing at her in a way Scott's never would. "Maybe it was never over between *us*," she says, "whatever we started all those years ago out on Foley's deck that night. Remember?"

"Remember?" For the first time all summer, she sees a spark in his eyes. "You'll have to refresh my memory." A slow grin spreads across his face.

"Huh. You wish," she says, grinning right back.

Jason unfolds the red and white checked cloth from the breadbasket and butters a slice of warm Italian bread. He speaks so softly, she almost misses his words. "I never forgot that kiss. Through it all, I never forgot you, sweetheart." He hands her a buttered slice of bread.

Maris doesn't realize just how hungry she is until she feels the warm, doughy bread in her mouth. "Mmh. Heaven."

"No. I don't think so."

She follows his gaze around the restaurant, seeing the golden light of late day slant into the dim room, seeing the tables and flowers and red candles. Paintings of piazzas and olive orchards hang on the walls. The aroma of fresh tomato sauce fills the air and the taste of wine lingers in her mouth. Her eyes stop when they meet his.

"Because I'm in heaven," he says. "Sitting right here with you."

⁓

For the first time in years, pregnancy tests sit on her bathroom counter. Eva bought two, knowing that whatever the outcome, she won't trust its results and will try again. She looks at her reflection and sweeps a stray eyelash from her cheek, expecting a change in her appearance other than the layered haircut. Expecting that sense of familiarity to come to her, that spark of recognition now that her hair is shorter and off her face. She looks into her reflected eyes, searching for someone else, for her mother to talk her through this. To smile for her and be happy, whether it is yes or no. She picks up the package and reads the bold print for the second time. *White – Not Pregnant. Pink – Pregnant.* After a few minutes, she checks again and sees that she is not in the pink.

What surprises her is the feeling. She'd thought she'd be relieved. She'd thought her life and family had passed the baby stage. And yet, it is hard setting down the test and turning away, glancing in the mirror and not seeing a smile.

The white result shifts everything. It shifts her focus. It shifts her mood. White means instead.

Instead the house is still. And quiet.

Instead of calling Matt at work with good news, her voice is sad. She wonders if he hears it through the relief she forces over her words. "At least now we can move ahead. Taylor will be in high school before we know it."

Instead of looking for Taylor's old baby things in the attic, Eva climbs the ladder to empty the contents of the old trunk so Matt and Kyle can move it downstairs and repaint it a sand color. She'll stencil starfish on it and use it in her office for extra storage.

She pauses at a carton of Christmas decorations and lifts the cover to see glass ornaments and window candles and velvet bows. For the past week, her thoughts have moved along the timeline of a pregnancy. When Taylor begins eighth grade in September, she'd be two months along. When her latest sale closes, she'd be three months. The baby's movements would start to be detected. Looking at the Christmas ornaments now, everything has changed. She will *not* be five months pregnant in December. Baby items will *not* be collecting in the extra bedroom.

Knowing there will never be another baby in their home makes her think back fondly to when Taylor was a baby. Opening the trunk, there are candlesticks inside, and Taylor's Communion Dress wrapped in tissue, a shoebox of loose photographs, tablecloths and doilies. Memories, memories, all of them, to be taped up in a cardboard box now as she empties the trunk. In a way, she's missing, too, the new baby memories that'll never come to be.

When the trunk is empty, Eva presses the lid closed until the old latch clicks inside. Crouching in front of it, her hand runs across the surface. The finish feels dry and cracked and it will need to be carefully stripped. She wants to see the back surface, and pulls one end of the trunk away from the wall. Sunshine comes through the attic window and catches on a sliver of gold thread snagged on the back hinge. The space around her swims with dust particles floating in the afternoon sunlight, like some sort of dream. The thread is twisted and so she carefully unwinds it and lifts a dusty, faded blue velvet pouch. It looks like it has hung there for years, long forgotten.

Eva sits on the closed trunk and leans into the sunlight shining in through the attic window. She gently slips her fingers through the golden threads and opens the velvet fabric. In a moment filled with wonder, she tips the bag sideways, catching in her other hand its glimmering contents.

A beautiful etched star hangs on a braided gold chain, which doesn't make any sense. It looks like the exact same necklace that Maris wears, the only one of its kind, designed purely for her. Eva's finger lightly traces the gold star, a thought playing games with her heart. The circumstances of her adoption, according to Theresa, though very sad, are filled with love.

Maris also lived very sad young years. She suffered a terrible loss when her mother died. Could they have possibly suffered the same tragedy? Is that why Maris is a part of her life, under the guise of being a summer friend? A thought comes, but no. No. It can't be. No way. Someone would have told them. Could their two lives have started in the same home, with the same mother? She closes her fingers tight around the necklace, unwilling to look on the back of the star yet. Various thoughts float like stardust, coming together brilliantly.

If there are two identical star necklaces, custom-made

and tailored with significance to a lost mother, then there must be two daughters. Two nieces with an aunt in Italy. Two separated nieces with inscribed stars.

She moves her touch around to the back of the pendant and feels it on her fingertip, the engraving in the gold.

Everything in her life suddenly comes together in that one, clear instant. She knows.

Sitting alone beneath the rafters, she knows. She knows as she looks down at the star, as she closes her eyes, as she folds her hand around the pendant, the chain hanging loose. She knows when she holds it to her heart.

Sitting in that attic with dust and joy and regrets and happiness all around her in the memories, she turns the pendant over and reads the delicate script inscribed there.

Evangeline.

Time suddenly moves differently, faster than just an hour ago when life stretched long before her with emptiness. She rushes downstairs to her dresser, rummaging over the top of it, through her jewelry box, searching for the telephone number where Theresa and Ned are vacationing this week. She yanks open drawers. Her hand skims for the slip of paper with the Martha's Vineyard number on it, because no surprise, the little cottage they're staying at has no cell service. For the life of her, she cannot remember where she put it. Not in the kitchen, on the top of the refrigerator, beneath fridge magnets, in the cabinet, in the junk drawer, in her handbag on the counter.

"Damn it," she finally says as she sits at the kitchen table. Between the wallpapering and painting and thinking she was pregnant and searching adoption registries, the telephone number is just gone.

So she grabs her phone and quickly dials Maris' cell,

impatiently waiting for her to answer. "Come on, come on," she says, pacing the kitchen, disconnecting and dialing again. "Answer the damn phone." She leaves a quick message on her voicemail, then disconnects and tries again. "Maris, call me." She takes a long breath, wanting to say everything, and unable to say anything. "We really need to talk, it's important. Call," she says before slamming down her phone.

When she hangs up, she looks at her gold star necklace. She, too, has an aunt, far across the Atlantic. Someone who must think of her, from time to time. And the thought leaves her feeling so purely connected to Maris and Elsa, the three women linked together through the years with a simple braided chain, that she puts on her sandals and heads off, half-running, to Maris' cottage. She has to see her, to tell her, to hug her.

After waiting endlessly on Maris' doorstep, she returns home. Matt finds her later sitting in their kitchen on the window seat, her knees pulled up in front of her as she watches out the window, hoping to see Jason's SUV drive by further down the street. Maris has to be with him.

"I knew you were upset about the baby," Matt says when he sits beside her and sets a bouquet on the table. He wears his uniform, his polished boots, his firearm still, in his rush to get home. "You're shaking," he says, wiping away her tears. "You'll feel better in a few days."

"It's not the baby." She takes off the pendant and holds it out to his hand, watching his gaze move from it up to her face. "It's true," she says. "And no one ever told me." The flowers lay on the table in front of them, the summer day grows warm outside the window, the scent of the sea reaches in.

Jason had forgotten that he could feel happiness in the wind brushing his face, in the damp sea mist settling on the night, in the darkness itself. At the water's edge, Madison bounds ahead of them, occasionally barking into the sea breeze.

"Sometimes it feels like I've never left here," Maris says as she brushes back strands of hair.

"What do you mean?" Jason asks.

"It feels like I've always been here and Chicago and the past twelve years were only a dream somehow."

"There's a reason for dreams, Maris. We work things out in them." A cool ocean breeze skims across the water. "Cold?" he asks. His suit jacket hangs draped over her shoulders and he lifts it higher, closing it around her arms while pulling her near.

"A little. Do you want to go back?"

"In a minute. There's something I have to do first."

"What's that?" Maris asks, looking up at him.

His fingers touch her hair, brushing wisps from her cheek. Standing at the edge of the sea, night and water are as black as one, broken only by a swath of pale moonlight falling from the sky, by the rhythm of the waves breaking close by. In that darkness, he kisses her and his world becomes just and only that, for one long moment as the waves continue to reach up on the beach. When he stops, his hand traces every curve of her face. "I couldn't love you and not tell you about that day."

Her fingers touch his lips. "I love you, too," she whispers.

"Come on," he says, and they turn back toward the road with his arm around her, holding her close. Madison lopes past them holding a stick of driftwood in her mouth, her tail swinging with happiness. They walk slowly behind the dog, lingering with the night. Time is finally, finally sweet.

Beneath his bedroom window, with the rhythm of the breaking waves carrying to them, Jason's hand stops hers from reaching for the bedside lamp. Moonlight allays the darkness instead, looking almost liquid, Maris thinks. The edges of the room are softly blurred by it, much like her sketches blur beneath fresh watercolor paints, the water dissipating clarity. And that blend of pale light from above, along with the sound of the waves breaking on the beach, makes the night itself watercolored. Sea colored, she thinks, with the evening's breeze bringing the sense of the sea close. Sometimes life is all about that, about how the waves continue to reach the shore no matter where we are. Bent over a sketch pad in a city studio, with denim samples strewn about. Or lying twisted on a hot summer pavement, it doesn't matter. The waves come. Once you've heard them, and walked beside them, they are always there.

Maris touches upon his scars, her fingers softly slipping along them. His breath catches at her first trace of his face and she stays there, close, her eyes searching his as she moves her hand along his neck to the gnarled skin of his back where his body met the road. Her touch comes in those waves, gentle but endless, down his side to his leg, tracing the scarred web along his thigh ever so slowly before reaching back to find the ridge above his jawline. Time is fluid, the night is fluid, life is fluid, and at the sea, one heals.

Maris knows this day has been like a silver cap on one of those sea waves, changing the direction and force of his life, bringing him gently to shore. She heals him then, completely, moving on top of him and leaving tender kisses along his jaw. His hands move over her back and up through her hair, touching her neck until he turns and cradles her beneath him. She whispers words that he stops with his kisses, so she brings the affection to her hands that stroke his arms, cling to his back, not letting him slip back into that sea of darkness.

What she is most glad for, more than anything else, is this. Summer, for him, will have this moment in it, too. She wants that for Jason, wants him to remember it drifting in through the open window, the starry sky above, the sea breeze moving the white curtains, bringing a hint of the sea itself. His hands frame her face. "Maris," he says quietly, searching her eyes. She senses, somehow, that this is how he has to love her, his eyes have to see the moment, hear the night. Sight and sound, sight and sound, keep him present.

When she answers softly, "I love you," it is the way his mouth tastes the soft of her throat before moving to her face and kissing her cheek, her eyes. It is the way his hands frame her shoulders close that tells her he hears the sound of her words. She presses her lips against his ear, letting him feel even her breath as she says his name, hoping he feels the possibility of life again, shimmering like a summer sea.

⁓

Later, Jason lies awake in the night feeling Maris beside him, her arm draped over his chest, her head on his shoulder. It is very late, all the world still. He hears Long Island Sound in the distance. It blurs motion and time and is a sound that can summon a lifetime of memories.

But there is something more. He holds Maris close and feels the rise and fall of her breathing. The waves reach up on the beach while he stays absolutely motionless, the sea breeze floating in, the moon's glow illuminating them, and he considers, unsure, just what he senses. After a minute, or ten, or waking from dozing, Maris turns her face up toward him and he feels her gaze. Out of the darkness, her hand reaches to his face and touches the moist streak slipping along the side of his cheek.

He takes her hand, then, and cups it in his, to his chest, before slipping his arm around her shoulders, lying close, the waves outside continuing to break.

twenty-six

IN THE LIGHT OF MONDAY morning, Maris sees Jason's life more clearly. She sees the ordered furniture in his beach home, everything in its place, meticulous. She sees a second, spare prosthetic leg beside his dresser. Crutches lean in the corner of the bedroom, and she sees him put a second pair of those in his truck. His day will be long and there might come a time when he'll have to remove the artificial limb. Sitting outside on his deck, she listens to him talk in the kitchen, hearing his inflections, his pauses, as his day lengthens with each phone call: an appointment with a building contractor, with a wholesale window supplier and with two clients at their cottages, followed by an evening meeting in Eastfield. Finally he needs to stop at his condominium to work on research papers still there for a new cottage restoration. They won't see each other until late that night.

While waiting outside for him, she checks her cell phone and calls back Eva, leaving her a message when there is no answer.

"Who you talking to?" Jason asks, bringing his coffee onto the deck.

"Evangeline."

"Eva?"

"She left me a couple tense messages."

"What did she want?"

"I'm not sure, she didn't really say. Something's up, though."

"Do you want to stop by and see her?"

"I just can't, there's so much going on today. It'll keep till I get back later."

"I'll come with you to your attorney's office," Jason insists then, his coffee on the table before him, his barn rising behind him, mid-restoration. He's already been moving in his pencils and shields and T-squares and design rolls, along with Neil's volumes of cottage scrapbooks. Without Neil's presence, she sees that he couldn't do it.

"I'll be okay, really. I already know most of what he'll tell me. Besides, your schedule is booked."

"I'll cancel." He says it without hesitation; she takes precedence.

"No, I'll be fine." She sips her coffee, thinking. "Do you know what you could do though? My appointment is at one o'clock and it's an hour drive each way. Could you stop by and take Madison out for a while? I hate to leave her alone for long."

Jason agrees and Maris gives him her extra house key while he writes his personal cell phone number on the back of his business card. "I have to take off now. But you call me if you need me." She takes the card from him and lets him fold her into his arms, talking into her ear. "Anytime, okay?" They kiss then and she misses him already when she feels his hands leaving her shoulders.

It is one of those crystal clear summer mornings, so she walks around his yard, looking into the barn and lingering alone on his deck with her coffee. Forty-five minutes after he leaves, she turns over his business card and dials the number. "Don't talk," she says, knowing he is with a contractor. She doesn't want her words to compel him to respond, possibly embarrassing him. "Just listen."

"Okay," he answers. There are noises in the background: workers' voices calling out, a power saw whining and a construction vehicle backing up. She imagines he bends into the call, maybe blocking his other ear to hear her over the sounds of the job site.

"There's just something I wanted to tell you."

"Go on."

She smiles, picturing him at work. "I love you," she says.

"I love you too, sweetheart. I'll call you later."

Only then does she feel ready to take care of something else pressing on her mind. She straightens up the kitchen and goes back to her cottage to make the other phone call that is long overdue.

"I can't compete with someone you've known your whole life," Scott says. "Especially someone from Stony Point."

"It's not about competition, Scott." She opens the ring box and looks at the diamond as he talks, slipping it on her finger, then taking it off again.

"For you, it's not. You've made your choice. But it is for me. Or it was, until you told me his name."

"I'm sorry, I never planned for this to happen."

"I know you didn't. And I know it's over. And it's not just Barlow. It's where he's from. It's Stony Point, Maris. I can't compete with whatever hold that little beach has on you."

She sets the engagement ring on the dining room table along with everything else wanting her attention. Her office at Saybrooks is anxious for her new fall designs, Eva needs to talk, and there's that pending job offer. Surrounded by denim sketches spread across the table, she opens her laptop and sends off a couple messages to her assistant, letting her know she'll send along the sketches in a few days. Then she opens the other email that has been idle in her inbox. The Manhattan design house needs an answer this week. Will she accept their offer for a position to expand their denim line, with free design rein and a substantial salary increase? The lace curtains behind her puff out like wind in the sails, then fall back limp. Her fingers tap at the keyboard declining the offer, pausing to place a stone paperweight on the sketches lifted by the breeze slipping in, before hitting the delete key as she erases her response and keeps the email as New for now.

Too much else is pressing in on her, including Eva, who she tries calling again, wondering what has her so upset. Still no answer. "I'll stop by after my appointment today," Maris says in a voicemail. "We'll have coffee and talk."

She shuts off her phone then and sets it aside on the table so there won't be any interruptions as she prepares for her attorney's appointment. The secret of her own family challenges her like no design assignment ever has, so she turns to the old box from her father's house. Everything in it is some sort of hint. Slipping her hand into the folds of a soft baby blanket, she pulls out the snapshots there. Their edges have begun to curl with age, but even though so much time has passed, Maris recognizes the rooms: the kitchen where something always simmered or baked, the formal living room for family visits, the paneled family room where chairs were meant for curling up on with good books.

Even though the prints are faded, she knows the colors:

the green appliances, the rich cherry wood of the mantel clock, the gold brocade sofa, the honey pine walls.

And even though she can't remember her, Maris knows the woman in them. She searches her mother's face, her eyes, her expression, and craves something she might see with her own eyes, some truth that explains a second child, a daughter who she had to love as much as she did Maris. But the photographs hold their secret well.

She turns back to the box. Everything in it is evidence of a second baby's life: the knitted baby cap, the family christening gown, a swaddling blanket, the home movie film, the empty small box from an Italian jeweler. Someone didn't want this child forgotten. She collects the photographs and reaches for the baby blanket to tuck back in the box. While fussing with the blanket over the table, a small manila envelope she missed before slides out from a fold.

And suddenly nothing is more important as she drops the blanket, carefully opens the envelope clasp and slips out the contents. Two items fall to the table ... another photograph, this one an old five-by-seven black and white print, and a yellowed identification card.

Maris picks up the photograph and angles it beneath her table lamp. A ship deck is crowded with people off to one side looking out over the water at a distant view. Far in the background, behind a misty veil, rises the Statue of Liberty. The photographer, standing to the stern, frames the picture to capture a large portion of the bow of the boat.

And one person on deck catches Maris' eye. A young girl of about fourteen turns her back on the crowd and faces the camera. Her clothing is plain and drab: a long gray dress over which a heavy black coat falls to below her knees. On her feet she wears a scuffed pair of black leather hightop boots. Her thick, dark hair is pulled back in a loose bun and a knitted wool scarf drapes over the back of her head with the ends wrapped loosely at her throat.

The resemblance is clear. She sees the wide-set eyes and prominent jawline of her mother, though it isn't her squinting into the early light of day decades ago. In one hand, the girl grips the handle of a leather travel trunk, while the other hand clutches a large paper, some sort of travel authorization. Maris knows, before turning the picture over, that this is her mother's and Aunt Elsa's mother. This young girl, her dark eyes gazing steady at the camera, is her maternal grandmother. On the back of the photograph, her mother had written the notation *Mama waiting for the ferry at Ellis Island.*

Why would this be saved? What significance does it have in the baby's life? She scans the crowds of immigrants dressed in dark clothes, the women's heads wrapped in shawls and scarves against the damp harbor air. They lean on the rails of the ship looking to New York. The planks of the deck's floor are wood and a staircase rises to a second level where the ship's uniformed crew mans the operations.

The answer jumps out at her then. The ship's name is painted directly below the rails of the upper deck, on the far side of the boat. She squints and angles the photograph to read it clearly.

This is the ship that brought her grandmother to America. Surprising tears burn her eyes as the one word says it all. It explains why the box of mementoes was kept, the photograph saved, the baby named.

Evangeline.

She drops the photograph on the table and picks up the yellowed identification card. Her eyes race over it, searching out more details. The heading is in bold print …

Inspection Card. Beneath that, in smaller letters, it reads ... *Immigrants and Steerage Passengers*. It lists her grandmother's name as well as the *Port of Departure*, Naples, Italy. But it is the next line that confirms everything.

Name of Ship ... Evangeline.

Outside, a robin sings and the cicadas buzz in the trees. She turns to look out the window, to know the truth of this one moment. She is here, at Stony Point. The sea breeze stirs. Summer lingers. But the card holds the other truth, the one that changes everything. That shifts her world. Information about medical and quarantine inspections have been stamped on it, dates and numbers.

But none of that matters to her now. Only one thing does.

The baby she's been looking for hadn't died.

Maris just found her. She'd been given up for adoption and is very much alive.

No one responded to Eva's birth parent search, nor would they ever, because her parents are Maris' parents. And they have both died. Theresa and Ned are somehow involved, too, bringing Maris into their home during all those years the two sisters were separated.

And no one ever told them. Not one word. Ever.

Eva is her sister. Evangeline.

Maris stands and backs away from the mess on the table, from the evidence, from the random sketches she'd finished up, from her cell phone off to the side. She's seen enough and figured out enough. Attorney Riley will fill in the rest. It is time to leave.

Upstairs, she splashes cold water on her face, pats it dry and runs a brush through her hair. She lifts the blue velvet bag from her dresser top and slips out her gold pendant, the evening star rising above the sea. Her hands shake as she tries to clasp it behind her neck. Elsa, a world away, had at least tried to hold on to *two* little girls. For certainly the empty jewelry box from the attic once held a similar pendant for Eva. Where is it? What ever became of Elsa?

A large black denim duffel sits on her closet shelf and it doesn't take long to open her dresser drawers and throw in enough necessities and a change of clothes to get her through a few days. She hurries back downstairs to the dining room with the tote over her shoulder, slips her laptop into it, grabs her purse and leaves the rest, the photographs and sketches and diamond ring and Identification Card and cell phone, leaves it all behind.

twenty-seven

MARIS SITS ACROSS FROM ATTORNEY Tom Riley in a comfortable seating arrangement, a low round table between them. She is dressed in black, black denim bell bottoms with a crochet inset in the bell and a black halter top. She wears a wide gold watch, sea glass earrings and her pendant. Her eyes follow the attorney's moves as he sorts through papers in front of him.

"Renee called me on my vacation," he begins. "She told me you were upset and we assumed it could be only one thing."

"I know that Eva is my sister," Maris answers. His eyebrows move, just barely, but she registers his surprise that she knows.

"We thought it had something to do with that. So I asked Renee to get some papers together that might help."

Maris sits on an upholstered chair, crossing her legs in front of her. "Why was Eva's identity kept from me?"

"Let's start here. You might want to look at these before I begin." He sets a bundle of correspondence on the table. "Your father thought that these might mean something to you. And to Eva. He asked me to hold onto them, and I think it's time you had them."

Maris thumbs through the envelopes stamped with international postmarks. They are letters from Italy, mailed to her and Evangeline, that her father intercepted over the years. She slips one out of its envelope and reads a flowery card celebrating her name day. Inside, in lovely script, Elsa had written a friendly note. *I have a big garden and the plants love the summer sun. I think of you when I'm in my garden, you must be growing so quickly. Enjoy your special day! And God bless you.* The cards came in birth years of significance … a few when they were children, then one each as they arrived at sixteen, eighteen and finally twenty-one. Maris glances at two or three, then sets the bundle in her lap, her fingers wrapped around it.

Elsa had never given up. Never.

"Why did my father keep these from me? I would have loved corresponding with her, receiving her letters from Europe. My God," she says, shaking her head. "I can't believe this."

Attorney Riley speaks slowly. "Attorney Fischer worked with your father on the adoption back then. When he retired, he filled me in on the case details. Apparently after your mother's death, your father was overwhelmed, especially with the idea of raising two young children alone. You were older, three years old. But a baby was too much. He didn't see how he could manage it."

"So what does that have to do with Elsa?"

"A lot. She was furious with his decision to place Eva up for adoption and even offered to come here from Italy to stay with him for six months or so, to help."

"She would have done that? Given up her life for all those months?"

"Without a doubt. Elsa was very close with your mother and knew she wouldn't want her two daughters separated."

Attorney Riley stands then and walks to the large paned window, leaning against the tall sill before continuing. "Your father wouldn't budge, Maris, and arranged a semi-open adoption. That way he could place the baby with a family who would take good care of her instead of have her suffer under a very trying situation with him working full-time and raising two babies, essentially."

"Semi-open. What does that mean?"

"He had a choice in selecting the adoptive couple, and did meet them before the adoption. Everything was on a first-name basis only and he also arranged to receive updates on Eva's life, on her health and milestones, at least once a year. The Lanes would send these via Attorney Fischer. But other than that, he relinquished all contact with Eva. You and Eva were so young, he thought your memories of each other would fade. You'd never know the difference and would have better lives this way."

"So you're saying that he did this out of love?"

"Absolutely. He may have been misguided by his grief. Don't forget the horrible way he lost your mother. But he loved Eva."

"But we were *sisters*."

"I know, and you had two people who cared about you in different ways. Louis and Elsa. As your father, Louis had the legal right to make his decision. The argument was so heated between them that Elsa finally *did* come to the States to try to stop the adoption. But she got here too late. Eva was gone."

Maris glances at the cards in her hands, feeling the heavy defeat Elsa had suffered.

"She was devastated," Attorney Riley continues. "Words were spoken that could never be taken back. You know how things get said in the heat of the moment. Elsa wanted the adoption reversed and your father cut ties with her then. He also might've been afraid she'd one day tell you the truth about Eva. But he couldn't stop her cards from coming. I think Elsa always hoped for a letter back from you. You can see by the cards addressed to Eva, too, at your home, that she never accepted the adoption."

"Is my aunt alive? I've looked online, but can never find her, no name, address." She glances at the envelopes. "But I never knew her married name."

"Renee did a little research. She still lives at the address on those envelopes. From what I understand, she's lived there in Milan for several years now."

"Milan?"

"Yes. She owns a clothing boutique there. It's very well-established."

"Did Renee speak to her?"

"No. She was discreet. Any communication is up to you."

Maris looks out the window beside her, out onto the old town green dotted with barrels planted with geraniums and zinnias, a wishing fountain in the center of it. Elsa had never stopped reaching out to her from her home across the sea. She turns at a knock at the door then, seeing Theresa and Ned Lane walk in.

"Maris," Theresa says, rushing over to kiss her on the cheek.

"Theresa?" She looks to Attorney Riley, then back to Theresa and Ned. "I thought you were on vacation."

Theresa pulls a chair beside her. "We are. But when Renee called us right before we left, we arranged to be here today."

"Maris," Attorney Riley begins. "Maybe the Lanes can help you understand. But you have to realize that they came into this thirty years ago as an innocent couple seeking to adopt a child. Circumstances drew them into your life and they did what they could to sustain a relationship between you and your sister."

At those words, *your sister*, Theresa takes Maris' hand and she knows that the story is just beginning.

~

The appointment passes over the next hour with questions, hesitations and answers. Attorney Riley sits with them, mediating the talk. He asks Maris if she needs a glass of water; motions to Theresa to stop when she goes on too long about how Louis gave them keepsakes from his home for Eva; asks for further details when Ned says Louis thought he saw Maris in her window that morning, watching him drive off for the very last time with Eva.

"It was very early. Louis arranged for a babysitter to stay with you while he brought Eva to us at the agency. The doorbell, he thought it must've woken you up when the babysitter arrived."

Maris looks from one to the other.

"Evangeline was the ship that brought your grandmother to America. We agreed to keep her name, but called her Eva instead of Angie."

From Ned to Theresa.

"We didn't live at Stony Point when we adopted Eva, but moved there a few years later. Never knowing your family vacationed there. You were playing on the beach one summer, flying a kite, and," Theresa pauses. "Well. You made friends with Eva, completely unaware that she was your sister!"

They speak faster, wanting her to hear everything at once now.

"We met with Louis on the beach, so surprised he'd rented a cottage there, and we made the summer visit arrangements after that."

"We wanted to keep you in each other's lives."

They interrupt each other, and she watches Theresa, then Ned, then Theresa again.

Secret, it was the only way he'd do it. Louis wanted the truth hidden … Children wouldn't understand … More harm than good … We agreed … To keep you together … Sisters … So we gave our word, silence.

Every muscle in her body tenses. A chance summer meeting on the beach changed everything. A cold November day—braking caused a slight melting of the thin ice, producing an even thinner layer of water between the tires and the ice, there was no traction. Time shifted. The view swung violently around: sleet, sand, ice, sea, Eva, Theresa, her mother grappling with a steering wheel, *Angie* she whispered, hands turning the wheel, this way, that way, the force of it all changing everything. Life reeled, her view spun, floating in the beach tubes together, water sparkling on the waves, a baby seat strapped beside her in the car, glistening icicles hanging from a split rail fence, sandcastles, her mother wearing a wool cap, looking over her shoulder, panicked, sitting on the boardwalk hooking pinkies, Foley's, crabbing, the jukebox, a gray sky spinning past, dances, Scott, a ship, Jason.

It is all a blur, her life, scenes spiraling in a sickening vertigo: an oak tree, the huge truth, looming in sight, overtaking, still, quiet, a photograph dropped on the table, the soft hiss of freezing drizzle sprinkling the roof of the idled car, beginning it all.

"Maris, wait," Theresa says when she stands and picks up her handbag and the bundle of envelopes. Theresa stands too and reaches for her arm. Maris glances at the hand holding her back before looking at Theresa's face, the face of the woman who would never have been in her life if it weren't for the wilting flowers set yearly at the base of an old oak tree. The accident never stopped in Addison. It skidded ceaselessly. Even now, every day at Stony Point would always be the result of a car skidding on black ice.

She turns and walks out of the office, slipping the cards into her handbag, hearing Renee call her name as the door closes behind her.

twenty-eight

SHE CALLS KYLE AND LAUREN, Jason at work, Maris' cottage and her cell. Eva keeps checking in with them once Theresa and Ned show up unannounced at her house, telling her things are bad. By dinner, everyone worries. Food and coffee and dishes and glasses and talk fill her kitchen. Someone brought grinders and Matt comes home with a pizza. Extra chairs are pulled from the dining room and squeezed around the mahogany kitchen table. Theresa and Ned repeat the details of the attorney's meeting and Jason sits beside them, listening carefully. Kyle asks Eva where Maris' favorite haunts are. Someone can check them out.

Eva looks at him blankly. "Well, here I guess. I mean, she likes the secondhand bookstore and to stop for a coffee. But Stony Point is really her haunt."

"Particularly this kitchen," Matt says. "It's weird with her not being here."

"I knew it. I just knew it," Eva says. "It's too much for her to handle alone. She needs us with her."

Lauren comes back from a quick walk along the beach and shakes her head *no* when everyone turns to her. "She's not there." She moves behind Kyle and sets her hands on his shoulders.

"This just isn't like her," Eva insists.

"Maybe it is," Jason counters. Everyone turns to him now. "How do we know? If she was really upset—"

"But we had plans today," Eva argues. "No. No, she wouldn't not show up without calling. She knows I'll worry, that I'll think her car broke down on the side of the highway somewhere."

Theresa moves to the counter, pouring a decanter of water into the coffee pot. "You might be wrong, Eva."

Eva turns and looks over at Theresa. "Well my God, just how bad was it there today?"

"She was really, really quiet," Ned says. "I've never seen her like that before. She just stopped talking."

"Why the hell didn't you ever tell us? Do you know how crazy it drove me all these years, wondering about my birth mother?"

"I was going to, I swear. Right when you graduated high school, Eva. I was up in the attic, getting things ready. I had the star necklace with me, it was time. And then." Theresa takes a quick breath. "And then you climbed into the attic that rainy morning telling me you were pregnant. Well. I quick dropped the necklace, closed that old trunk, and that was that. You were eighteen and having a baby? I couldn't tell you the rest, it was too much for you."

"But for all these years?"

"It was a trying time, then, with Taylor. Don't you remember? And well, years went by and then I didn't know where I put the necklace, I couldn't find it anywhere, and Maris moved away, so I let it go. I just never knew how bad this situation could get."

Eva stands then, runs out of the kitchen and up the

stairs into her bedroom, not caring if they hear her slam things around. A minute later, she storms back into the kitchen and drops a large carton on the table, shoving aside the food and dirty plates. "Well now you'll know how bad the situation got."

"What's going on?" Matt asks. "Eva?"

"I don't get it," Eva begins, her hands on her hips. "They keep protecting Maris' father, who happens to be my father as it turns out. They swore themselves to secrecy so no one would know, so he wouldn't be looked down upon and his stupid decision wouldn't be criticized."

"Eva, we were afraid he'd end the summer arrangement if we told you," Theresa tries to explain.

"Well what about Maris now? And what about me? Okay?" Eva takes the carton and tips it over on the table, its contents spilling across it. Monogrammed coffee cups, a beach umbrella spoon rest, tubes of lipstick, a silver pocket mirror, the illustrated *Alice's Adventures in Wonderland*, amethyst stud earrings, a small teddy bear, a picture frame, fashion scarves, a child's beaded bracelet, a ballerina music box, fancy pens, stationery, Christmas ornaments of red and silver, a digital camera, sunglasses. "Are you happy now?" she yells at Theresa and Ned.

"Hey, hey," Matt says, standing and turning her to him. "What is all this?"

She looks at him for a long second, her eyes brimming with tears. "I stole it, okay?"

"What?"

Nobody moves. Their eyes silently look from Eva to the loot on the table. Kyle looks back at Lauren then, while Jason and Matt watch Eva closely.

"Eva," Theresa says, still standing at the coffee pot. "What do you mean you stole it? I don't understand."

"What? What's not to understand?" she asks, crying now. "Louis didn't want anyone to know he gave me up, maybe because it was the wrong decision after all. And for all these years, you're protecting him and this is how crazy the whole secret made me. I was always searching, searching for my roots. I stole all this, okay? Every time I listed a house, or showed a house and saw something that could be a part of my birth mother's life, or could be a memory from the life I did *not* have with her, a life I only imagined, I took it. I *built* a life." She picks up the spoon rest. "The meals we might have cooked together," she says, then sets it gently down. "The pretty lipstick she wore, that I never got to see her put on." She opens a tube of lipstick, then drops it and shuffles through the items. "The birthstone earrings she picked out, special for me," she says, holding the amethyst studs up for everyone to see. "Here, look at this." She turns on the camera and shows them pictures stored on the screen, images of a woman and young girl sitting on a picnic table bench, having an ice cream together, the sun shining behind them, a lake in the distance. Then she reaches for the book. "Stories she never had a chance to read to me," she whispers, still crying.

"Oh, Eva," Theresa says, sitting beside her now, looking at the mess. "I'm so, so sorry."

Matt reaches over and begins putting the things carefully back into the carton.

"It's too *late* for apologies," Eva insists. "Way too late. If this is what happened to me, who the hell knows where Maris disappeared to. This is big stuff to handle. Big. And it's getting late now, and we always check in with each other. Where is she?"

Lauren hurries around the table and hugs Eva close. "It's all right, hon," she says, stroking her hair. "We'll find her. Maybe Jason's right. I mean, she's had a lot to deal with lately. Maybe she needs a little time alone."

Eva backs up and looks through her tears from Lauren to Jason, then turns and stacks the dirty plates on the table. Matt continues setting the items back in the box while Theresa gets the coffee cups from the cabinet and begins pouring coffee.

"Eva," Jason says, and she turns to him. "I totally get this." He motions to the box. "But Maris, well, I can't just sit here waiting. Where's her father's house in Addison?"

"Do you think she'd be there?"

"It's worth a shot. I'm going to take a ride there."

"Okay." Eva sets the pile of dishes on the counter near the sink and wipes her eyes with a napkin. "Okay. You call me right away if she is."

Jason nods and stands to leave.

"Do you want a coffee for the road?" Eva asks.

"No, I'm good."

Eva jots down the address and takes his cell number. She and Matt both walk him to the front door. "You know how to get there?" Eva asks, handing him the slip of paper.

"I'll put it in the GPS."

"Okay. And call me either way," Eva says.

"The night shift's keeping an eye out for her car," Matt tells him.

"Thanks, man. I'll check in later."

⁓

The air changed during the past few days with a coolness lifting off the water. Jason stops home to throw on a long sleeved shirt loose over his tee, turning up the cuffs while standing in his kitchen. A flash of annoyance rises when he checks his cell and has no messages. "Come on, Maris," he says, switching on the light over the sink and grabbing the flashlight from the cabinet on his way out. "Call me already."

Before picking up the highway, he stops at Maris' cottage. Maybe she left a note, something. He stands in her living room, his eyes scanning the furniture for clues. "Where are you?" he asks, rushing up the stairs to her bedroom and opening her closet. Her clothes hang in place, but a suitcase lays open on the floor. The bed is made, the window opened above it. A breeze moves the lace curtains and lifts a paper off her bedside nightstand. He pulls open the little drawers in the table, searching for a telephone number, an address, a name, anything. His business card is there, the one that he'd written his cell phone number on. So does she have any way of reaching him now? With Madison shadowing his every move, he goes back downstairs, nearly tripping on the dog following right at his side.

"God damn it, Maris, what are you doing?" he asks, randomly moving though the dining room. He sees then why she hasn't answered her cell all day. It sits on the table alongside all her fashion sketches and the velvet ring box. He opens it and takes a look at the diamond. Apparently she doesn't want any part of her life with her. Not Scott, not a phone, not the jacket slung over a chair, not her designs, not his cell number. She has walked clean out.

Before leaving, he switches on her kitchen light and rifles through a few drawers and cabinets, slamming some, leaving others half closed, silverware in disarray, pieces of paper on the floor. Madison sits, watching him closely. He finds her food, feeds her dinner and turns to go when the ache in his leg begins to throb. It'll feel good to sit and drive for an hour, but first he grabs three aspirins from her medicine cabinet, trying to stall the pain.

In Addison, the headlights sweep the lawn like a searchlight when he pulls in to her father's driveway. The small Garrison colonial, with its multipaned windows, is dark. He rings the bell, tries the door handle, then moves behind thick shrubs to the living room windows and shines the flashlight inside the house. The white light slices a narrow path through the living room into the empty dining room and halfway up the dark staircase, following the maple banister as far as he can. The balusters throw thin shadows on the stair wall behind them as he moves the light.

"What have they done to you?" He snaps off the light and makes his way out from behind the bushes. The warm SUV engine clicks as it cools down. Crickets chirp slowly. The street seems pleasant enough with lots of trees, with colonials and cape cods tucked back onto deep, shadowy lots. Lampposts throw circles of welcoming yellow light. He can picture her growing up here. How many times had she walked out this front door, meeting a friend, going to school, a job? He glances over his shoulder. Where would she go now?

He looks out over the front lawn. Someone has been keeping it mowed while the house awaits a sale; the realtor's For Sale sign stands near the street. Then he turns back to the front doorway. She said something to him recently, and he tries to think of her words.

Her drug of choice. Her tranquilizer. And he knows where he has to go. She lost herself, and her past, in the big city. If he's right, he only hopes she hasn't boarded the plane.

Maris stares out the window onto the night, studying the maze of runways below. Twinkling lights lead the eye to the end of each runway, then into the black sky. It looks like the sea at night, the water and sky inky, punctuated with buoys and lighthouses. She can picture a slow moving barge crossing Long Island Sound, its lights trailing across the horizon like the runway lights.

A big jet crawls along, taxiing into position until she loses sight of it maneuvering away far down the runway. When she has nearly forgotten about it and turns her attention elsewhere, the jet screams out of the darkness as it returns and climbs into the sky. She watches it go until it joins the stars far above, and she turns to the next jet preparing to fly.

~~

It doesn't happen often, but when it does, you are pulled up short, coming upon a familiar face in an unfamiliar setting. It is the neighbor you can't, for the life of you, place when you see her in the checkout line. Or the co-worker you don't recognize buying movie tickets ahead of you.

Damn it, her face has been in his mind all afternoon and still he nearly walks right past her, not *seeing* her until he looks twice. Dressed in black, she seems simply a shadow, standing near the window looking out at the night.

She is still here. Slivers of pain shoot through Jason's leg as he walks a wide circle around her, lost in a throng of travelers. He keeps moving, turning back, never letting her out of his sight, wanting to calm down before talking to her.

Finally, he can't walk any longer and finds a seat in a cluster of chairs in a waiting area. Leaning forward, his elbows resting on his knees, he watches only Maris. The rest of the airport, the commotion, the travelers walking past, the sporadic broadcast announcements, the lights, they all form a kaleidoscope, swirling out of focus beyond her. Tension knots his shoulders and so he rolls them, stretching his neck to the side. He can't talk to her yet because as much as he wants to take her into his arms, he also wants to take her shoulders and demand to know why she is leaving.

In time, Maris wraps her arms around herself, looking cold, and he finally thinks he will take his long sleeve shirt, come up behind her and drape it over her shoulders, until his eyes fall on the airline ticket packet visible in the slash pocket of her shoulder bag. She has reserved a seat, has planned to board a plane out of here, away from him. He almost misses Maris turning to the bank of telephones along a far wall, adjusting the shoulder strap of her black duffel as she walks to an empty phone.

She'd gotten the long distance number from Information and dials it carefully. This time she hopes to stay on and speak, to not change her mind and hang up. She focuses on the phone in front of her while waiting for the call to go through, willing him to be home. On the second ring, a hand reaches over her shoulder and firmly disconnects the call.

"Unless you're calling me, you don't need to be on the phone."

Without turning around, Maris closes her eyes. He takes the receiver from her hand and returns it to the telephone cradle, his hand staying on the receiver, reaching around her and blocking her in.

"Maris. Hey, what are you doing?" Jason asks quietly.

He steps close behind her. She can't move at all unless she turns into his arms. But the anger, and disbelief, comes through in his words and it stops her.

"I've been out of my mind worrying about you. What did you think," he asks from behind her, his mouth close to her ear, "that I wasn't waiting to hear from you? To see you?" He takes a long breath before pressing his mouth against her hair. "To hold you? Jesus Christ, I've been all over the state looking for you."

She's glad he can't see over her shoulder, can't know her eyes close tightly against the thought of him panicking.

"Talk to me," he tells her.

"I was calling your house," she begins, fighting the burning tears. "I didn't have your cell number." She turns, but he keeps his hand on the telephone, walling off the other callers. There is no room between them. She can only look at his eyes. "Please believe me."

"To say goodbye? Is that it? You were going to see me off over the telephone?"

"No," she says, crying now as his arm moves around her and pulls her closer. "I was afraid. I didn't know what to do."

He hesitates before holding her head to his shoulder and rocking gently, embracing her tighter until she feels like he'll never let go. "Do you know there's an A.P.B. out for you?" he asks, gently stroking her hair.

It seems like he still doesn't believe that she is here in his arms, with the insistent way his hand moves over her head. That, and the thought of her friends searching for her, worrying about her, has her give up on the tears. They keep coming. She feels Jason shift his stance, feels his head lower, his mouth near her ear. "Don't go, Maris."

She can't talk. She can only feel him move closer still, turn his head away and take another deep breath before he turns his face back to her.

"Don't leave me," he says.

"No," she whispers. She pulls back and touches his face. "I'm not. I'm not leaving."

His fingers tangle in her hair. "Do you know how scared I was?" he asks, searching her eyes. "For you?"

"I thought I had to get away, it was all too much. Just too much. Do you know what I'm saying?"

"Shh. It's okay, sweetheart. Of course I do." His thumb catches a tear on her cheek. "Let's go sit down."

When she nods and steps back, he picks up her duffel and slips an arm around her shoulder, glancing down at her and speaking quietly. His gait shows fatigue. They walk to a coffee shop at the other end of the airport. Inside the café, an entire curved wall of windows faces the wide airfield. Dreams and lives take flight there, she knows. Hers have in the past.

It takes a moment for Maris to compose herself in their booth. She sets down her handbag, twists her watch into place, wipes her face with a tissue. When she looks up, Jason leans across the table and slips her hair behind an ear, then takes off his long sleeve shirt and hands it to her to put over her shoulders.

"Jason," she says from behind more tears. "I'm sorry. I am so sorry for doing this to you today, for making you worry."

He reaches for her hand and holds it on the table. "Don't apologize, sweetheart. I've been there, too. Just let me help you."

"You know, earlier I was thinking how I couldn't stay, that every single day here was all because of my mother's car skidding on black ice. That everyone I know at Stony Point I sadly only know because of that one November afternoon when my mother died, and I wasn't sure how to handle it."

He doesn't speak, and she senses that he won't. Not until she's said everything.

"And then, I knew. Somehow, I knew that you, and everyone at the beach. You know. The whole gang." She smiles through her tears then. "You're all what saved me."

Jason leans over the table, holds her face and kisses her then. "Have you eaten at all?" he asks when he sits again.

"Not since breakfast."

"We'll have a coffee here. Then you need something good to eat. But first a hot coffee," he tells her as the waitress sets down a silver carafe and two large mugs.

"How did you know I was here?"

"It was something you said about Chicago, remember?" He lifts the carafe and fills her mug. "That troubles can't find you there?"

Maris nods and adds cream to the black coffee.

"I thought that whatever went down at your attorney's office shook you up pretty bad. Bad enough to chase you back to Chicago."

"It almost did," Maris says quietly. "But what it really did, after I thought about it, was make me realize how much things have changed this summer." She touches her star pendant. "How things can really change in an instant. Life can pivot on one moment. I just didn't know how to face all that I learned today. Everything, I mean. It's too huge."

"About Eva?"

"Yes. I still can't believe it. I have a *sister*."

"She knows." He takes a long drink of his coffee, then

313

tops off his mug. "Everybody's pretty surprised. And we thought the worst about how you'd taken the news."

"Oh I love the idea, but it hurts to think about what I've lost, too, for the past thirty years. I mean, thirty years!"

"I know. But it could have easily been so different. Imagine if you'd never known Eva."

"How is she?" Maris asks, taking a sip of her steaming coffee.

"Eva?"

"My sister." She smiles then. "I can't say it enough. My *sister.*"

"She's worried sick about you," he tells her. "Everyone is, really. Kyle, Lauren, Theresa and Ned. They're all at Eva's house." He pauses, his thumb stroking her hand.

"What do you think of it all?" she asks him. "Isn't it crazy?"

"I think it's amazing. Theresa and Ned are to be commended. So they made some mistakes, okay, but look what they accomplished, too. You're one lucky lady, and so is Eva."

"I have to talk to her."

"It's late now, and you're tired. I'll call and let her know you're all right and you can rest and think about things tonight. We'll go have dinner somewhere quiet, okay?"

She nods. "What about my car?"

"I'll come for it tomorrow with Matt. That'll give you the afternoon with Eva. But I want you with me tonight. I thought I'd lost you, Maris."

Maris looks across the room at a jet lumbering into the sky, climbing slowly past the large windowed wall, the sounding might of its engines pressing its way into the room.

"Your flight?" Jason asks.

314

She reaches into her handbag, slips out her airline ticket and slides it across the table without explanation. "Read it," she says.

He picks it up and scans the details. It clearly notes her destination. JFK Airport. "New York?" he asks, looking up from the ticket.

"I know it's close enough that I could've driven, but being on a plane, with that sense of being removed from everything, well, I thought I needed that."

"What's in New York?"

"That design job I told you about? They've offered it to me but are holding it open only till the end of the week."

He looks at the ticket again, longer this time.

Maris waits for him to realize what she's done. The airline and flight number are listed, as well as her departure time. It passed two hours ago. She had never gotten herself aboard the plane.

"Don't close the door on this," he says, and hands her the ticket back.

"On the job?"

He pauses for a long moment. "There's room for two in that barn of mine, you know."

"Well I just might take you up on that, because seriously? I'm never leaving you," she says, tucking the ticket into her bag. "Never," she whispers.

Jason stands and reaches for her hand again. "Come on, sweetheart. I'll bring you back."

As Maris turns to leave, catching a glimpse through the window of the diminishing lights of a jet, or of starlight in a vast sea of constellations and wishes, wishes from hearts opening to the stars while standing below on earth and looking up, longing for something, or someone, a voice, a touch, a memory, she knows.

These stars are the very same stars above Stony Point. The same stars she rises to each time she boards a plane. The same stars she looked at with her mother, thirty years past, caught on an 8mm home movie. The same stars where her mother is now. Stars, stars all around us. Celestial stars above and ocean stars on the water. Silver threads of stars stitched onto denim. Stars on gold chains. In the end, they are mere glimmers of light. Hopeful and illuminating, as we're wanting still another day.

The beach friends' journey continues in

THE
DENIM BLUE SEA

The next novel in The Seaside Saga from
New York Times Bestselling Author

JOANNE DEMAIO

CONTINUE WITH
THE SEASIDE SAGA

1) Blue Jeans and Coffee Beans

2) The Denim Blue Sea

3) Beach Blues

4) Beach Breeze

5) The Beach Inn

6) Beach Bliss

7) Castaway Cottage

8) Night Beach

9) Little Beach Bungalow

10) Every Summer

* And more in The Seaside Saga . . .

FROM NEW YORK TIMES BESTSELLING AUTHOR
JOANNE DEMAIO

Also by Joanne DeMaio

The Seaside Saga
(In order)
1) Blue Jeans and Coffee Beans
2) The Denim Blue Sea
3) Beach Blues
4) Beach Breeze
5) The Beach Inn
6) Beach Bliss
7) Castaway Cottage
8) Night Beach
9) Little Beach Bungalow
10) Every Summer
—And More Seaside Saga Books—

Summer Standalone Novels
True Blend
Whole Latte Life

Winter Novels
Eighteen Winters
First Flurries
Cardinal Cabin
Snow Deer and Cocoa Cheer
Snowflakes and Coffee Cakes

For a complete list of books by *New York Times*
bestselling author Joanne DeMaio, visit:

Joannedemaio.com

About the Author

JOANNE DEMAIO is a *New York Times* and *USA Today* bestselling author of contemporary fiction. The novels of her ongoing and groundbreaking Seaside Saga journey with a group of beach friends, much the way a TV series does, continuing with the same cast of characters from book-to-book. In addition, she writes winter novels set in a quaint New England town. Joanne lives with her family in Connecticut.

For a complete list of books and for news on upcoming releases, please visit Joanne's website. She also enjoys hearing from readers on Facebook.

Author Website:
Joannedemaio.com

Facebook:
Facebook.com/JoanneDeMaioAuthor

Made in the USA
Middletown, DE
27 May 2023